continued . . .

"A fun small-town drama starring a delightful . . . lead couple and an eccentric but likable supporting cast."
—The Best Reviews

"LuAnn McLane makes the pages sizzle. . . . *Dancing Shoes and Honky-Tonk Blues* is one of the better romances out there this month."
—Roundtable Reviews

Dark Roots and Cowboy Boots

"An endearing, sexy, romantic romp that sparkles with Southern charm!"
—Julia London

"This kudzu-covered love story is as hot as Texas Pete, and more fun than a county fair."
—Karin Gillespie, author of *Dollar Daze*

"A hoot! The pages fly in this sexy, hilarious romp."
—Romance Reviews Today

"Charmingly entertaining . . . a truly pleasurable read."
—*Romantic Times*

Wild Ride

"A collection of sensual, touching stories . . . *Wild Ride* is exactly that—a thrilling, exhilarating, sensual ride. I implore you to jump right in and hold on tight!"
—A Romance Review

Also by LuAnn McLane

Trick My Truck but Don't Mess with My Heart
Dancing Shoes and Honky-Tonk Blues
Dark Roots and Cowboy Boots

A LITTLE LESS TALK AND A LOT MORE ACTION

LuAnn McLane

A SIGNET ECLIPSE BOOK

SIGNET ECLIPSE
Published by New American Library, a division of
Penguin Group (USA) Inc., 375 Hudson Street,
New York, New York 10014, USA
Penguin Group (Canada), 90 Eglinton Avenue East, Suite 700, Toronto,
Ontario M4P 2Y3, Canada (a division of Pearson Penguin Canada Inc.)
Penguin Books Ltd., 80 Strand, London WC2R 0RL, England
Penguin Ireland, 25 St. Stephen's Green, Dublin 2,
Ireland (a division of Penguin Books Ltd.)
Penguin Group (Australia), 250 Camberwell Road, Camberwell, Victoria 3124,
Australia (a division of Pearson Australia Group Pty. Ltd.)
Penguin Books India Pvt. Ltd., 11 Community Centre, Panchsheel Park,
New Delhi - 110 017, India
Penguin Group (NZ), 67 Apollo Drive, Rosedale, North Shore 0632,
New Zealand (a division of Pearson New Zealand Ltd.)
Penguin Books (South Africa) (Pty.) Ltd., 24 Sturdee Avenue,
Rosebank, Johannesburg 2196, South Africa

Penguin Books Ltd., Registered Offices:
80 Strand, London WC2R 0RL, England

First published by Signet Eclipse, an imprint of New American Library,
a division of Penguin Group (USA) Inc.

ISBN-13: 978-0-7394-9745-6

Copyright © LuAnn McLane, 2008
All rights reserved

SIGNET ECLIPSE and logo are trademarks of Penguin Group (USA) Inc.

Printed in the United States of America

PUBLISHER'S NOTE
This is a work of fiction. Names, characters, places, and incidents either are the product
of the author's imagination or are used fictitiously, and any resemblance to actual per-
sons, living or dead, business establishments, events, or locales is entirely coincidental.
    The publisher does not have any control over and does not assume any responsibility
for author or third-party Web sites or their content.

This book is dedicated to my aunt Pat.
Thanks for your support and enthusiasm.
It means the world to me.

ACKNOWLEDGMENTS

I would like to thank the country music fans who have discovered my books, especially the Toby Keith Warriors. The colorful world of country music continues to influence my writing.

Thanks to Liza Schwartz for your hard work and friendly deadline reminders that keep me on task. I appreciate all that you do to make these books happen. I want to extend a special thanks to my editor, Anne Bohner. Your belief in my writing, even through the rocky road of revision, has made me a better, more confident writer. I can't thank you enough.

As always, I want to give a big thanks to my agent, Jenny Bent. Your encouragement, support, and knowledge are valued and appreciated.

1

Bittersweet

Just how is it that one of the happiest days of my life can also be one of the saddest? It just doesn't seem right. A big fat tear slides down my cheek, making me really glad that I had the foresight to fortify my eyelashes with several coats of waterproof mascara. I simply knew I'd be crying buckets at my best friend's wedding.

"Jamie Lee looks beautiful, doesn't she?" observes gruff old Irma Baker, who is standing next to me on the church steps. Irma's wearing a lavender linen suit smelling faintly of mothballs, and a matching pillbox hat perched slightly askew atop her silver curls.

"Yes . . ." A sigh escapes me and my lips tremble. "She sure does." Jamie Lee is radiant in a soft white, simply cut wedding gown. She's a no-frills kind of girl but right now she looks elegant.

"Whoo-hoo! That there Griffin Sheldon sure is a mighty fine specimen of a man. Jamie Lee's one lucky girl. I'm sure gonna miss watchin' him build my deck. I think I might have to add on."

"Miss Irma, you've already added on to your deck twice."

Irma gives me a sly grin. "I know. Purty soon my danged deck is gonna be bigger than my house!" she admits, and tosses a handful of rice at the newlyweds. "But just lookie at him, all tall and studly in his tuxedo. I betcha he's gonna rock Jamie Lee's world. He sure could rock mine, doncha know." Miss Irma crooks one eyebrow. "You need someone to rock your world, Macy. I'm thinkin' bodacious Luke Carter could be your ticket. That man's got a butt you could bounce quarters off."

"Miss Irma!" I hiss, and hope no one heard her. Luckily all the attention is on the newlyweds. "Hush!"

"I'm just sayin'." She shrugs her narrow shoulders and then twists open the gold clasp on her lavender patent-leather pocketbook to dig out her Virginia Slims. "Dang, I need a cigarette just thinkin' about it. You'll have to excuse me," she apologizes, and at least has the grace to walk away from the church before lighting one up.

While shaking my head, I have to grin as I watch her puff curls of smoke skyward, but my focus goes back to Jamie Lee and Griff, who are being showered with rice and hugs. I'm happy for them, really happy, but it also hits me hard that my best friend since my sandbox days is *married*, and while I'm certain we'll always be as close as sisters, realistically I know that her marriage changes everything. I toss a handful of rice a little too hard, hitting Jamie Lee in the back of the head. Some of it sticks to her golden hair, which was artfully arranged by me. We tried about a dozen different updos in our salon but in the end the simple knot at the nape of her neck was perfect.

As if reading my mind, Jamie Lee turns and gives me a reassuring smile that says she knows and understands. That's the way it's always been between us. My throat tightens and my eyes well up as I toss another handful of rice, a bit more gently this time. Tears spill over and slide down my cheeks, dripping onto my bouquet of wildflowers. I dearly need a tissue, but of course I don't have one.

"Hey, are you okay?" asks a deep voice that will forever make my heart skip a beat. Without turning around I know that Luke Carter, Jamie Lee's brother and the unrequited love of my life, is standing on the step behind me. "Here." He comes down to the step beside me and reaches in his breast pocket. "Looks like you could use this." He offers me a snow-white handkerchief that I gratefully accept.

"Thanks." I look up at him and try for a smile but all I can manage is a wobble of my lips. Even though I'm wearing three-inch, dyed-to-match-my-dress heels that are already killing my feet, Luke towers over me, six foot four inches of masculine beauty. Before today I had never seen him in a tux and I have to say that it is a sight to behold. Holding my bouquet with one hand, I daintily dab at the corner of my eyes. I dearly need to blow my nose, but I'm afraid of the dreaded honking noise that sometimes plagues me when I blow. When Luke reaches his hand toward me I'm confused, but then realize he's offering to hold the bouquet. With another lip wobble that comes closer to a smile, I hand the flowers to him and continue my dabbing, this time at my nose.

"Hope Griff knows what he's getting himself into." Luke nods his dark head toward his sister and best friend.

"Oh, if there's anyone who can handle her, it's Griff."

"Yeah, he'll keep her in line."

My head snaps up and I momentarily cease my dabbing. I get a little feisty when it comes to comments like that but since it's Luke I bite my tongue, although I do sort of narrow my eyes.

"Whoa there, I'm just teasin'." He grins down at me and I try not to blush like a schoolgirl. "Griff worships the ground she walks on."

"I know," I say wistfully, wishing someone would worship my ground . . . like maybe *him*.

"Ready to kick up your heels at the reception?"

I nod and brighten a bit at the thought of the evening of fun ahead of us. "Hey, speaking of heels, were you the one who wrote *Help me* in white shoe polish on the bottom of Griff's shoes?"

"Who, me?" He jabs his thumb at his chest and tries for an innocent expression but the laughter in his blue eyes gives him away.

"Jamie Lee's gonna kill you when she sees the video tape! Luke, it wasn't right to make light of such a serious event." I give him a stern frown.

Luke leans down and says close to my ear, "Oh, come on, it was priceless. Admit it."

I would admit that it was pretty darned funny and in truth Jamie Lee is going to laugh, but with his mouth so close to my ear that his warm breath causes a tingle to travel down my spine all I can manage is a mute nod.

"Thought so," he teases, and straightens back up. The sleeve of his jacket brushes against my bare arm and I shiver even though it's a warm summer evening. I wonder if the man has any idea what he does to me. "You want to ride to the reception with me in the limo?"

I swallow hard. Except for the flower girl and the ring bearer, Luke and I were the only ones in the wedding party. Unlike her mother, Jamie Lee wanted things small and simple.

"Jamie Lee and Griff are going to take the traditional ride in rocking chairs in the back of Dad's pickup truck. We might as well use the limo since the driver's still on the clock."

Luke looks at me expectantly and I realize that I'm supposed to answer. A tight ball of nervousness clenches at my stomach. "Um, okay, but then I won't have a car." The reception is a buffet on the lawn of Jamie Lee's family's farmhouse.

"Don't worry." He hands me the bouquet. "I'll drive you home."

"All right," I agree, hoping that my voice doesn't sound as breathless as I feel.

"And if we drink too much I'm sure Mama won't mind if you crash at the house."

"Oh, that won't be necessary," I assure him with a wave of my hand.

Luke arches one eyebrow down at me. "I know you better than that, Macy McCoy."

"Well okay . . . it probably will be," I admit with a grin. Not that I hadn't stayed over at Jamie Lee's many times over the years. With the passing of my own mama early on and my daddy busy working, the Carter household was my home away from home. Jamie Lee's mama would be pleased as punch if I ever hooked up with Luke.

She even drops hints, but that's not going to happen, so I don't know why I'm letting my mind wander in that direction. Luke Carter was a hometown football sensation here in Hootertown, went on to play college ball, and now, after coaching the Payton Panthers to the NCAA Division II Championship, has risen to a new level of hometown hero. Why, they recently had a big parade for the Panthers and then named a street after Luke! There's buzz around town that Division I colleges are courting him, so it's likely he'll be moving up to bigger and better things soon anyway.

"Ready?" Luke asks, and politely puts his hand on my elbow, guiding me across the church lawn to where the limo awaits. I have to walk on my toes so my narrow heels don't sink into the soft ground. When we pass by Miss Irma, she gives me a wink and a thumbs-up, drawing a questioning glance from Luke. "What was that all about?"

"Darned if I know," I tell him, hoping my cheeks aren't flaming. The driver opens the door and the silky material of my green dress slides across the smooth leather seat. Jamie Lee chose the color to complement my auburn hair, which has been my color of choice for at least a while, although I have been contemplating blond highlights. As hairdressers, we (especially me) frequently change our color and cut. Right now my hair is shoulder length and slightly wavy from the remains of an earlier perm that I dearly hated. Today I opted for a classic French twist, letting a few tendrils trail down my neck. Jamie Lee told me that I looked amazing, and if I were only twenty pounds lighter I would have believed her.

"Would you mind taking this?" Luke removes his jacket and hands it to me through the open door.

"Sure." The jacket is warm from his body and smells of his spicy aftershave. It's all I can do not to bring it to my nose for a better whiff but he's already sliding onto the seat beside me.

"Thanks, I was burning up in that thing. I really want to loosen this tie but Jamie Lee warned me that there will be even more pictures over at the house," Luke complains with a good-natured shake of his head.

"I know! My face was starting to hurt from smiling."

"You always seem to have a smile on your face, Macy. It's one of the things I like about you."

"Thanks," I tell him, glad that the driver shuts the door, putting us in muted darkness so he can't see the blush that's surely heating my cheeks. "I'm trying hard these days to look on the sunny side." I sneak a peek at him through my eyelashes. Maybe Jamie Lee's right and Luke has stronger feelings for me than I thought . . .

But then he reaches over, pats my knee, and says, "That's a good attitude, Macy. Never change."

Well, hellfire. He might as well have patted me on the head like a puppy. Luke will forever think of me in a protective, brotherly way. Of course the devil on my shoulder whispers in my ear that this is the way it once was with Jamie Lee and Griff but I shake it off. I don't care what anyone says; I'm just not Luke's type. "Okay, I'll try." My goal is a light, breezy reply but to my dismay it comes out gurgled with emotion.

"Hey," Luke says in a voice that's low with concern, "I know that Jamie Lee's marriage is going to be a little tough on you sometimes." He gives my knee a reassuring squeeze and I have to smile. Luke really is a good guy and a squeeze *is* a bit better than a pat. I make the mistake, though, of looking down at his tanned hand, which is a stark contrast to his white cuff and looks so masculine next to the silky material of my dress.

"Thank you, Luke. I'll admit that today is bittersweet. It's one of the happiest moments . . . ," I begin, but falter and have to dab at my eyes with Luke's handkerchief.

"But it's a loss of sorts for you too. It won't be quite the same for Griff and me, so believe me, I get it. I'm about the only one left in my circle of buddies who isn't married. You'll find someone though. You're too much of a sweetheart not to get snapped up by some lucky guy." He gives my knee one final squeeze and then smiles down at me.

With a small nod I smile back but I'm gripping my bouquet so hard that I'm surprised the flowers aren't wilting. Luke just gave me a nice compliment but my brain isn't really processing it that way. For a moment I stare out of the tinted glass at the passing landscape without really seeing it. Luke's lack of romantic interest is no surprise, so it shouldn't bother me; yet his comment also makes me feel like a loser who is just hoping and praying for my prince to show up and whisk me away. Well . . .

My feisty nature is bubbling to the surface. Gripping the bouquet even tighter I swallow and try to tamp it down. If Jamie Lee were here she'd sense the signs and give me a warning look. Once I shift into feisty gear it's sometimes hard to rein myself back in, so I take a deep breath and in a firm and almost calm voice mutter, "I don't really feel the need to have a man in my life to make me happy or fulfilled."

"I—"

"There might be pressure for women to still feel this way even in this day and age but I'm not about to get out there and troll for a man just to get married."

"I—"

"Oh no, I'm not about to settle." I try to keep my head from bopping but fail. "If and when I ever *do* decide to get married it will be all or nothin'."

"You—"

"Like the Sugarland song says, 'I ain't settlin' for anything less than *everything*.' I mean, why should I? And if it never comes my way, then I'll be just fine and dandy." I shift in the seat and give my bouquet a little shake, dislodging some daisy petals, which swirl in the blast of cool air coming from the overhead vent. There's a moment of silence that I'm not sure how to fill. Lowering the flowers to my lap I quietly say, "I guess I went a little overboard. When I get on a roll, sometimes there's no stopping me no matter how much I just want to shut my mouth."

"It's okay. Emotions are runnin' high today." Luke gives me a slow smile filled with amusement but in my mind it is so doggone sexy that I just want to grab him by the lapels and kiss him silly. I refrain, thank the Lord.

"It—it might be low blood sugar," I hasten to explain. "I haven't eaten since breakfast." Of course I want to clamp my hand over my big mouth. Sure Macy, bring attention to the fact that you have to stuff your face on a regular basis or you turn into a crazy person.

"Macy, there's no need to apologize for speaking your mind. Especially to me." Expecting a response, he looks at me with those blue eyes of his but I'm distracted by a curve in the country road that has me sliding so close that my shoulder and thigh press up against him. "And you're entirely right."

"I am?" Wow, his thigh is as hard as a rock.

"Yeah, you are." His eyelids lower and a tender expression crosses his face. I'm still pressed against him but I pretend not to notice even though my heart is pounding like a jackhammer.

I've, of course, totally forgotten the point I was making, so I merely nod.

"There's no reason whatsoever that you should ever have to settle, Macy."

"Right."

He flexes his fingers, and for a breathless moment I think he might take my hand in his but he doesn't. "So don't, okay?" When I nod again he opens his mouth to say something else but we both suddenly realize that we've arrived at the family farm. The serious moment passes and he smiles. "Ready to have some fun?"

"You betcha."

2

Wedding Bell Blues

Without waiting for the driver, Luke scoots out of the limo and then offers his hand to assist me. Hooking his finger in the back of his jacket, he flips it over his shoulder and curves his other hand lightly around my elbow, making me feel almost as if we're a couple. I've felt like that a lot lately, since with all of the wedding plans over the past few weeks we've frequently been thrown together socially. Another sad thought hits me—after today our relationship will go back to normal, which translates to me hoping for attention and Luke oblivious to my needs.

"Hey, why the frown?" Luke asks as we circle the big white farmhouse to the backyard, where the reception will take place. "The hard part's over. Now we get to cut loose."

"You're right." I flash him a smile that I hope doesn't appear forced, since it is.

"That's better."

My smile widens when I give my sorry-ass self a mental shake. This is a once-in-a-lifetime occasion and I'm not going to ruin it by having an emotional meltdown. Jamie Lee and I have dreamed of this day since we were kids . . . Of course, in our imaginations it was a double wedding to whatever celebrity crush we'd had at the time and Vince Gill would be singing at the reception. "Oh, my . . ." I come to a halt and put a hand to my chest. "This is *beautiful*!" I dab at the corners of my eyes with Luke's handkerchief which is wadded up in my hand.

Luke nods. "Yeah, we might have insisted that Mama hire everything out but she's still managed to work nonstop. She was still flittin' around fussin' with the flower arrangements on the tables this mornin'." He glances my way. "You should be proud too, Macy. You had a hand in the planning *and* more importantly kept Mama and Jamie Lee from stranglin' each other."

"Oh, it wasn't that bad."

Luke arches an eyebrow.

I have to laugh because he's right. Jamie Lee and her mama don't always see eye to eye. There's been many a time when I've been the buffer between those two. "Well, the endless hours of planning were worth it," I admit as I gaze at the round tables covered in white linen and topped with fresh flowers scenting the air with sweetness. Fluffy paper wedding bells strung overhead are bobbing in the breeze as if trying to chime. "Oh goodness! The cake is lovely!" I exclaim as it's wheeled past us to a place of honor beneath a huge tent erected for the occasion. Handmade, white gum-paste roses and white petals adorn a rolled butter-cream cake decorated with whimsical hearts and a pearl border. It was one of the few details

Jamie Lee and her mama actually agreed upon. Later, after dusk there will be thousands of twinkling lights and flickering candles casting a soft glow over the festivities. For simple country folks, I do believe we've outdone ourselves.

"Why, this could be featured in *Southern Living* magazine," I gush.

"Oh no, here comes trouble," Luke says fondly as his mother rushes out the back door. "Every detail has been taken care of, but you just watch, she'll find something to fiddle with."

Luke's right. Daisy Carter surveys the backyard with a critical eye. She doesn't see us since we're off to the side of the yard and not directly in her line of vision.

"Thirsty?" Luke asks as he reaches into a decorative tub filled with ice, beer, water, and pop.

"Parched," I admit, and I'm about to ask for a bottle of water when he unscrews a longneck and hands it to me. When I hesitate he says, "Go on—you've earned it."

"You twisted my arm."

"That's my girl," he says with a wink, and then reaches into the tub for another one. "The guests will be arriving shortly, and then, heaven help us, more picture taking before I can shed this jacket for good."

His girl . . . I smile but hide my sigh behind a swig of cold beer. *If only.* We drink in companionable silence while watching his mama give orders like a drill sergeant. It's weird since she's so soft-spoken but she somehow has the ability to make people listen. "You think there's somethin' we should be doin'?"

"I'm not goin' anywhere near my mama. Oh no, here comes Dad." Tipping back his bottle, Luke takes a long pull of his beer. "He shoulda stayed inside where it's safe."

"Daisy, you need any help?"

Luke slowly shakes his head. "Wrong question, Pop."

"Do I look like I need help?" Daisy puts her hands on her slim hips and stares him down. Despite the heat she looks cool as a cucumber in a lovely, shimmering gold tea-length dress that showcases her deep red hair and ivory skin. I don't think I've ever seen her break a sweat.

Instead of being intimidated like the servers seem to be, he slowly walks her way, looking quite handsome in his tux. The thought occurs to me that Luke will age just as gracefully. Even at this distance I can see that his deep tan from hours spent working outdoors makes his eyes appear bluer.

"You look delicious." He leans in for a kiss that has Daisy pushing at his shoulders but then giving in and kissing him back. He sticks the pink rosebud back in the arrangement and takes Daisy's hand. "Enough, woman. The guests are arriving, including our beautiful daughter and new son-in-law."

"They're arriving?" Daisy gasps. "Why didn't you tell me?"

"That's precisely what I came out here to do . . . well, that and to sneak a smooch."

Luke grins. "I sure wish I were as smooth as my pop. I think he's the only man alive who knows just how to handle Mama." But then Luke raises both hands in the air. "I meant that fondly, just so you know."

I feel heat creep into my cheeks. "I'm sorry, Luke. I overreacted before."

"Yeah, you're a little firecracker just like my mother."

He pauses for a second and angles his head at me. "I wonder if there's a man out here who can handle *you*?" Luke teases, but then he taps his beer bottle to his head. "There I go again, heading into dangerous territory."

His half grin makes me suddenly wonder if . . . ohmigod *if he's flirting*. I wish I had the nerve to say, *What about you, Luke? Think you could handle me?* But of course I don't, even with the beer buzz that went straight to my head. I'm saved from answering since everyone seems to be arriving at once. What am I thinking anyway? Luke was teasing, not flirting. Right?

Griff's brother, Brandon, is directing cars into the grass field to the left of the house and guests are swarming into the yard like honeybees on a mission. Here in the country, past the city limit signs, people work hard and play hard. Luke gives me a crooked smile that I can't quite read and says, "Okay, maid of honor, you ready to party?"

"Yeah, I am, best man."

And party we do. After Reverend Jacobs has us bow our heads in prayer, Jamie Lee and Griff lead us to the buffet line. The table is laden with mounds of food. Roast beef, country ham, and fried chicken are the main attractions but there's also every side dish known to Southern man. Even though Daisy had the whole thing catered, that didn't stop neighbors from bringing covered dishes, but it's a good thing because although half the town was invited, it looks to me like the other half are wedding crashers.

Since this is a special occasion I pile my plate high with my favorite foods, refusing to worry about carbs or calories. I'm seated at the head table next to Jamie Lee with Luke to the other side of me. Ever the gentleman, he pulls out my chair and is so attentive that I have to remind myself that this is a Cinderella evening and that he's not really my date, however much it feels that way. After tonight my maid-of-honor duties will be over. I'll go back to styling hair at Jamie Lee's Cut & Curl with her mama who will be filling in while the newlyweds are on their honeymoon . . . two weeks in Hawaii! I won't lie, I'm more than a little jealous.

"Can I get you anything?" Luke asks. "I'm going for a beer."

"Yes, thanks." It will be my third but I tell myself that it's a wedding reception for goodness's sake. Jamie Lee's been telling me to loosen up and tonight I plan on letting my hair down a little. It's been a long time since I've whooped it up and maybe it will pull me out of my blue mood.

"Luke sure seems to be stuck at your side, Macy," Jamie Lees says, and wags her eyebrows.

"Oh stop! It's part of the best man's duties for Pete's sake," I say with a wave of my hand, but give her a look that says, *Do you think so*?

"I think he's going over and above the call of duty."

I roll my eyes at her. "Yeah, well, I think the champagne is goin' to your head. Luke's just bein' polite, just like always," I protest, fully expecting Jamie Lee to argue her point right back like we always do, but she frowns thoughtfully instead and stays quiet. I know she's waiting for me to prompt her, so I stubbornly don't. Well, for a few seconds anyway. "Okay, *what*?"

Jamie Lee leans in closer to me, which is a sure sign that I'm not going to like what she has to say. "You should make your move." She pauses for drama, and then whispers, "Tonight."

"What?" I squeak, but I already know what she's alluding to.

"You should make your move on Luke," she repeats in a stage whisper.

"That's it. I'm cutting you off." I reach for her flute of champagne but she puts her hand over mine.

"I'm *serious*!" she insists. "Stop pussyfootin' around, Macy, or it'll be too late. You and Mama pushed me with Griff and look what happened."

"That was different. It was plain as day that you two were in love. Luke isn't into me that way."

"And you know this, how?" She shakes a dinner roll at me.

"Because . . . because I'm . . . me."

Jamie Lee's eyes narrow, "Don't you dare go puttin' yourself down!"

"I'm just statin' the facts. You can put your boots in the oven but that doesn't make them biscuits." I pick up my dinner roll as a prop. It's not a biscuit but close enough.

"Now what in the world is that supposed to mean?" Jamie Lee asks in a bit of a heated tone. She shakes her head at me but her hair stays in place thanks to my liberal dousing of shimmering hair spray.

"No matter what you say, the fact remains that I am what I am and nothing can change the fact that your brother is way out of my league, especially since he took the Payton Panthers to the NCAA championship, raising his hero status to a new level!"

Jamie Lee opens her mouth to protest but the photographer pauses to snap our picture, so we smile momentarily and then go back to our argument. Griff, who is used to our heated discussions, concentrates on his meal. I dearly wish that Luke would get his butt back here so we could end this pointless conversation but I spot him chatting with Brandon.

I chew up a bite of my dinner roll and then say, "They just named a doggone street after your brother, Jamie Lee, and the Welcome to Hootertown sign now says, Home of Luke Carter!" I'm trying to keep my voice down to a whisper but two beers on an empty stomach are making it difficult for me to do so. I shove another bite of roll into my mouth, thinking that food will help the situation.

"Macy, this is Hootertown, Kentucky, for goodness' sake, not . . ." She leans closer to my ear and whispers, "Hollywood." She gives me a pointed look. "It's not where you're from or what you do for a living that matters. It's what's in here." She taps her heart and her eyes mist over. "Just promise me that you'll follow your dreams and listen to your heart."

"I promise," I tell her gruffly, and have to dab at my eyes once more. Pretty soon my waterproof mascara is going to give up the fight.

"And this ring on my finger doesn't mean I won't be here for you."

"I know." We do our secret handshake that we've been doing since we were kids. I know she means what she says but things *have* changed. Griff is her first priority now, as he should be. Soon she'll be having babies and driving a minivan. I start to tear up again for both sad and happy reasons but when I spot Luke heading back to the table I rein in my emotions. He's removed his jacket and has his cuffs turned back to reveal tanned forearms. The black fitted vest shows off the fact that he's as fit and trim as his football days but without the overly bulky muscle. With his neatly trimmed dark hair and a five o'clock shadow he could easily grace the cover of *GQ*. Luke might be a country boy at heart but there's a polished way about him that I find insanely attractive but intimidating at the same time.

"Here's your drink," Luke says as he slides into the seat beside me. "Sorry I got sidetracked."

I accept the cold bottle with a smile. "No problem. I needed to slow down anyway."

"The offer's still open to stay here, you know."

I nod after taking a sip. "I appreciate that."

"Then just plan on it and don't worry."

Jamie Lee, who is eating but I know darned well is listening to every word, nudges me with her knee. I turn and give her a he's-just-being-polite look but she shakes her head.

Lucky for me Griff distracts her. "Jamie Lee," he says, "your mama has been gesturing toward you."

"I know. I've been ignoring her."

"I think she's getting pissed," Griff warns in a she's-now my mother-in-law way. "What's that all about?"

"She wants me to get up and mingle."

"That include me?"

Jamie Lee leans in and kisses him. "No. You finish your meal. I'll handle Mama. But don't wander off, because in a little while we'll have the cutting of the cake, which you will not shove in my face and up my nose," she says firmly. When Griff gives her an innocent nod, I snicker. "And then comes the throwing of the bouquet,"

Jamie Lee adds, and gives me a pointed I'll-be-tossing-it-directly-at-you look. "By then Wet Willie's band will have arrived and we can finally let our hair down and get this party started." After eating a few more bites she gives Griff a peck on the cheek and says, "Okay, off to do my mingling duties."

After Jamie Lee leaves, Griff shoots me a grin. "How you holdin' up, maid of honor?"

"Fine," I tell him, but of course my eyes start to leak because I think he is such a great guy and Jamie Lee is going to be so happy. "You're a lucky guy, Griff. Jamie Lee is one of a kind," I say, and my voice cracks. Oh crap, now my nose is starting to run. I'm going to have to break down and blow here in a second.

Luke tips his chair onto its back legs, bracing his hand on my chair so he can lean and say, "Yeah, she's one of a kind, all right. They broke the mold after Jamie Lee. I tried to warn ya," he jokes. I would have laughed but I'm too zoned in on the fact that Luke's arm is brushing against my bare shoulders. "Don't come cryin' to me after the honeymoon is over."

Griff laughs. "Jamie Lee is gonna be pissed when she finds out that you wrote *Help me* on the bottom of my shoes."

"Did you know it when you put them on?"

"Yeah," Griff admits, but puts his fingers to his lips when I give him a wide-eyed, openmouthed stare. I was about to give the groom a piece of my mind about the seriousness of the occasion but Luke leans in closer and his chest touches my shoulder, and my brain goes into Luke overload.

"Yeah, Griff, it's all honey-do from here on in."

"Yeah, right," Griff scoffs, but when Jamie Lee crooks her finger from over at the cake he immediately jumps to his feet and heads her way.

"That boy is whipped." Luke lowers his chair back down to the ground but his arm remains on the back of mine. "Not that there's anything wrong with that," he amends with a grin.

"Glad you added that part." My tone is deceptively breezy since my heart is thudding wildly. Does he realize that his arm is practically around my shoulders? Does he want it there? Or is it just casual . . . friendly in an I've-known-you-forever-this-means-nothing kind of way? I look in Jamie Lee's direction to see if she's observing the arm-around-me gesture but she's busy posing like she's cutting the cake with Griff.

"Any bets on whether Griff shoves the cake in her face?" Luke asks.

Trying to ignore the way the hair on his arm is causing a tingling sensation to slide down my spine I say, "Griff will be gentle but Jamie Lee will have no problem shoving a bite in his face."

"Naw, he'll get her good."

"No way."

"Wanna bet?"

"Sure, cause I know I'm right."

"Okay then, what's the wager?"

"If you win I'll give you a free haircut," I offer.

"Fair enough," he says with a grin.

"Okay then, if you're right, what'll you give me?" I automatically ask. My heart pounds when he doesn't im-mediately answer and I swear his gaze drops to my mouth. If he says *a kiss,* I'm going to slide right out of my chair.

"How about lunch?"

"What?"

"If you win I'll buy you lunch anywhere that doesn't have a dollar menu."

"Oh," I say with a nervous chuckle. *A kiss . . . Who am I kidding?* "Sure, okay."

"Come on then, let's get closer."

"Closer?"

"To the cake. I need to egg Griff on."

"Oh, right." *Close to the cake . . . not closer to me.* God, I'm officially losing my mind. It's all Jamie Lee's fault by telling me to make my doggone move. Here I am reading something into nothing. But then Luke puts his hand on the small of my back, gently leading me through the crowd. I know that it's a gentlemanly gesture but right now it somehow feels intimate and possessive. Inhaling a deep breath I try to clear my brain and remind myself that this is not a date, but a doggone wedding.

The guests part the way not because we're the best man and maid of honor, but more likely because it's hometown hero Luke. When we reach the front of the crowd, Luke eases me in front of him since even in my killing-my-feet heels, he towers over me. Again, this is the mannerly thing to do but that doesn't change the fact that I can feel the heat of his body standing so close. And then he lightly rests his hands on my shoulders and it's all I can do not to lean back against him.

Jamie Lee and Griff slowly cut the first piece together, allowing for pictures to be snapped. He says something in her ear and she laughs. I think again just how perfect they are for each other and sigh.

"You ready to lose?" Luke teases in my ear when Griff lifts the small slice of cake to Jamie Lee's lips, pausing for photos. The crowd is cheering him on, of course hoping for him to get her good. Griff grins and waggles his eyebrows . . .

3

Holes in the Floor of Heaven

When Jamie Lee narrows her eyes in warning, Griff's grin gets wider and the guests get louder. I remember reading somewhere that tradition dictated that the bride feed the groom first, but I bet Jamie Lee wanted to see if he would smash the cake in her face before getting her turn to retaliate. Griff feeds her a delicate bite while the crowd boos. I give Luke a joyous little jab with my elbow.

Then Jamie Lee takes a slice of cake and puts it to Luke's mouth. She pauses for a picture, smiles sweetly at him, and proceeds to feed him a tiny bite . . . but then shoves the heel of her hand upward, squishing icing over his chin and cheeks. The crowd roars, but just when Jamie Lee thinks she's had the upper hand, Griff grabs her and kisses her, smearing icing all over her face as well. At first, Jamie Lee pushes at his shoulders but then wraps her arms around his neck and kisses him right back. Griff picks her up and spins her around while cameras flash like strobe lights.

With a triumphant smile I turn to Luke and jab my thumb at my chest. "I win."

"Did not," he responds.

With my hands on my hips I shoot a frown at him. "How do you figure that? It went down just like I said it would."

"Griff got her back and then some."

"Yeah, but—"

"He knew what she would do and planned the whole thing."

"Nuh-uh."

Luke angles his head. "Be honest, Macy."

If only I could, I think to myself but then say, "Okay . . . you're probably right. I guess it's sort of a tie although I was more right than you." I jab my thumb at my chest but then feel as if I'm pointing at my boobs and quickly lower my hand.

"How about if you give me a haircut and I take you to lunch afterward? Deal?"

"Deal," I agree, and extend my hand to shake on it but he gives me the high five, side slap, knuckle bump.

"Hey, how'd you know the secret handshake?"

Luke scratches his chin. "Well, hmmm let me see . . . I've only seen you and my sister do it a few thousand times."

"Right. I guess it's not so secret. You probably know a lot more about me than you want to know," I say with a laugh.

Luke looks at me rather thoughtfully but his reply is lost in the noise of the crowd when it's announced that it's time to toss the bouquet and then the garter. Jamie Lee goes over to the back-porch steps but before she turns her back to the single women gathered in a group, she gives me a discreet little elbow point to the right. Everyone else probably thought she was flexing her tossing arm but I know she wants me to stand *there* so I can catch the doggone thing. I nod and rub my hands together but these shoes weren't made for running so I have my doubts.

"Okay! On the count of three!" Jamie Lee raises her bouquet in the air and shouts, "One, two . . . *three!*" and she lets 'er rip. Unfortunately, her throw goes cockeyed and way, *way* up in the air, flipping a few times before beginning to descend as if in slow mo. I try, I really do, but I'm no match for single women on a mission for marriage. Pushing, shoving, and squealing ensue. Rose Jenkins slips in the grass and lands on her butt in an unladylike spread eagle. Miss Irma knocks me sideways, almost bowls over a six-year-old whose mama should not have let her into the fray. I blink in wonder when Miss Irma elbows Lorna Mae Sweetwater out of the way and then jumps higher than I think is humanly possible for a woman her age, especially with her skinny legs. She makes a single-handed sideways catch that should be replayed on *Sports Center* tomorrow morning.

"Woohoo!" Miss Irma shouts in her smoker's voice, and does a victory dance as if she were in the end zone after a touchdown. Lorna Mae purses her lips and gives Miss Irma a glare, but Miss Irma juts her chin out in a you-want-a-piece-of-me challenge. Lorna Mae gives her a disgusted wave of her hand, turns on her orthopedic heel, and marches away, mumbling beneath her breath. I spot Miss Irma's purple pillbox and scoop it up before Lorna Mae stomps all over it.

"That was amazing, Miss Irma." I pin the hat back on top of her stiff, hair-sprayed curls.

"Yer, not mad at me, are ya? I know Jamie Lee wanted you to catch it but you've got a lot of years ahead of you to git yerself a man. My days are numbered." She pulls me close and says in her gruff way, "'Sides, I think that Luke is sweet on you, Macy. Caught him eyeing your hiney."

"You did not!" I gasp, but think, *Wow, was he really?*

"Did too!" she insists. "You are boo-ti-licious, girl-friend."

"Miss Irma, you really need to stop watching MTV."

"Why? Makes me feel young . . . and fr-*isky*. I'm tellin' ya, Luscious Luke was ogling yer backside," she insists, but her eyes are twinkling with humor so I'm not quite sure if I should take her seriously. I don't have time to wonder because it's time for Griff to take the garter off Jamie Lee and toss it to the bachelors.

Whooping and cheering erupt when Griff lifts Jamie Lee's dress and dips his dark head beneath the white folds.

Griff makes a big show of sliding the garter down Jamie Lee's leg with his teeth while Wet Willie's Band plays a striptease tune in the background. Jamie Lee fans her face and laughs with the crowd. Finally, Griff stands up with the garter dangling from his mouth and then twirls it around his finger shouting, "You ready, boys? Who's brave enough to risk catching this thing?"

Jamie Lee's jaw drops in mock horror and when Griff turns around, she gives him a quick kick in the butt with the toe of her shoe, not hard enough to make him stumble but he pretends to almost fall down. Cameras are clicking and I'm thinking that the retelling of the events will surely be embellished.

"Wish me luck." Luke winks and then joins the circle of single men. Griff counts to three and then fakes them out. The guys boo and then jockey for position.

Jamie Lee brakes and comes over to stand by me. "Hoping Luke catches it?" she teases.

I shrug. "Makes no difference to me."

Jamie Lee gives me a yeah-right look. "I tried to get the bouquet to you but my aim wasn't too good."

"That's okay. Miss Irma is thrilled. Can you believe she could jump that high?"

Jamie Lee laughs but our attention is diverted when Griff flings the garter into the rowdy crowd. I watch as Luke jumps high but just when I think he has it, Griff's brother, Brandon, snatches it from the air with a triumphant whoop! I have to grin when I hear a collective sigh from the younger girls in the crowd. With his shaggy hair, stud earring, and armband tattoo, he has *bad boy* written all over him and the girls in Hootertown eat it up. Griff tries to keep him on the straight and narrow but it's a challenge.

"Whoo-wee," Miss Irma says with a sigh. "The boy sure would be a walk on the wild side."

Jamie Lee laughs. "Miss Irma, he's supposed to put the garter on you since you caught the bouquet." She points to the chair. "Go sit yourself down."

To my surprise Miss Irma shakes her head so hard that her hat slides even more cockeyed. "You want me to have a heart attack right here and now?"

"Oh come on!" Jamie Lee coaxes. "You're made of stronger stuff than that!"

"Yeah, right. The moment that boy would slide his hand up my bony old leg my heart would explode. If nothin' else I'd slide right outta that chair and break a hip."

Jamie Lee laughs. "Okay, we'll skip it." She hooks an arm in mine and the other one in Miss Irma's. "Let's go get us some cake before the dancin' begins."

We never do make it as far as the cake before it's announced that the wedding party is supposed to come forward for the first dance. This makes my heart pound harder since of course this means a slow dance with Luke.

When I'm sort of frozen in place Jamie Lee grabs my hand and tugs me forward. We head over toward the barn where Wet Willie's Band had set up a small stage and a fairly large, raised wooden dance floor. By this time the sun is sinking low in the sky, sending streaks of pink through the warm orange glow. Tiki torches have been lighted to keep the bugs at bay but I'm wondering if someone has forgotten to hook up the twinkling lights. I'm surprised since Daisy is so on top of everything.

When we reach the barn Griff is standing solo in the middle of the wooden floor. As soon as he sees Jamie Lee, he extends one beckoning hand in her direction. As soon as her fingers touch his, thousands of twinkling lights illuminate the night, making the simple country setting suddenly seem magical. Wet Willie is a great big, rough-looking guy but he has a velvet voice made for love songs. His smooth rendition of John Michael Montgomery's "I Swear" has tears sliding down my cheeks and I'm not the only one.

Halfway through the song Luke comes to my side.

"Mama just informed me that we're supposed to join them." When I nod my head in agreement he gives me a tender smile and wipes away a tear with the pad of his thumb. With a shaky laugh I swipe at my cheeks and then take his offered hand. Jamie Lee's mama and daddy join us and I'm pleased that Brandon asks his mama to dance too. He might be a hell-raiser but he's a good kid.

My heart thumps as fast as the wings of a hummingbird as we move in a slow circle to the beat of the music. Even though I'm in heels, the top of my head still comes only to his chin . . . not that I'd have the nerve to dance cheek to cheek anyway. His hand feels warm and possessive on my bare back and I really, *really* want to press my body to his. Of course I don't have the nerve, especially in front of all these people.

By this time Luke's Windsor tie is missing and the first few buttons of his shirt are open, giving me a nice view of tanned skin. I'm suddenly nervous not only from dancing with Luke but I'm in front of an audience, no less. When my hand trembles in his I'm totally embarrassed.

"Dance like no one is watching," Luke says in my ear.

I look up and smile, thinking, *Yeah right, that would mean plastering myself against you.* But I'm pleased that he sensed my mood and cares enough to try and calm my nerves. Trying to clear my head, I inhale a deep breath but the spicy scent of Luke's cologne only makes me want to fling my arms around his neck . . . but of course I don't.

As we sway to the music, though, his hand slowly slides up from the small of my back to meet bare skin. And it's probably my imagination but it suddenly feels as if he's holding my hand a bit tighter, pulling me in a tad closer. When my breasts brush against Luke's chest, a hot tingle shoots all the way to my pinched toes. His chest expands when he takes a deep breath and then he splays his fingers more firmly against my cool skin in what feels, *holy cow*, almost like a caress. Could he be experiencing some of the same feelings that are washing over me like warm summer rain? Do I dare move my hand from his shoulder to his neck and curl my fingers into his hair?

I'm thinking about this so hard that at first I don't realize that the song has ended until Luke starts leading me off the floor. "Thanks," he says when we reach the edge of the wooden planks.

"Anytime," I tell him, and then want to bite off my tongue. Stupid answer, I'm thinking but he smiles and leans down to give me a kiss on the cheek.

"I'll keep that in mind," he replies, and I wonder if he's flirting or just being polite. If I weren't such a wuss I would find out . . . make my move like Jamie Lee suggested. The problem here of course is that if I make my move so to speak and I get shot down, not only does it dash my dreams but it would make things forever awkward between Luke and me, and I'm not sure I want to risk that.

My pathetic musings are interrupted when Wet Willie announces that the next dance is for fathers and daughters beginning with Jamie Lee and her daddy. I look around and spot my own daddy chatting with his fishing buddies but he excuses himself and heads my way. Being a trucker means he's gone a lot, so I treasure the time I get to spend with him. He's a gruff man of few words who didn't always know the right thing to say to a young girl who lost her mama too young, but he tried his best and I love him to pieces.

"May I have this dance?" he asks with a twinkle in his eye.

I incline my head and tuck my arm in his. "You may."

"I haven't gotten the chance to tell you how lovely you look, Macy. More and more like your mama every day," he says with a warm smile edged with sadness.

"And you look handsome in your suit." I'm thankful that my voice only cracks a little.

"You know I'm not much on gettin' gussied up."

"You wear it well," I assure him. Wet Willie starts singing Tim McGraw's "My Little Girl" and I swear my gruff old daddy's eyes tear up.

"Won't be long and I'll be walking you down the aisle."

"Daddy, I have to get me a boyfriend first."

He winks at me. "Any boy would be lucky to have you, Macy-girl."

"Oh, thank you, Daddy."

"I'm not just runnin' my mouth. I mean it," he says while dancing surprisingly smoothly. When the song ends he gives me a hug. "Have some fun. I'll be leaving with the older folks in a bit. If you're drinkin', don't be drivin'."

I nod. "Luke said that I could stay here."

"Luke, huh?" he says, and rubs his chin. "Solid young man, that one. Seems to me you're gettin' on pretty good with him. You two make a fine-looking couple."

"Daddy!"

He shrugs. "Just an observation," he says as we walk to the edge of the crowd. "Don't go gettin' riled up."

"Maybe that's my problem."

Daddy stops in his tracks and gives me a questioning look. "What do you mean?"

"I tend to get all fired up once in a while. Maybe it scares the boys away," I tease.

"Don't you go changing a thing about yourself," he says with surprising firmness.

"Daddy, I was really only kiddin'."

"Were you?" he asks with more insight than I realized he has about me. "You know, your personality is a lot like your mama's too. Quiet as a church mouse but I could get her goin' in a heartbeat." He chuckles. "Used to love to get her all riled up."

"You still miss her, don't you?"

He rubs a hand down his face. "Not a day goes by . . ."

My throat closes up and I have to swipe at another doggone tear. Pretty soon there won't be a drop of moisture left in me.

"Aw, Macy, I didn't mean to get so melancholy."

I reach up and cup his chin. "Daddy, I love it when you talk about Mama. Keeps her memory alive."

"I was lucky to have her if only for a little while." He grabs my hand and squeezes it. "You go on back up there on the dance floor and kick up your heels."

"Okay." I lean in and give him a kiss on his cheek. "You all right to drive?"

"Yeah, just had a couple."

"'Kay." I watch him leave and have to wonder about his mood. I suppose weddings are hard for him. I never thought about it until now. *Oh, Mama,* I think to myself, *why'd you have to leave us so soon?* I look skyward and think of the song "Holes in the Floor of Heaven," hoping that she is looking down seeing Jamie Lee get married and me dancing with Daddy. Oh, wow . . . I inhale a shaky breath and let out a long sigh but then the thought occurs to me that even knowing what he knows now, Daddy wouldn't change a thing. Squaring my shoulders, I decide that from here on in I'm going to start living my life with no regrets. With that thought in mind I kick off my toe-pinching shoes and head to the dance floor to start whooping it up.

Dancing in a bridesmaid's dress isn't an easy task but I manage. As the night wears on the older crowd heads home, except for Miss Irma, who has amazing stamina for a woman her age. Deciding it's time for a cold-beer break, I head for a tub and fish my hand into the melting ice. A moment later Jamie Lee joins me.

"Ohmigod, Jamie Lee, look!" I point to Miss Irma, who is busting a move with Brandon, who is being good-natured about the whole thing, bless his heart.

"The crowd's thinning out," I observe. "Just the die-hards remain."

"Yeah, even Mama and Daddy called it a night."

I take a sip from my longneck and then grin. "Oh, I don't think they're calling it a night . . ."

"Ew!" Jamie Lee says in mock horror. "My parents do not have sex."

I raise my eyebrows.

"Okay, they did, but only twice. Right now they're in there snorin'."

"I think it's cute that they're still so in love."

Jamie Lee's expression softens. "Yeah, if Griff and I can be as happy as the two of them, I'll be blessed." She swallows hard and I give her a little shove.

"Do not make me cry again! My tear ducts are plumb wore out."

Jamie Lee laughs. "Hey," she says a little too casually, "have you seen Luke lately?"

I shrug.

"You gonna make your move, Macy?"

"No!"

She waggles her eyebrows. "I'll get Wet Willie to play a slow song."

"Don't you dare!" I protest, but of course it's pointless. I stand there for a minute but then think about my daddy who only had Mama for a short while. If Luke is the one for me, why wait another day? Maybe it's high time that I really do make my move.

4

What Was I Thinkin'?

With a lift of my chin I decide to locate Luke and ask him to dance. Fueled by more alcohol than I usually consume, I thump my bottle down and decide that it's about time to take matters into my own two hands. Trying not to be too obvious, I glance around but I don't spot Luke anywhere. I'm thinking I'll go in search of him, pretending to head to the bathroom, which isn't such a bad idea anyway. My heart starts to pound at the prospect of finally doing what I've wanted to do for a long time but when Jamie Lee has Wet Willie play "Stairway to Heaven," I start to lose my nerve. With a defeated moan I pick up my beer bottle, and I see Miss Irma snag Brandon again. Now, if she has the nerve to ask a guy a good fifty years her junior, then surely I can ask Luke, right?

Right! I thump my bottle down again and as if on cue I see Luke walking my way. My heart starts beating faster when I see that he's approaching me. I smile, letting him know that I was thinking the same thing and search my beer-soaked brain for something pithy to say when he asks me to dance to one of the most notorious make-out songs of junior high dances . . .

But my thumping heart sinks to my toes when I realize that Luke isn't coming toward me, because he pauses to speak to Mindy Morgan. I swallow a groan. *Mindy Morgan*. Tall, blond, and of course *skinny*, she's everything I'm not . . . Oh and did I mention she's the type of arm candy that Luke has always dated?

"What was I thinkin?" I mutter darkly, and take a long slug of beer that suddenly no longer appeals to me. If Jamie Lee were over here instead of dancing she'd tell me to get a grip and to think this situation through. But Jamie Lee's wrapped in Griff's arms . . . As a matter of fact, it seems like everyone except for me has a dance partner, including Miss Irma!

I start thinking how to remedy this intolerable situation and then it hits me. *I'll cut in.* Yeah! The doggone song lasts like ten minutes. I'll just wait here for a reasonable length of time, like a few seconds, and then politely tap skinny Mindy on her bony bare shoulder. There now, I feel pretty good about taking control of my destiny. I'll just wait a few more polite seconds before making my move. My hands are trembling a little but I can do this! After taking a deep breath I take a step toward the raised floor but just as I'm ready to step up, skinny Mindy presses her cheek to Luke's cheek, because of course, unlike me, she's tall enough to do so, and now that my feet are bare I'm even more vertically challenged.

So what, I tell myself. I consider putting on my shoes but my toes curl at the mere thought. Gritting my teeth I remain on task and take another step up until I'm actually *on* the dance floor. But then I see Mindy say something in Luke's ear, probably something flirty and sexy because he tips his head back and laughs. All-righty then . . . my bubble is burst, my nerve is gone, and to make matters even worse I see Luke look my way. God, how pathetic I must appear hovering at the edge of the dance floor, all short and sweaty.

Well . . . hell.

I decide to head to the bathroom instead of standing here looking like I belong in Loserville. But on the way I pick up my purse, scoop up my painful shoes, and head to the makeshift parking lot, hoping to catch a ride home. I know that Jamie Lee will be disappointed that I left but I'll call her and make up an excuse that I suddenly felt sick to my stomach, which unfortunately isn't far from the truth.

As luck would have it, Fred Farmer is leaving and offers to give me a ride home. Fred's name would have been funnier if he truly was a farmer but he owns the hardware store in Hootertown that's unfortunately being financially threatened by the big chains. I rent the apartment above his store from him but as soon as my lease is up I plan on moving to Jamie Lee's flat above the Cut & Curl, making my commute to work a mere walk down a flight of stairs. I haven't told Fred yet and since he's kind enough to give me a lift, I decide that now is not a good time to bring it up. He's such a nice man and always reminded me a lot of Fred Rogers. He even wears Mr. Rogers–style sweaters, moves and talks real slow, except, of course, with a Southern twang.

"You okay?" Mr. Farmer asks as we drive down the road in his big diesel truck. I know . . . it's a far cry from my earlier limo ride, when the evening held so much promise.

"Tired is all," I lie. "Mind if I open a window?" Suddenly I'm feeling a bit queasy. God, do not let me toss my cookies in Fred's truck!

"Go ahead," he says, but shoots me a worried glance. "You sure you're okay?"

"Yes, just worn out," I assure him, but then mutter a mental prayer and make a few deals with God if he will help me refrain from barfing. I will never again drink another beer as long as I live. No really, *never.* "And my feet hurt," I feel the need to add.

Fred glances at the shoes in my lap and nods but I must look a bit peaked because he steps on the gas, throwing me back against the seat. "I'll get ya home in a jiffy."

I'm a little afraid to open my mouth, so I merely nod. The twists and turns of the country are a challenge to my stomach but the wind whipping in my face helps. I take big gulps of hay-scented air and in record time Fred pulls up in front of Farmer Hardware.

"Thanks, Mr. Farmer." As I reach for the door handle I give him a smile since I'm actually feeling a teensy bit better. He looks so relieved that I almost laugh but I suddenly don't have the energy.

"No problem, Macy-girl. You take care, now. You want me to walk you up?"

"No, I'm fine."

"Okay, then." He gives me a kindhearted Mr. Rogers smile as I shut the door.

I walk up the side entrance stairs in a sad, defeated, and not quite steady way. It's not a surprise that I've forgotten to put my keys in my tiny purse but there's one be-

neath the pot of purple petunias that look about as wilted
as I feel. After tossing my purse onto the tiny kitchen
table I pour a glass of water and go back onto the landing
to water the droopy flowers, wishing it were as easy to
perk myself back up.

After slipping out of my bridesmaid's dress I carefully
hang it on a special cushy hanger and smooth out the
wrinkles. Even though I'm in a funky mood I have to
smile. "Jamie Lee is married," I whisper. I shake my head
in wonder because in some ways it's hard to believe since
she almost messed things up with Griff, but I guess sometimes things have a way of working out even though it did
take a bit of meddling on the part of her mama and me.

After slipping a Payton Panthers football shirt over my
head I sit down on my bed, thinking that I really should
call Jamie Lee and let her know what happened . . . well,
not the Luke part, but that I wasn't feeling well and all
that hogwash. With a groan I get up from the bed and
head to the kitchen and locate my phone in my purse, but
before I hit speed dial Jamie Lee is already calling me. I
can't count the number of times that's happened. Knowing that I'm going to catch some hell for leaving without
seeing her off on her honeymoon I flip my phone open
because I really do deserve to be bitched at a little anyway.

"Hello?" I say, careful to sound under the weather. I
decide to add a cough for added drama.

"Just what do you think you're doin' leavin' my wedding reception without saying good-bye?"

"I was feeling icky, Jamie Lee," I protest in a sickly
tone.

"You seemed fine earlier," she says skeptically. It's very hard to pull one over on her.

"I drank a bit too much," I explain in a whisper as though someone might overhear, even though I'm the only tenant Mr. Farmer has other than field mice that like to slip in uninvited.

Jamie Lee pauses as if she might challenge my excuse but then says, "Well, I hope you don't feel too hungover tomorrow. Hydrate and take an Advil or two," she advises in a mature I'm-married-now tone. I'm about to get a little snippy with her but then she says, "I really wanted to give you a hug good-bye."

"Don't go gettin' her upset," Griff says in the background.

"My God, Jamie Lee, you two already sound like a married couple," I tell her, and chuckle weakly. "I'm sorry that I left. I truly wasn't feeling well."

She pauses again and I just bet Griff is giving her the message not to go where she wants to go, mainly talking about Luke. "We'll discuss this later," she finally says. "By the way, you were a beautiful maid of honor." Of course her voice cracks.

"Don't you dare call me on your honeymoon, Jamie Lee! Give Griff your undivided attention, you hear me?" Of course she can since I've raised my voice to nearly shouting.

"Good advice!" Griff says loud enough so that I can hear.

"Go see to your man," I tell her.

"Macy . . ."

"I'm fine!"

"Okay, but just one thing. Mindy Morgan has been

after Luke forever. I'm sure that she asked him to dance and not the other way around."

I should have known that she had the whole thing figured out. I want to tell her to give it up but I play along. "Yeah, I shoulda shoved her skinny butt right out of the way."

"There's the attitude!"

"I would have too if I hadn't been feeling so crappy."

"Damned straight," Jamie Lee says, even though we both know that I'm telling a big fat lie.

"You know—if I hadn't been feeling crappy," I reiterate. Telling her about my actual aborted cut-in of Luke's dance would upset her on one of the most important days of her life so I decide to go for some humor. "Well, y'all make sure you get to sleep early since you have an early flight out. Jamie Lee, maybe you should take a sleeping pill, you know, to make sure you go out like a light."

Jamie Lee laughs. "Yeah, I think I'll do that." She goes quiet for a second and then says, "You know I love ya, Macy McCoy."

"I know," I answer gruffly. "Just don't go sending me a postcard sayin' that you wish I were there, you hear me?" Griff hears me too and they both laugh before she hangs up. I have to smile thinking how happy they sound. I think that Daisy might get a grandbaby sooner than she thinks. With a sigh I head into the bathroom to wash up for bed but after slipping beneath the covers, I know I'll just toss and turn while reliving the day's events. My thoughts turn to Luke and I cringe when I recall that he actually saw me hovering at the edge of the dance floor. I'm so deep in my ponderings that when my cell phone rings it startles me and I yelp. Reaching over to the night-stand I grab my phone.

Holy crap . . . it's Luke.

I contemplate not answering but it dawns on me that he's probably worried, so I pick up. "Hey there," I say a little too perkily since I'm supposed to be feeling sick.

"Macy?" Luke says. "Where are you?"

"Home." I feel a twinge of guilt at the concern I hear in his voice. "I wasn't feeling well."

"Oh, you shoulda said somethin'. Mama has a whole cabinet full of medicine for about every ailment known to man."

"It was just an upset stomach." *From seeing you dancing with Mindy Morgan.* "No biggie."

"How'd you get home?"

"Mr. Rogers . . . I mean Farmer," I admit, wishing I could say some hot guy instead.

"Oh, good, because there weren't many guys who were still okay to drive. I had a slew of 'em bunk down in the barn."

"I would never get in a car with someone who was drunk," I assure him, forgetting all about my sickly tone.

"I wouldn't think that you would."

"You just did." Oh why am I being so mean? He's just worried. I know why! I don't want his big brotherly con-cern. But still, I have no reason to be rude. "I'm sorry, Luke. I should have let you know I was leaving but when Mr. Farmer offered a ride, I took it. I think the strongest thing he had to drink was a cup of coffee."

"I was just worried. When I noticed you were gone I went inside the house looking for you, and when you weren't in Jamie Lee's bed I"—he pauses and clears his throat—"realized that . . ."

My heart starts pounding a little harder and I lean back against the headboard for support. When he fails to finish his thought I can't help myself and prompt, "You realized *what*?" My beer buzz fizzles and I suddenly go on all-systems alert. I hear Luke take a deep breath and blow it out and it suddenly hits me that he too has been drinking and that I shouldn't put too much stock in whatever he's about to tell me. Still, I want to know. "Luke?"

"I realized how much I . . ."

I grip the phone tighter but refrain from prompting him again. I can picture him running his fingers through his dark hair like he always does when he's tired or upset.

"I realized how much I care about you," he unexpectedly blurts out. My heart skips a beat but then I remind myself again that he has been partying all night.

"Thank you," I say in a silly breathless voice while wondering where he's going with this. When he fails to elaborate I decide I should try to get to the bottom of what he's really trying to say to me . . . if anything. "I care about you too."

"And you looked very . . . pretty. I don't know if I ever said that to you . . . tonight, I mean." Even though his words are a bit slurred, his voice is low and sexy.

"Th-thanks." I grip the phone tighter and swallow.

"I should have told you that before now."

"We were busy . . ."

"No, I mean before tonight."

"Luke . . ."

"Oh God. No, Macy. What am I doin'? I should shut my mouth."

"Why?"

He sighs. "Because you're *Macy.*"

Frowning, I ask, "What does that mean?"

"Everything," he says, explaining absolutely nothing.

"Luke, if there's something you want to say to me—" I begin, but he cuts me off.

"So, anyway, I'm glad you're safe and sound," he says, completely switching gears. "I'm guessin' you already talked to Jamie Lee? She was worried too."

My heart plummets and I swallow the words that were on the tip of my tongue. "Oh, so *she* sent you looking for me?"

"Yeah, but—"

"Well, I'm home all in one piece." I make a show of yawning. "So you can rest easy. Sorry for the worry. Night, Luke." Before he can say another word—and I can embarrass myself making something out of a simple *You looked pretty*—I flip my phone shut and then sit there in the darkness. "There you go again trying to read something into something that simply isn't there, at least for Luke," I whisper. After another long sigh I lean over and place the phone on my nightstand, telling myself that I have everything under control. Still, for a minute there I thought he was going to say something . . . wonderful. "Ahhh! Stop!" With an exasperated groan I punch the pillow. "Just *stop*!"

My eyes tear up but before I can start wallowing once again I remind myself that I love my job and have friends and family who care deeply and a daddy who might be on the road a lot but who adores me too. I need to quit feeling so doggone sorry for myself.

The Carters have been like family, and I love them to

pieces but it's high time I start living my life on my own terms. Jamie Lee is my best friend but she's moving on with her life. After snuggling beneath the covers I vow to give up this obsession I have with Luke as well.

Surely there's got to be some adventure out there for me too?

With that thought in mind I close my eyes, hoping that fatigue and alcohol will put me fast asleep. My last thought though is that if adventure doesn't come to Hootertown, then maybe I need to go out there and find it. Yes, I do believe that it's high time for a little less talk and a lot more action.

5

The Sooner the Better

"Hey Macy, are you coming over for chicken dinner?" Daisy asks as I'm walking out of church. I'm trying to hurry to my Blazer so I don't have to face Luke.

"Mrs. Carter, aren't you worn out after last night's festivities?" Not that she appears tired. No, Daisy Carter looks lovely in a crisp buttercup yellow dress. Not one strand of auburn hair is out of place and her makeup is a tad over-the-top but perfectly applied. I marvel at how she does it.

"Oh, I'm fine." She waves a dismissive hand. "A crew came over and cleaned everything up."

"I don't want you to go to any trouble. You need to relax today."

"A person still has to eat." She pats my shoulder.

"I appreciate your offer," I tell her with a warm smile. "But I'm still a bit tired." I pick up my pace trying to put some distance between Luke and us.

"Are you feeling okay?" Daisy inquires with a frown.

"Luke said that you were under the weather and left the reception early."

"Oh, I'm okay. I just overdid it a bit," I assure her, and force another smile. "But I think I'll just watch a movie and be lazy today."

"Okay." Daisy relents but looks at me a bit more closely, as if she doesn't quite believe my story. "But my offer stands if y'all change your mind. And you know your daddy's always welcome too."

"I believe he's fishing today but thank you." I lean over and give her a quick kiss on her powder-soft cheek but then quickly dig in my purse for my keys since I see Luke and Mr. Carter heading in our direction. Luckily Daisy spots Rose Jenkins and excuses herself. My keys of course are hiding from me somewhere in the mess in my purse. I make a mental note to clean out the junk this afternoon.

I'm so intent on my task and getting a little perturbed that I don't notice Luke approach me. "There you are, dammit," I snap when my fingers finally find the illusive set of keys.

"Well good morning to you too," Luke says, startling me into dropping the key chain. When I bend over to retrieve them Luke does as well and we bump heads. "Sorry!" he says while rubbing his head. "You okay?"

That's a loaded question but I give him a polite smile while rubbing my head as well. "I'll live. Maybe I needed some sense knocked into me," I tease, proud that I'm holding myself together.

"Me too," he says, but instead of laughing, his blue eyes seem serious. I'm wondering if he's remembering our confusing conversation from last night and I'm not sure what to make of it but then give myself a mental shake not to go there again. "Are you comin' over for Mama's chicken?"

Wow, he sounds hopeful, I think to myself but then shake my head. You know, I really wish I could kick my own butt. When he hands me my keys I totally ignore the tingle when his fingers brush against mine.

"Oh, I thought Mama invited you."

For a second I'm perplexed but then realize that Luke thought I was shaking my head in answer to his question and not at my own stupid self. "She did but I'm still a bit under the weather. I think I'll pop a movie in and chill for the day."

"You want company?"

I'm so unprepared for this question that the keys slip from my fingers again and land with a jangle in the parking lot.

"Got 'em," Luke warns so we don't bump heads again. As he hands them back to me he says, "Well?"

"Well, what?" I ask like an idiot.

"Would you like some company watching a movie?"

I grip my keys as though they're suddenly a lifeline. A big part of me—well okay, all of me—really wants to shout *Yes!* but I know or at least I *think* he's doing this out of concern and not the need to spend time with me, so I force myself to shake my head. "That's okay, Luke. I'll probably just end up falling asleep on the sofa anyway."

"Okay," he says quietly. Something flickers in his eyes that I can't read . . . hurt? Disappointment? Regret pools in my stomach and I almost change my mind. As if sensing my indecision he says, "I'll bring over some leftover chicken."

Be strong, Macy. "I appreciate the offer." I hate that I might have injured his feelings. "But I'm fine, really," I assure him, and place my hand on his forearm that's leaning against my Blazer. The sensation of his sun-warmed skin beneath my hand sends such a thrill through me that I snatch my hand away and feel the heat of a blush warm my cheeks.

"All right, then," Luke says, but threads his fingers through his hair, making me wonder if he's trying to think of a reason to change my mind. I don't probe, however, since I've vowed not to obsess over him any longer. It's just not healthy to moon over a guy whom I have no chance with. I'm too darned old to crush on my best friend's brother but when he hesitates for another fraction, my heart betrays my vow by beating fast. "If you change your mind give me a call," he offers as I slide behind the wheel.

"Thanks, Luke. I'll remember that," I assure him, knowing full well that I would never muster up the nerve to call and invite him over. When he nods slowly and then turns away I feel an odd sense of loss. I'm struck again with the notion that there's something going on here that I'm missing and I suddenly feel as if there's an important reason that I should call him back. But then I close my door with a click while muttering hotly, "Macy McCoy, you are one crazy chick. Luke is just a nice guy with a Southern sense of polite concern for a family friend." The sooner I get that through my thick skull the better off I'll be.

After arriving back at my apartment I take off my church clothes and slip into my favorite ratty jeans shorts and a hot pink T-shirt that reads WHATEVER. Jamie Lee bought it for me when I used that word so often that it drove her crazy. I tend to latch on to a word and use it to death. *Whatever* . . .

But after trying my best to relax on the couch with a Diet Dew and baked potato chips—I know, ew, they just don't cut it—I get antsy. Telling myself to chill, I channel surf but nothing captures my attention for more than a few seconds. Maybe it's because the devil on my shoulder keeps telling me to call Luke and invite him over. Finally I give up and decide to drive down to the Cut & Curl and do something constructive even though it's a Sunday afternoon. There probably won't be much for me to do since the part-time stylist we hired, Daisy, will be there. She usually works only one day a week to keep her longtime clients happy, but will still be filling in during Jamie Lee's absence.

The familiar beauty shop smells make me smile when I open the door but the shop feels almost eerily quiet, so I turn on some country music to fill the silence. While humming along with Dierks Bentley, I'm trying to remember if I've ever been in here by myself as I tidy up the shelves of hair products and tanning lotions. We added tanning beds last summer and Jamie Lee is even toying with the idea of having Griff build on to the shop. I feel proud of the business we've created and I enjoy what I do, but I'll never be more than the hired help.

Odd that this never really bothered me until now but I suppose it's just the mood that I'm in. With a sigh I start arranging nail polish by color. Luckily the sassy Tammy Turner song "Just Watch Me" comes on and starts to lighten my mood. At first I just hum but then really get into the song and begin to sing rather loudly. I grab a nearby broom and use the handle for a microphone while belting out the refrain. My eyes are closed as I bring the song home, do a little booty shake for good measure, and then add my own little whoop with my fist in the air at the end.

When I hear applause, at first I think it's a fantasy in my head that I'm singing before a large adoring audience. This wouldn't be the first time I've had this particular wishful thinking. But when I open my eyes I grip the broom tighter and mouth, *Ohmigod* since my voice totally fails me. All I can manage is a little squeak. I blink and think that maybe this is the aftereffect of a night of heavy drinking.

"Well now, that was pretty doggone good! I loved that move at the very end."

"T-T—" I squeak, I point, I swallow, and then mouth, *Ohimgod* again.

"Tammy Turner," she says, and extends her hand.

"M-Macy McCoy," I manage to stutter.

"Are y'all open for business? I have a bit of a hair emergency," says the one and only Tammy Turner who is standing right here, right now in the Cut & Curl! I glance out the window and there's a huge tour bus parked out front. Two big men who must be her bodyguards are standing just outside the door. Their tree-trunk arms are folded across massive chests as they watch from behind mirrored sunglasses. Not that there's likely to be a ruckus on Sunday morning in Hootertown but *wow* wouldn't it be cool to have a bodyguard? A person could say whatever they felt like and let the big burly dudes take care of the matter with a flex of muscle and a steely-eyed glare.

"Well?" Tammy asks in a patient tone but I'm trying

unsuccessfully to make my brain and mouth work together. "Look, I know it's Sunday but I'll be *ever* so grateful if you could help a girl out."

Thankfully I manage to nod—kind of a nervous jerky nod but I get my point across because Tammy raises her hands upward and says, "Ah, praise the Lord." A white cowboy hat is hiding her jet-black hair so I'm not quite sure what I'm getting myself into. All of a sudden my palms start to sweat.

Okay, I take a deep breath, give my head a little shake, and attempt to put on my professional face. "What exactly is your emergency, Ms. Turner?" I ask in a crisp tone that's only a little bit shaky.

"You mean just what am I hidin' under this here hat?" Tammy asks with a grin. She's gorgeous in a don't-mess-with-me Gretchen Wilson kind of way and, like Gretchen, her songs are both in-your-face anthems for women and sweet love songs that bring tears to your eyes. She whips the hat off her head, and I don't mean to yelp but I instinctively do. Embarrassed by my outburst, I clamp my hand over my mouth.

"I know," Tammy says with a grimace. "Damned hair extensions! I cheated and used regular shampoo and half of the damned things fell out! And the kicker is that I have to be in Nashville to do an interview on *Country Music Minutes* in a little over two hours." With her eyebrows raised she holds up her index and middle fingers. "Please help me, Macy. I'll make it worth your while."

Lowering my hand from my mouth I confess, "We don't do hair extensions here." Jamie Lee and I looked into it but hair extensions run hundreds, sometimes thousands of dollars!

Tammy shoves her hands in the back pockets of her low-rise jeans. "You don't need to replace them. Just remove the rest and then style my hair. Think you can hop on the bus and do that for me?"

"H-hop on the bus?" I glance out the window.

"We don't have time to do it here."

"May I take a look?"

"Sure." Tammy nods and then dips her head since she's a few inches taller than me.

"Oh, my, they're like glued on with hard little suction tips."

Tammy sighs. "I know. It took the stylist three and a half hours to put the doggone things in." She raises one dark eyebrow. "I'm not good at sittin' still, let me tell ya." With another long sigh she rocks back on the heels of her boots. "I was supposed to use this special shampoo so the extensions wouldn't slip off my real hair, but the stuff didn't lather, you know?" She wrinkles up her nose. "Felt like I wasn't getting my hair clean so I broke the rules and used real shampoo." She grins at me and explains in a low tone, "I tend to break rules. Not always a good idea." Her grin is infectious and I find myself relaxing just a tad. "Well, whad'ya think?"

"I don't have the product they use to get them out but I think soaking your hair in deep conditioner will loosen the connection and allow the extensions to slip off with minimal damage to your hair. Although I have to tell you that I'll need to trim up the damaged ends. Do you trust me to cut your hair?"

"Well sugar, I'm in a bit of a pickle. My hair and makeup chick had the nerve to go into labor," she explains with a laugh. "If she had been on the bus I wouldn't have gotten away with using regular shampoo. You're a licensed beautician, right?"

I nod. "We're small but we keep current."

"Good enough for me. I'm a small-town girl myself. I'd be right at home gettin' my hair done here. Don't tell anybody but I would rather have my hair done here than by some of the snooty people I have to deal with." She jabs her thumb over her shoulder toward the tour bus. "You ready to go?"

I glance down at my worn shorts, my WHATEVER T-shirt, and my flip-flops.

Tammy waves a hand at me. "You're fine. Looks like something I'd wear. Just get the tools of your trade and hop on the bus. Oh, you might want to pack an overnight bag. Just in case. Or do you have to get back tonight?"

"N-no," I answer as I gather up my things. "We're closed on Mondays so I'm good to go." *Holy crap!* "Just let me run into my apartment and I'll throw some stuff in a bag. It's just right down the street on the way out of town."

"Fair enough," Tammy says as she puts her hat back on. "Let's get a move on."

When I stand there with my duffel bag sort of dumbfounded and wondering if this is really happening, Tammy links her arm through mine. "Oh, *quit*. I grew up in a town about the size of Hootertown." She laughs and says, "Hootertown. What a name, huh?" While hauling me toward the door, she adds, "Listen, it's hard when you make it in this business to stay grounded. I do try to remember my roots but if I start to act like a spoiled diva, just give me a good whack upside the head."

"Okay," I assure her, knowing full well there's a snowball's chance in hell of my actually doing that. I lock up and give a tentative smile to the big burly guys. The bald one takes my duffel bag and carries it for me. Cool. Protection *and* service, not to mention that they're both really hot in a badass kind of way.

"You think I'm kiddin', don't ya?"

"Um . . . yeah."

"Well, okay, I am. But I do try to stay grounded," Tammy says, climbing up the steps and entering the bus.

"Yeah right, she's a demanding diva," counters a cute little blonde who looks up from a tabloid. "Says here that you're dating Jason Aldean." She snorts. "Yeah right, in your dreams."

"In *his* dreams," Tammy shoots back, and then turns to me. "Macy, meet Lilly Mason, my friend since forever and backup singer. Maybe you can do something with *her* hair."

Lilly reaches up and pats her short layers. "Not everyone has to fall into the stereotype of big Southern hair."

Tammy rolls her brown eyes. "She always did march to the beat of a different drummer. Speaking of which—"

"Don't even go there," Lilly warns.

"You mean you and Keith haven't kissed and made up?"

"When hell freezes over," she says, and starts rapidly flipping through the magazine.

Tammy turns to me. "She might not have big hair but she's big on drama."

"Bite me," Lilly says without looking up.

While shaking her head Tammy grins. "Her sister is much nicer."

"Bite me again."

"Prettier and younger too."

"Yeah well, I'm a better singer than her. Better than you too."

I look at Tammy, wondering if she's getting angry but she just laughs. "Where is Sam anyway?"

Lilly shrugs. "Sleeping, I think."

"Stayed up late workin' on that song, didn't she."

"Yup. I told her to give it up but you know how well she listens."

"Okay, Macy, follow me to the bathroom where you can fix this mess that once was my hair." She wrinkles her nose. "Well, it was someone else's hair too. I never could get used to the idea of havin' somebody's hair hangin' from my head." With a drawn-out sigh she adds, "Sometimes I can't believe the things I let myself get talked into."

"You ready to push off, Ms. Turner?" asks the driver.

"Yep, Pete. Let's hit the road."

"Everyone accounted for?" he asks, looking up into the rearview mirror.

Tammy gestures for me to follow her down the aisle. "Anyone not here raise your hand," she says, getting a laugh or two. I notice that most of her crew's sleeping in the cushy seats. We're almost to the bathroom when Tammy stops and turns to me. "Oh, you need to stop and pick up a few things at your apartment, right?"

"Yes, thanks, I almost forgot."

"Go tell Pete when to stop. I'll be waiting in the bathroom until you get back, but hurry. We're kind of in a rush," she says calmly, but I guess she's used to this kind of pressure.

"I'll make it quick," I promise, and walk on rather

wobbly legs back to the front of the bus. This whole thing feels surreal and I keep wondering if I'm dreaming and suddenly going to wake up. "Here, Pete," I tell him a moment later when we're in front of Farmer Hardware. "I'll be back in a jiffy."

While digging my keys out of my purse I hurry up the steps to my apartment. Once inside I dash to my bedroom and toss fresh underwear, my best jeans, and a nice white blouse into an overnight bag. As an afterthought I add a white skirt and leather sandals in case I need to get more dressed up for whatever reason. After grabbing some toiletries I slip them into a cosmetic case and run for the door but pause to catch my breath at the top of the landing. When I see the big bus parked out front my heart skips a beat.

"Wow," I marvel beneath my breath. "Maybe my adventure I've been wanting has just begun."

6

Big Timin'

The bathroom is small yet bigger than I expected, but then again this bus is total luxury. Although I'm still in an I-can't-believe-this-is-happening-to-me state of mind since here I am slathering intense conditioner on Tammy Turner's head while she sits on her closed commode, I concentrate on the task at hand. Tammy carries on a constant stream of conversation, asking me about my life and acts as if my boring, normal existence is interesting. I know she's trying to calm my nerves and I think it's real sweet of her. It's natural for me to talk while I work, so I try to forget who she is and to treat her as I normally would any client, so I tell her all about Jamie Lee's wedding. I'm kind of amazed at how easy she is to talk to.

"So, tell me more about Luke," Tammy says while I slide my fingers through her slippery hair.

"Luke?" I ask casually. "There's not much to tell."

"Bull feathers. I can tell by the way you say his name that you're into him. Spill, Macy."

My fingers go still for a moment. "Am I that transparent?"

With a small shrug she says, "Mmmm, probably not to most people. Because I write most of my own songs I try to be perceptive, especially where relationships are concerned. I want listeners to be able to relate to the words, ya know? There's been many a time when a certain song has helped me through a rough patch in my life. It's my fondest wish that I do that for others."

I nod because I know exactly what she means. "I bet that writing the lyrics is cathartic too."

"Oh sure," she agrees with a grin. "Definitely. I'm thinkin' it's what kept Sam up all night long."

"Lilly's sister?"

"Yep. She's five years younger than Lilly and me." She shakes her slathered head. "That girl is hell on wheels. She always goes for the bad-boy types and you can't tell her any different. Most of her songs end up being like Miranda Lambert's 'Kerosene'."

I chuckle as some of the extensions start to slip off. "Yeah, those leather-jacket types are hard for some girls to resist. Griff's younger brother, Brandon, is like that. He's got trouble written all over him and the girls in Hootertown eat it up with a spoon."

"Yeah, I tend to go for the rough-around-the-edges types myself," Tammy admits. "I think I'm gonna go after a nerd next time around," she says with a laugh. "Hey, that just might make for a fun song. 'Next Time Around I'm Goin' for a Nerd.' Whad'ya think?"

While wiping drips of conditioner from her neck with a fluffy white towel I say, "I think it would be a riot. Just think of the hilarious music video you could do."

"My God Macy, you're so right," she says, tilting her head so that she can grin at me. "I just might have to keep you around. Think I could steal you away from . . . what was your beauty shop called?"

"The Cut and Curl." I know she's just teasing but a little thrill shoots through me when I think to myself: *What if she wasn't?* But then I give myself a mental shake, knowing full well that I could never leave Hootertown. Just who am I kidding? With a deep intake of breath I slip the rest of the extensions from Tammy's hair and toss them in the sink. "Okay, I need to rinse your hair and then trim up the ends but not with the bus moving. Could you ask Pete to pull into a rest stop for just a few minutes?"

"I can see how that might not be wise." Tammy pulls her cell phone from her pocket and glances at the time. "Okay, but we need to make it quick. Just shape me up the best that you can so I'm presentable for the interview." She calls Pete on an intercom and tells him to pull over at the next rest stop, which I know will be coming up as soon as we cross over into Tennessee. "I think I'll wear my hat so you don't have to be too concerned about my hair."

"Okay," I tell her with a smile, but I wonder if it's a polite way of telling me that she doesn't trust my skills. While running my fingers through her conditioned tresses I decide to give her a few more layers to add some lift and bounce. She has thick, beautiful hair but I would love to texturize it a bit to thin it out. The problem is that I don't know if I have the nerve to suggest it to Tammy. Holy cow, what if I messed up? I would just die! After another deep breath I clear my throat. "You have nice thick hair,"

I comment while squeezing excess conditioner from her extension-free locks.

"Thanks. It tends to get unruly on me though."

My heart starts pounding but I force myself to say, "Would you mind if I style it a bit? Give you some lift and bounce?" I scoop the extensions out of the sink so I can rinse her hair. I'm sure she has some fancy-pants stylist and here I am giving her advice.

Tammy laughs. "Can you add some lift and bounce in a couple of other places while you're at it?" she asks before dipping her head beneath the stream of water.

"Oh stop. You're gorgeous!" I tell her while rinsing her hair in the small sink.

"Yeah, well, I have a personal trainer who works me like a dog and I still struggle with my weight." The running water muffles her voice, but I understand her frustration. When I'm satisfied that her hair is rinsed clean I squeeze the excess water and then begin towel drying. "It doesn't help that I eat and sleep at odd hours."

"Yeah but you must burn about a million calories performing."

"True enough," she says with a nod, "but don't ask Pete how many times I make him stop at an IHOP for strawberry pancakes at about two thirty in the morning. When it comes to eating I like real honest-to-goodness, stick-to-your-ribs food. Unfortunately, it tends to stick to my butt instead."

"I hear ya. My willpower just isn't that strong." I nod in sympathy. "I've tried every diet that comes down the pike but nothing seems to work for me."

Tammy makes a shooing motion. "Come on, you have a cute shape, Macy. Bein' skinny as a rail is overrated.

Now give me a high five," she insists with a grin. "And I do believe that Pete's stopped the bus. Get out your tools and start snipping away."

"Oh, okay." Even though Tammy is doing her best to put me at ease as I unzip my duffel bag, I notice to my horror that my hands are trembling. Not a good thing when working with scissors. "Um . . . I'm not so sure I can do this."

"Macy McCoy," Tammy says firmly, "just how many haircuts have you done over the years?"

Shrugging I say, "I don't know . . . lots."

"Why am I any different?"

"Because you're Tammy Turner. I sing your songs in the shower."

Tammy laughs. "In the shower, huh?"

"Okay, that was awkward," I say with a nervous snicker. "I sing in my car too. Really loud." I flex my fingers, hoping to stop the trembling. From outside of the bathroom I hear bantering, laughter, and music, and I remind myself that to these people this is a business, their life. I also know that this is an opportunity not to screw up.

"Look Macy, I might be Tammy Turner, country singer celebrity, but in reality I'm just a small-town girl like you. While I know I'm lucky as hell to be where I'm at, I miss being . . . *me*, if that makes any sense."

I nod because it does. "Fame comes with a price," I say as I tie a towel around her shoulders and then start combing her hair.

"You betcha. Pretty much as you might imagine. Friends walk on eggshells around me. Long-lost cousins have come out of the woodwork. And ya know what I'd dearly love is a date with a regular Joe. But do you think men will approach me?"

"Um . . . I suppose not. They must be intimidated by your success."

"Yeah, I guess," she says with a tired sigh. "Plus I'm on the road so much. I don't mean to sound like a poor little rich girl but I fully admit that sometimes it just blows. Sometimes when I've been on the road forever I wonder if it's all worth it."

"Really?"

Tammy lifts her towel-covered shoulders in a shrug. "Nah," she jokes with a grin, but something in her expressive brown eyes suggests differently. "Now quit your sniveling about bein' nervous and cut my doggone hair. Make me bea-u-ti-ful."

Of course I have to laugh and before long Tammy has me relaxing again. After trimming the damaged ends from her shoulder-length hair I add layers and texture while hoping that she will love the end result. While I'm not doing anything revolutionary and I'm still anxious as hell, I do know with a measure of pride that even though I'm just a small-town beautician, Jamie Lee and I have always strived for excellence. I might not work in an upscale salon but I'd pit my skills up against just about anyone . . . well anyway that's what I bravely tell myself as I trim Tammy's split ends.

Knowing that time is of the essence I work swiftly, forgetting to be aflutter about who she is until I'm finished and it's time to do some styling. "I'm done trimming, so you can tell Pete to head on down the road."

"Excellent." Tammy pushes an intercom button and instructs Pete to get a move on. She scoots around on the commode lid and looks at her reflection while running her fingers through her hair. "God, it feels good to be rid of those extensions." She shakes her head as she meets my eyes in the mirror. "Never again!"

I laugh as I slide my fingers to the ends of her hair, making sure she's cut evenly on both sides of her head. "You want me to blow-dry and style you?"

"Yeah, why don't you do that? Maybe I won't have to wear the cowboy hat after all."

"Okay, I'm going to give you some volume but flip it out a bit on the ends. It's a little different look for you but I think it's fun and sassy just like you." I meet her eyes in the mirror. "Sound good?"

"Go for it, girlfriend."

"You got it." As I spray some root boost and then start styling, it occurs to me that Tammy would be an amazing friend to have. It must be hard to be on the road so often, but I suppose the band and crew become a family of sorts. "Lilly seems like she's a lot of fun," I comment after turning the blow-dryer off.

"Yeah, she keeps me grounded. I'm lucky to have a close friend on the road with me. Believe me, it takes us both to keep Sam in line."

"Stop talking about me," protests a husky voice that belongs to a petite blonde who pops her head in the door. "Hey, cool haircut. It's about time you did something different."

Tammy looks up at Sam. "Hair extensions weren't different?"

Sam rolls her big blue eyes. "All those did was make your hair longer. You needed some updating. I like this a lot. Makes you way younger."

"Then I must look twelve, right?"

Sam snorts. "Yeah right."

"I love your cut," I tell her. She has the Posh Spice long, swept-over bangs and hair layered short on the sides and back.

"Thanks," she responds in her husky voice. I notice dark smudges beneath her eyes as though she's indeed had a sleepless night. "See Tammy, my haircut isn't goofy."

"I didn't say it was *goofy* . . . I said *different*."

"What*ever*," Sam responds, and then points to my WHATEVER shirt. "Ahh . . . love the shirt. I need one of those."

"Would be better than some of the ones you wear." Sam opens her mouth but Tammy points a finger at her. "Don't you dare say *Bite me* like your sister did."

Sam's dark blond eyebrows shoot up and she points at her own chest. "Me?" she innocently squeaks. "Would I do that?"

"In a heartbeat."

Sam's low chuckle sounds tired. "Hey, you gonna be outta here soon? I gotta go."

Tammy glances at me in question.

"Almost done. I just need to find my hair spray." After digging around in my duffel bag I find my favorite fine-mist spray. "This stuff is awesome. Holds the style without the stickiness and adds a bit of shine." I fluff her hair, add a few more touches, trim here and there, and then mist her hair to hold the style. "What do you think?" My heart pounds while I wait for her answer.

"Sexy," Sam says from the doorway. "Maybe you'll finally get—," she begins, but Tammy stops her with a look.

"Don't even go there."

"Colin is so into you, Tammy . . ."

"He's not my type and you know it," Tammy argues, but she fidgets a little, making me wonder if Sam hit a nerve.

Sam raises her palms in the air. "Right . . . he's talented, smart, polished, and nice as can be."

"Really, now. This is coming from the queen of bad-boy chasers."

"We're not talking about *me*."

I'm watching this like a game of tennis while wondering who is going to win the match.

"We're not talking about me either." Tammy shakes her head and I'm pleased to see that her hair swings nicely just brushing her shoulders. Bounce and lift . . . I did my job.

Sam leans against the door frame. "The man is crazy for you, Tammy."

Tammy rolls her eyes. "Colin Reed doesn't know how to get crazy. Come on, Sam, the man is much too laid back for me. And he's so . . . I don't know . . . *sensitive*. I mean, look at the lyrics he writes!"

"Right, love songs. The last one made even *you* cry." Sam sighs. "God, I bet he'd be amazing in bed . . . all caring and *giving*." She nods. "Yeah, I'm certain he'd be a giver. I just bet he'd make sure—"

"Sam!"

"What?" she asks, palms up in the air. "You know you've thought about it."

"I have not," she protests hotly, but a light pink blush

stains her cheeks. "You know me. I like rugged men. Colin's long hair and little hoop earring just don't do it for me."

"Yeah well, he'd do it for me," Sam says casually, and Tammy flashes her a look of warning. "Ha! I knew that'd get ya. Quit kiddin' yourself. Don't lie. You want him."

"Are you finished badgering me?"

Sam pushes away from the door frame. "For now. Hey, y'all finished? My bladder is about to burst."

Tammy looks at me. "All done?"

I nod and then hesitantly ask, "Do you really like it?"

"Yeah," she says with a slow smile. "I do. You know your stuff, Macy McCoy."

"You're not just sayin' that, are you?"

Sam snorts. "Believe me, if Tammy hated her hair you'd know it."

"Just shut *up*," Tammy says while I remove the towel tied around her neck.

"Bite me," Sam says in a singsong voice, but then squeals when Tammy jumps up and grabs for her.

"I'm gonna kick your butt!" When she chases Sam down the center aisle I poke my head out the bathroom door and watch while shaking my head. No one pays much attention to the two of them, making me think that this is a common occurrence.

"You and what army?" Sam laughs as she ducks into a seat. "Stop, you're gonna make me pee my pants!"

"Would serve you right!" Tammy says, but laughs as she lets her go.

"Yeah, well, I don't wear Depends, like you," she says, and then squeals when Tammy acts as though she's coming after her again.

Ducking back into the bathroom I quickly scoop up my tools while I hear Sam thundering down the aisle. "Ohmigod, lemme in," she pleads with a giggle. "Too many Mountain Dews!"

I quickly brush past her knowing full well the effect that too many Dews have on a person. Tammy heads in my direction and says, "I'm going to change my clothes. We're almost to Nashville. I want you to come into the studio with me, okay? Someone there will do my makeup but I want you to touch up my hair." I nod but my eyes must be as big as moon pies because she says, "Don't look so freaked out, Macy. Relax and have some fun. Just have a seat until we arrive. Oh, and if you need a snack or a drink, just help yourself, okay?"

"Sure, thanks."

"I should be thanking *you*. I sure would've hated to arrive with half a head of hair. Someone would have snapped my picture and rumors would have started that I went off the deep end like Britney Spears. I'd have been thrown into rehab and I barely drink."

I laugh. "Glad to be of service."

When she disappears into the back bedroom I slide into a seat and stare out the window without really seeing the landscape pass by. It suddenly occurs to me that no one really knows where I'm at, but then again I can't think of anybody who is expecting me anywhere today anyhow. It's kind of a bummer that no one is really going to miss me, but I don't want to ruin my adventure by dwelling on anything crappy. For a moment I consider calling Jamie Lee but I don't want the crew to overhear my conversation, so I decide to wait until later when I know I'll be bursting with news to share. It might be her honeymoon but she'd want to know about my little . . . okay *big* adventure.

Wow . . . I woke up this morning just like any other morning and yet somehow I ended up on Tammy Turner's tour bus doing her hair. I suppose it goes to show that you just don't know what life's going to throw at you, so you had better be ready.

Well, I'm ready!

I think . . .

7

Ready or Not

Rushing into the Country Music Channel studios with only thirty minutes to spare has me a nervous wreck but Tammy and her entourage are perfectly at ease with the situation. With my heavy duffel bag hefted over my shoulder and my short-legged stride I'm struggling to keep up. My flip-flops slap against the hard marble floor and when I start to breath rather hard, Boone, the bald bodyguard says, "Here, gimme that."

"Oh, thanks!" My big bag looks amazingly small in his clutches but when I look up to give him a grateful smile he's got his I'm-a-badass-bodyguard expression going on, so I only get a sharp nod in return. I get the feeling that he's a big teddy bear beneath the I-could-crush-you-like-a-twig exterior . . . but if I were a dude I wouldn't want to cross him. Boone takes his job very seriously. We're hurrying way too fast for me to take it all in, but the chrome, glass, and lush green plants remind me that I'm not in Kansas anymore. Although I managed to change from my tattered shorts into my jeans, I wish I were wearing something more professional. At Sam's insistence I'm still wearing my WHATEVER T-shirt and now I wish I were in my skirt and blouse.

"Right this way!" A no-nonsense receptionist leads us to a waiting room that she calls the green room even though the walls are painted a soft yellow. I don't have time to ponder this because Tammy and I are whisked down the hallway for her hair and makeup session.

"Hey, Tammy!" says a perky woman with a warm smile. She looks to be thirty-something but her skin is so flawless that it's hard to tell. She gestures toward a tall director's chair surrounded by a three-way mirror illuminated by large round bulbs. "Have a seat."

"Make me pretty, Carrie," Tammy says with a wink.

"You're already pretty."

"Then make me gorgeous."

"She's not a miracle worker," Lilly comments dryly as she enters the room.

When Tammy flips Lilly the bird, Carrie merely laughs, so I suppose she knows them all well. "Guess you came in to get some much-needed pointers," Tammy tosses back.

"Actually, I did," Lilly admits, and then turns to me. "Carrie is an amazing makeup artist. I learn something new every time we come here."

"Where's Sam?" Tammy asks.

Lilly rolls her eyes. "Curled up on the sofa in the green room, fast asleep."

"Wow, who did your hair?" Carrie asks Tammy as she starts applying brown eyeliner.

My heart starts beating hard when I wonder if she

means *wow* in a good way. Tammy jabs her thumb in my direction. "Oh, I forgot to introduce you to Macy McCoy. She came to my rescue when I had a bit of a hair emergency."

Lilly snickers. "Yeah, I'd say so."

Tammy pauses to pull a face at Lilly. "Cindy, my regular stylist who goes on the road with me, went into labor. Without her around I cheated and washed my hair with regular shampoo. Low and behold my extensions started slipping off and well, let's just say I was quite a sight."

"Oh my!" Carrie makes a tsk-tsk noise with her tongue. "Doesn't sound pretty." She looks over at me. "Hi Macy. Nice to meet you. Love, love, *love* the cut you gave Tammy. Fun and flirty! The flipped-out ends are too cute. What salon do you work for?" she asks as she turns back to her task.

"Um . . . the Cut and Curl in Hootertown." I nibble on the inside of my lip, waiting for her reaction.

"Oh, what a quaint little town." She snaps her fingers and says, "Y'all had an amazing football team last year. I remember reading about some hotshot coach who turned the program around." She flicks me a glance. "What was his name? Luke something or other?"

"Your Luke, Macy?" Tammy asks with a gasp.

"The Panther's football coach is your BF?" Carrie asks while smoothing blush across Tammy's cheekbones with a big, fat brush. "I heard rumors that Vandy is after him."

"He's my best friend's brother. Not my BF."

"Hmmm . . . I seem to remember from his picture that he's quite the hottie," Carrie comments. "You lucky girl!"

"Yeah, he is," I admit in a small voice. "But he's just a friend. Luke's a legend in Hootertown. Way outta my

league. I'm sure I never even cross his mind, you know,
like *that*."

"Whoa now, back up a minute," Lilly chimes in. "Did
you just say that you're not good enough for some guy?"

Well . . . ," I begin, but don't know what to say. "Not
exactly, but come on, you know what I mean."

"Watch out," Tammy warns. "You just got Lilly's
panties in a twist."

"Not exactly, huh?" Lilly angles her spiky head at me.
"Please tell me that you don't really believe that some
guy no matter who he is could be out of your league."

"Yeah, come on, Macy," Carrie says. "You're a cutie-
pie. What gives?"

"Nothin'." I lick my lips for a second. "He's just, you
know . . . *Luke*," I finish lamely.

"And what are you, chopped liver?" Lilly demands.

"Ew," Carrie says. "Chopped liver is gross."

"Exactly!" Lilly slaps her thigh.

"Stop badgering the girl," Tammy protests, "and let
her touch up my hair."

Glad to have something to do, I unzip my duffel bag
and locate my comb and hair spray. My phone that I
tossed in there startles me when it rings. I'm about to let
it go but Tammy says, "Hey, go ahead and answer it. I
don't want anybody to think you've gotten kidnapped."

"Ohmigod," I tell them as I pick up the phone. "It's
Luke!"

"Answer it!" they demand in unison.

I stare at the phone for a second, then flip it open.
"Hey," I say in a soft, shaky voice. I'm fully aware that all
eyes are on me.

"How you doin'?" Luke asks.

"Okay."

"Good, I'm glad to hear it. Say listen, I know you declined but I'd like to stop over and pick you up for dinner."

My heart beats faster. Maybe he cares more than I thought?

"Mama's been after me to get you over here."

"Oh . . . she has?" Okay, now my heart plummets. When will I ever learn?

"Yeah, and you know how she gets when she doesn't get her way. You don't want to put me through that, do you?" he says in a teasing tone. "Come on and say yes."

"Well, sorry but I'm, um, in Nashville." I glance over at Tammy who grins.

"Nashville? What for?"

"Well . . . I'm styling Tammy Turner's hair before her interview on *Country Music Minutes*."

Luke pauses and then says, "You're joking, right? You don't really expect me to tell Mama that, do you?"

"No, *really*, I'm in the Country Music Channel studio right now."

"Hand over the phone," Tammy says, and wags her fingers at me. When I hesitate Lilly pries the phone from my fingers and tosses it to Tammy. Carrie puts a hand over her mouth and looks at me with big eyes.

"Hey Luke. Tammy Turner, here. How's it goin'?" She pauses while he answers. "Good . . . good. Heard you're a helluva football coach." She pauses again. "Well the best of luck with this next season. I'd love to come to Hootertown and sing the national anthem if you'll have me." She grins and then winks at me. "No, I'm serious."

Lilly leans over and whispers in my ear. "She's not kiddin'. When she says something like that she means it."

I swallow and wonder again if I'm going to wake up here any second and be really pissed that this is all a dog-gone dream.

"Listen, Luke, I have a bit of a problem and I hope you might be able to help me out," Tammy says.

I glance at Lilly but she just shrugs. We all wait with bated breath to hear what she's up to.

"Macy was kind enough to hop on my tour bus and help me out." She pauses while he answers and then grins over at me. "So she's always helpful like that, huh? Not surprising. Anyway, I'm in a bit of a pickle. See, since she came on the bus, I have no way of gettin' her back to Hootertown. Do you think you could be a sweetie and come here and get her?"

I gasp and shake my head at Tammy. Lilly giggles and Carrie mouths, *Shut up* at me.

"You could? Awesome! I owe ya one."

Lilly pokes me in the ribs. I start to sputter but Carrie shushes me with her index finger to her lips.

"Okay, how soon can you leave? Great. I'll be here at the studio for about an hour. Then we're all gonna grab a bite to eat at Jack's Bar-B-Que. Yeah, the one on Broad-way next to The Stage. I think we'll be upstairs on the patio out back overlooking the Ryman." She pauses. "I know. Me too. I almost never visit Nashville without stopping there. Thanks, Luke."

"Tammy!" I hold my hand out for the phone but Tammy flips it shut, guessing that I might try to talk Luke out of coming here, and of course she's right.

"You can thank me later," she says with a grin.

I shake my head. "What have you just done?"

"Sorry for gettin' all up in your business." She gives me a small shrug and doesn't look at all sorry. "Can't help myself."

A young guy with a clipboard pokes his head into the room. "Five minutes, Ms. Turner."

"Oh!" I hurry over to fluff and spray her hair.

"You mad at me?" Tammy asks. At first I think she's teasing but her brown eyes appear serious. "Should I have kept my nose out of your love life?"

"I don't have a love life. Luke is doing this as a friend."

"Didn't he just ask you to dinner or something?" Carrie asks.

"Yes, but because his mama put him up to it," I say as I mist Tammy's hair and then play with her bangs a bit.

Lilly purses her lips. "Maybe not. Maybe he was using his mama as an excuse to sway you to come."

"No way . . ." I shake my head. "I mean why wouldn't he come right out and say that he wants me there?"

"Well . . . ," Tammy says slowly, "you've never let Luke know how you feel about him, have you?"

"No," I admit in a small voice.

"Then he might be just as hesitant to let you know too, Macy. Love is a two-way street."

"Oh my God—could that be the title for the new CD?" Lilly asks.

Tammy grins. "Love is a two-way street?"

"Yeah!" Lilly says with an enthusiastic nod.

While pursing her glossy lips Tammy nods slowly as if pondering the title. "Yeah, I think it could work." She grins at me. "Macy, I think I really do need to kidnap you from Hootertown."

"I think you're right," Lilly agrees.

While I know that they're teasing—at least I think they're teasing—the thought that I could be a part of this world is exciting. The funny thing is that I already feel as if these women are my friends, and I barely know them. We just seem to click.

"We're ready for you," the young man says as he enters the room to escort Tammy to the studio.

"I can't wait to meet your Luke," Tammy says over her shoulder as she exits the room.

"He's not *my* Luke!" I tell her, but she just waves her hand at me.

"You're blushin'," Lilly observes, and gives my shoulder a little shove. "If you really like this guy, then go for it, Macy."

"Yeah," Carrie chimes in, and then gestures toward her chair. "Want me to do your makeup?"

"Really?"

Carrie pats the chair. "Get your tush over here."

When I stand there dumbfounded that a professional makeup artist is going to hook me up, Lilly gives my shoulder another little shove. "Go on, Macy. This is going to be fun. Just wait, you'll knock Luke's socks off."

I smile but her statement sobers me a little.

"What?" Lilly asks with a frown. "Did Luke say somethin' to upset you that you're not tellin' us?"

I shrug. "No . . ."

"Spill," Lilly prompts.

"Well, I'm tellin' ya that he only asked me over for his mama's sake. It's a regular Sunday thing for me to go over for fried chicken after church but with Jamie Lee on her honeymoon I felt a bit awkward, even though Daisy is like a mother to me."

"Don't be so sure of that," Carrie comments as she looks at my face with a critical eye. "I think Lilly might have hit the nail on the head."

I breathe in deeply and then sigh. "He asked me only because his mother badgered him into it. Not because he wanted me to be there. See, I've got to get over this crush I have on him. He'll always be a friend and nothing more. It's not healthy. I've got to move on with my life."

Lilly comes closer and angles her head at me. "You don't know that, Macy. Why don't you just not think of it going one way or another and just let the chips fall where they may?"

"Lilly has a point," Carrie agrees as she tilts my head up to blend my eye shadow. "Don't overanalyze, and let things come naturally."

"I'm telling you guys, I'm *so* not his type."

Lilly arches one delicate eyebrow. "He's still single, isn't he?"

"Well then, he hasn't found his type yet."

"Yes . . . but Luke likes . . . arm candy."

Carrie gives me a slow smile. "Kinda like this?" She steps away from the mirror so that I can see my reflection.

I put my hand to my chest. "Oh my. My eyes are so blue. And wow, I have cheekbones."

Carrie laughs softly. "Yeah, you do. What do you think of the lip gloss?"

I rub my peach-tinted lips together. "I love it. It's so soft and feminine."

"And complements your hair color," observes Lilly.

"Here, take this." Carrie hands me the silver tube. "I get samples all the time. I'll write down the cosmetics I used so you can duplicate this look at home. Since you're a cosmetologist you know all about bone structure and colors. You won't have any problem recreating this look."

"So, still think you're not hot enough for Luke?" Lilly asks with a little head bop.

I shrug. "He's a hard body and I need to take off a good twenty pounds."

"Macy, you've got some curves . . . so what?" Lilly says with a more pronounced head bop. "Play up whatcha got, girlfriend."

"Lilly's right, you know," Carrie chimes in. "I do makeup for lots of famous country stars. Yeah, you've got your Shanias and Carrie Underwoods but there are plenty of stars who are incredibly sexy and yet not built like twigs. You're a gorgeous girl, Macy. You just have to learn to believe in yourself. Lilly's right. Play up whatcha got."

When she gives me a high five I slap her hand hard, as though I'm buying into all of this. But the fact of the matter is, now that it's sinking in that Luke is driving all the way here to Nashville to pick me up, I'm nervous as hell. I need to call him and let him know that he really doesn't have to do this.

"Oh no you don't!" Lilly says with a hard shake of her head.

"What?" I ask while innocently blinking my eyes.

"You're thinking about calling Luke off," Lilly says in a matter-of-fact tone that I feel the need to dispute.

"Nuh-uh."

Lilly arches one knowing eyebrow.

"Okay, how'd you know?"

"By the expression on your face and the fact that you were eyeballing your phone with longing."

"Okay . . . guilty," I admit with a groan. "But you know what?"

"What?" they ask in unison.

"If only I felt as if Luke were doing this for me and not somebody else, then I'd have a whole new attitude about the situation," I tell them, but then put my hands to my cheeks.

"What?" they ask again.

"I can't believe I'm tellin' you all of this."

Tilting her head, Carrie leans on the back of the chair and looks at me in the mirror. "You know, I firmly believe that things happen for a reason. Events, people you meet." She pauses for a moment as if waiting for me to roll my eyes or tell her she's full of baloney.

I glance over at Lilly, thinking that she might make a snide comment, but she gives me a small shrug and says, "Having Carrie do your makeup is like having her read your palm."

"Oh, shush," Carrie says with a wave of her hand. I get the feeling that Lilly is only half teasing, making me wonder if Carrie is going to give me a pearl of wisdom that I'll need to latch on to. I know, I'm probably desperate . . . reaching for something, *anything*, but I wait with bated breath to hear what she's about to tell me.

While playing with my hair she says, "I've lived near Nashville all of my life and I still love to go to the Honky-Tonk Highway and watch the wannabes. Since I've been doing this job for nearly ten years I've seen the difference between those who make it and those who never will."

I'm wondering what this has to do with me since I can't sing worth a lick, but I nod my head.

Lilly pipes in, "I can tell ya the difference. Hard work and luck . . . not necessarily in that order."

Carrie purses her lips. "Mmmm . . . yeah, not to mention talent. But what it really boils down to is believin' in yourself." She taps her chest. "You have to know yourself from the inside out before achieving success. Just think of Toby Keith or Reba McEntire. Sure, they have talent out the wazoo." Carrie pauses and holds up her index finger. "But so do a whole lot of others. It's the inner confidence of knowing just who you are and what you're all about that makes the difference. Reba is sexy as hell at fifty and is still tryin' new and exciting things like Broadway and clothing lines when she wouldn't have to lift a finger for the rest of her life. Toby said to hell with it all and started his own record label and starred in his own movie."

Lilly snickers.

"Okay, so Toby can't act." Carrie pauses and looks at me in the mirror. "You're wondering what my little speech has to do with you, aren't ya?"

Knowing it wouldn't do any good to deny it, I nod my head. "Sorta."

Carrie puts her hands on my shoulders and says, "You've got it in ya, Macy. You just don't know it."

"I've got what in me?"

"The ability to break out. Do exciting things. Go places."

A little shiver goes down my spine. I'm about to ask her how or why she thinks this when Lilly says, "I'm tellin' ya she can read your face. It's spooky."

"Oh stop, Lilly. I'm just giving Macy a little advice."

Lilly leans closer to me and says in a stage whisper, "I'm telling ya . . . *spooky*." When she wiggles her fingers in the air, Carrie laughs. I'm not sure if they're kidding or serious and I suspect a bit of both.

I'm about to ask Carrie a few more questions when Tammy comes rushing into the room. "Done! Man-oh-man, am I ever ready for some Jack's Bar-B-Que. Y'all ready? Carrie, can you break away and join us?"

"No, I'm heading over to Greystone Record Studios to do makeup for a music video. I'd beg off but I've been moonlighting for them on occasion since they've been shorthanded," she explains, and then sort of frowns at me. "Hey . . . Macy, I know they're in need of a hair stylist too. Would you want me to put in a good word for you?"

"Whoa now, wait a doggone minute," Tammy says. "You're beating me to the punch. I was gonna ask Macy to fill in for Cindy while she's on maternity leave."

Carrie shrugs. "You're gonna be in the studio working on a new CD, right?"

"Yeah . . . but I have a few gigs."

"Then she could do both."

Lilly shakes her head. "Do you think they've forgotten you're standing right here in the room?"

I kind of chuckle but my brain is trying to process the fact that I'm about to be offered a job by Tammy Turner and Greystone Records.

Tammy ponders this for a moment. "I suppose she could." She turns around to face me. "Well, Macy, whad'ya say?"

8

Never Been Kissed

My mouth opens but of course no words come out. Realizing that I look as if I'm trying to catch flies I snap my jaw shut but then stand there blinking like a dork. "Um . . ." is all I manage, so I swallow, clear my throat, and then try again. "I don't know that I'm qualified."

With a grin Tammy reaches up and fluffs her hair. "I've already received tons of compliments on my flirty new do, Macy. I know your shop is small but I really don't think that being qualified is an issue. Truth be known, you would be better at the traditional styles that most of us want anyway rather than some of the off-the-wall cuts from the high-end stylists sent our way. Need I remind you of my recent disaster?" She raises her eyebrows at me and I try to grin but it comes off as more of a lip tremble. "But look," she says gently, "I know this is being thrown at you from out of left field. You don't have to give us an answer right now. Think on it."

"Okay, thanks. I will," I tell her while a voice in my

head is screaming that I should jump all over this opportunity. I suddenly remember what Carrie had just preached to me and shoot her a questioning is-this-what-you-meant-before look. Her answer is a slight shrug.

Lilly gives me a nudge with her elbow. "I know. Frustrating. She gives you just enough information to confuse the hell outta ya."

"What are y'all yappin' about? You know how I hate bein' outta the loop," Tammy complains, but then nods. "Oh I get it. Did Carrie give you one of her famous face readings?"

"I don't read faces," Carrie insists.

"Heck if she doesn't," Tammy argues. "It's uncanny." She snaps her fingers. "Had me pegged right off the bat."

Carrie sighs and looks at me. "I get . . . I don't know . . . vibes. What you read into it is your decision." She comes over and gives me a hug. "I hope we didn't overwhelm you, Macy. Think it over and I promise I'll put in a good word if you're interested. I can't guarantee the job but I do pull some weight."

"Thanks, Carrie. It was very nice to meet you."

She squeezes my shoulders. "Same here. Good luck in whatever you decide, sugar."

"Tootles, Carrie," Tammy calls over her shoulder as she breezes out the door. With two index fingers pointed in the air she says, "Look out, Jack's! Here we come!"

Lilly and I follow her out the door and are quickly joined by the bodyguards. I smile and Boone almost smiles back until he remembers to have his badass bodyguard face on. He holds the heavy front door open with ease but instead of the big tour bus, there's a black SUV waiting to whisk us over to the restaurant.

"Everybody else already over there?" Lilly asks as we slide across the cool leather bench seat.

Tammy nods. "Ready and waiting to chow down. My trainer's gonna have a fit especially since we have the music video shoot coming up, but I'm gonna splurge and eat whatever I want today."

Lilly gives me a look. "She kills me. Only fluctuated five pounds up and down easy as pie. All I'll have to do is smell the barbeque and I'll pack on a couple of pounds."

"I hear ya." I give Lilly a knuckle bump.

"Oh shut up." Tammy flips her phone shut and turns around in the seat to face us. "Quit your complainin'. You two are cute as Christmas!"

I have to smile at Tammy's comment. I can't believe how down-to-earth she is. Of course I'm having trouble believing any of this is truly happening.

But it is.

And then ohmigod, I remember that Luke is on his way to join us before driving me back to Hootertown.

"You thinkin' about Luke?" Lilly asks after Tammy turns around to answer her phone.

"How'd you guess?"

"You had a dreamy yet slightly panicked look on your face. Like this." She imitates my expression.

"Good Lord."

Lilly pats my leg. "Okay, not quite that bad," she admits. "But believe me, I know where you're coming from."

I'm guessing she's referring to Keith Connor, the drummer, but when she doesn't elaborate I don't have the nerve to ask her. Even though it feels as if I've known

Lilly for a long time I remind myself that I'm not really a part of this crew.

But I could be.

That thought hits me like a ton of bricks. Would I ever have the courage to uproot myself and leave Hootertown for Nashville? Could I leave the Cut & Curl, my daddy, my friends and start a whole new life amongst strangers?

Lilly taps her knee against mine. "Don't worry. You'll handle this thing with Luke," she says, mistaking my new panic attack for more Luke anxiety. "Are you wishin' Tammy had kept her nose out of it?" She lowers her voice an octave and continues. "Or are you secretly glad?"

I toy with the edge of my shirt before answering. "Both, I guess."

Lilly sighs. "It's scary to put your heart on the line, isn't it?"

"Oh . . . yeah." I wonder again if she's referring to her own love life but before I decide once again whether or not to go there, we turn onto lower Broadway, better known as Honky-Tonk Highway. Even though it's afternoon, there are wannabes performing in the hole-in-the-wall bars. My personal favorite is Tootsie's Orchid Lounge that stands out since it's painted purple. Looking out the tinted window, I notice that it's mostly tourists pointing cameras in all directions but when the sun goes down, the neon lights will flash and flicker, bringing Nashville alive with music and nightlife.

"There's nothing quite like this place, is there?" Lilly comments.

"You got that right," I agree with a nod. "I usually visit here a few times during the summer but with the wedding and all I haven't gotten the opportunity. I had forgotten how much I love this town."

"So Hootertown's only about an hour away?"

"Give or take depending on traffic."

"Then Luke should be arriving soon," Lilly points out with a glance down at her watch.

Holy cow, she's right. My heart skips a beat until I remind myself that Luke is doing this as a friend and I should keep this all in perspective.

"Here we are, girls!" Tammy announces when she finally snaps her phone shut. "I don't know about y'all but I'm famished. Pulled-pork sandwich here I come."

Boone comes around and opens the door for us. I blink in the sunlight as he politely offers his huge hand in assistance from the SUV that's pretty high up from the ground for a short person such as me. "Thanks," I tell him, and this time he forgets and smiles before quickly reverting back to badass bodyguard mode.

After stepping down to the sidewalk I look up at the JACK'S BAR-B-QUE sign and have to grin. When Jack lost his lease in a building that was torn down for the Hard Rock Café, he landed this amazing location in the heart of lower Broadway between the Ryman, Tootsie's, and the Ernest Tub Record Shop. The garish neon sign sporting flying pigs was Jack's answer to the controversial monster PLANET HOLLYWOOD sign erected without city council permission. I find it amusing that Planet Hollywood has since closed its doors but the flying pigs over Broadway remain.

"I'd love to eat out on the back patio," Tammy comments as we're being ushered upstairs to the private Nashville room.

"I know, Tammy, but you'd never get to eat a bite. All you'd be doin' is signing autographs."

She pulls a face. "I know. But it's such a pretty day and you never know who we might see goin' into the backstage entrance to the Ryman."

As we walk up the steps, Lilly curves her hand over her mouth but says loud enough for Tammy to hear, "She's the biggest autograph hound ever."

"Nuh-uh." I look over at Tammy to see if Lilly's pulling my chain.

With a grin she raises a clenched fist in the air. "I will get Toby Keith if it's the last thing I do."

"She means it," Lilly says. "I once saw her chase after Dierks Bentley like a crazed groupie."

"He's cute as a button. All that curly hair . . . !" Tammy says with a sigh as if that explains everything. "What I really love though is getting the legends like Loretta Lynn and Dolly Parton. Believe me, I still get starstruck at the CMA awards. Seriously, I have a little autograph book that I carry around with me. Remind me to show it to you."

"So, did you get Dierks Bentley?"

"No! He slipped through my fingers," she complains with a laugh.

"Did he know that it was you—you know, *Tammy Turner* chasing after him?" I ask as we enter the Nashville room that has a cool view of Broadway. The smoky aroma of ribs and pulled pork makes my stomach rumble.

"No! See, we were heading into, I don't know, Starbucks or something."

She looks at Lilly, who nods. "Sam needed some caffeine."

"I spotted him out of the corner of my eye. I turned to Lilly and Sam, who I knew would understand, and said, 'Hot damn, that was Dierks Bentley!' And we were off like three crazy fans!"

"Um . . . make that two crazy fans. I was roped into the whole thing by you and Sam just like I usually am." Lilly groans as if reliving the memory. "We were in high heels, for goodness's sake. I almost broke a doggone ankle. Sam is a huge fan as well. Oh yeah and did I mention crazy too? She slipped off her heels and sprinted down the street with Tammy huffin' and puffin' after her."

"I was *not* huffin' and puffin'. I do believe that was your own heavy breathing you're recalling."

I have to laugh as they continue to argue. I'm so entertained by their banter that I don't immediately realize Luke has already arrived until he stands up from where he's seated at the long table near the rear of the room. My heart pounds as he walks my way.

"Wow," Lilly whispers in my ear. "Those blue eyes are killer."

Thank goodness I swallow the nervous giggle that bubbles up in my throat—a horrible habit that's sometimes difficult to explain because it tends to happen at totally inappropriate times. Such as now. It bubbles up again, so I try to disguise it by clearing my throat, making for a weird low-pitched giggle/clear that thankfully everyone chooses to ignore except for Lilly. When she reaches over and discreetly squeezes my hand, her small gesture actually helps to calm my giggle attack even though the cat's still got my tongue.

Luckily Tammy takes control and extends her hand to

Luke. "Hey there, you must be Luke. Tammy Turner. Nice to meet ya."

"It's a pleasure to meet you, Ms. Turner," Luke says, and gives her what I know is a firm handshake. "I'm a big fan of yours."

"Why thank you, Luke. You can call me Tammy. Oh, and this is my friend and backup singer, Lilly Mason."

"Nice to meet you too, Lilly. I do believe I've met your sister, Sam."

Lilly smiles. "Once you've met her you're not likely to forget her," she announces loud enough for Sam to hear. "I mean that fondly of course."

I look over and see Sam mouth, *Bite me* at Lilly. If Luke notices, which I'm pretty sure he does, he politely ignores it.

"I understand. I've got a sister like that too," Luke jokes to Lilly, but loud enough for Sam to hear. He grins at me and while other men might have found this unusual situation with celebrities intimidating, he seems perfectly at ease. I remind myself that Luke is pretty successful in his own right and I feel a sense of pride. But it also reinforces the fact that although Luke and I might have grown up in the same town, he is polished and educated in a manner in which I'm not. He's come back to Hootertown while I've never been away. While he's thinking of taking a high-profile position at a Division I school, I've never even stepped on a college campus . . . unless you count watching football.

"Some women are just unforgettable," Luke adds.

"You mean that fondly too, right?" I finally manage to interject in a fairly normal tone, thank goodness. Wait, he wasn't referring to me with that comment, was he?

"Of course," he replies, and for a wild moment I feel as if he's reading my inner thoughts. When Luke's grin widens to a smile, a warm feeling slides down my spine but then I tell myself this isn't a Mel Gibson movie where he knows what I'm thinking. He's merely teasing like always. Right?

"I'm only joking, Macy," Luke says, freaking me out a little bit again, but then I guess he mistook my silent ponderings for getting ticked off at his teasing manner. I need to back off my continual wishful thinking and stop second-guessing everything he does so that I can simply enjoy his company. After all, an amazing day like this might never come my way again.

"Everybody help yourself," Tammy announces when trays of food start arriving. "We're getting a little bit of everything and I said to keep the barbeque comin'."

After Tammy waves her hand in a small circle over her head the crew cheers and noisily shoots chairs back from their tables. When Luke and I hang back from the rush to the buffet I put my hand on his arm and say, "I'm sorry you got roped into this, Luke. I'm sure you're tired after last night, and a long drive to Nashville was the last thing you wanted to do."

Luke looks at me long enough for my defiant won't-listen-to-my-head heart to go pitter-patter. "And maybe you don't know what I want as well as you think you do," he teases in a lighthearted tone, but there's something in those blue eyes of his that gives me pause. But when I'm hoping he'll say more we're suddenly at the buffet table, and my typical scared-to-go-for-it mode kicks into high gear.

"Have you tried the ribs?" Luke asks as we eat and

chat with the band and crew. He cuts one from his slab and puts it on my plate. "I love the sauce. We'll have to buy a couple of bottles as we leave. My favorite is the Tennessee Original," he says, holding up the bottle. "How about you?"

"Mmmm, I like the sweet, smoky one."

Luke nods. "Yeah . . . I like that one too. I believe it's called the Kansas City–style. We'll get a bottle of that one, as well. Your dad would like the Texas Sweet Hot."

"Yeah, he would. That man puts hot sauce on everything. Even his scrambled eggs."

Luke laughs. "Yeah, I remember that from fishing with him at his cabin. We'll pick him up a bottle of the hot stuff."

"Good idea," I tell him, and it suddenly reminds me again of how much we've felt like a couple over the last few months while planning Jamie Lee's wedding except, you know, that we've never had sex . . . or have even kissed for that matter. Mercy . . . that last thought causes an image of us in a lip-lock, causing me to choke on my sweet tea.

"You okay?" Luke asks with a slight frown. "Go down the wrong pipe?"

With my hand to my chest and my eyes watering, I nod. Lord, did I swallow the slice of lemon?

"You need a pat on the back?"

No, I need my head examined. "I'm . . . okay," I manage. Lilly, who is sitting next to me, doesn't help when she whispers in my ear, "I'd choke on my tea too if he were sittin' next to me." She bumps my knee with hers, reminding me of something Jamie Lee might do, causing me to choke and laugh at the same time. Luke, who obviously thinks I'm going into some kind of seizure, gently pats me on the back.

"Sorry," Lilly apologizes with a straight face, but the laughter in her eyes says otherwise. Unable to speak I bump her knee back letting her know I'm on to her tactics.

Laughter and easygoing chatter continue and I think to myself that I could definitely fit into this group of people, so I'm a little let down that after we've finished eating nothing more is mentioned about my coming to work for Tammy or the record studio. I tell myself that it's a good thing since I'd never have the courage to leave Hootertown anyway.

"Thanks again for comin' to my rescue," Tammy says as we stand up to leave. "You saved the day, Macy McCoy." She slips an envelope into my hand. "Sorry I was so busy during lunch or I would have visited with y'all more but it seems like I'm always on that doggone cell phone. Someday I'm gonna toss it right out the window."

"I was happy to be of service and I had fun," I assure her. Thinking that my short-lived adventure is over, I give hugs all around the room, even to Boone, who surprises me with a big hug in return.

Tammy hurries back over to us as we're heading out the door. "Nice to meet you, Luke. You two have a safe trip home." When Luke turns away for a moment, Tammy gives me two thumbs-up and a wink. I quickly shake my head but she mouths, *Go for it.* I mouth, *Oh stop* just as Luke turns back, causing us both to straighten up but I know we have guilty we-were-talking-about-you looks on our faces.

With one last wave and another hug for Tammy we exit the room to a hallway that seems so quiet after all of the boisterous conversation. "Thanks again for coming all this way to pick me up, Luke," I tell him to fill in the silence.

Luke stops in his tracks and turns to face me. "Macy," he begins, but then hesitates with a rather serious expression on his handsome face. This is unusual for Luke, who always seems so sure of himself.

My heart beats faster in anticipation but he remains silent. Wondering what's wrong I put my hand on his arm and somehow find the courage to prompt him. "Is something botherin' you? You do know you can tell me anything."

While nodding his head slowly Luke gives me a tender smile. "Yeah, I know that, Macy."

"Well then, what's on your mind?"

9

Unexpected

I wait for him to answer but he swallows and I swear his gaze drops to my mouth. For a heart-stopping moment I think he might lean in and ... *kiss me* right here in the hallway of Jack's Bar-B-Que. After the initial nonbeating shock, my heart starts thumping wildly ... but then again Luke might be staring at some barbeque sauce in the corner of my mouth or something, so I discreetly lick my lips in search of Tennessee Original.

When I don't encounter any tangy flavor I'm pretty sure that he's thinking about kissing me, so I step closer to give him easy access. I mean, why make it difficult, right? Because he's so tall, I tilt my head up and I'm thinking I should stand on tiptoe, but just as I rise to my toes Luke bends his head, tilting to the left. In that instant I realize that he's going to kiss me on the cheek as though I'm his doggone sister! Something in me snaps—from pent-up emotion or maybe just from the fairy-tale feeling of this incredible day. I think, *Screw this kiss on the cheek stuff* and turn my head so that Luke's lips land smack-dab against my mouth.

Luke stiffens as if surprised—*shocked? Oh God, what am I doing?* I want to kick my own butt for being so brazen. When a dreaded nervous giggle begins in the back of my throat, I swallow hard. Looking down at the floor I take a quick step backward while wondering how to explain my behavior. When my back meets the rough, exposed brick wall I clear my throat of giggles, but I refuse to look up at him while I rack my brain for something pithy to say to lighten the awkward moment. When nothing clever pops into my befuddled brain, I decide to simply apologize.

"Luke, I'm . . . ," I begin, but my words are smothered when he tilts my head up and covers my mouth with a sweet yet sexy kiss that sends a hot tingle shooting all the way to my toes. I swear that if the wall weren't right behind my feet, one would pop up just like in the movies. My hands take on a life of their own, first fisting in the soft cotton of his shirt, but when he deepens the kiss I slide them up and wrap my arms around his neck until my fingers are buried in the silky hair at the nape of his neck. His mouth is hot, his lips are soft, and when his tongue tangles with mine, my pent-up desire for him bubbles to the surface. If we weren't in a public place I think I'd have to jump up and wrap my legs around his waist while he pinned me to the wall and made wild and crazy . . .

If we weren't in a public place bangs into my brain and echoes in my head like a gong. Luke must have had the same sudden thought because he pulls his lips from mine and takes a step backward. He looks dazed and confused but then again maybe it's because I'm looking at him with half-lidded, dazed, and confused eyes.

"Wow," he says while threading his fingers through his short-cropped chestnut brown hair that I recently cut. He has great hair, by the way, thick and slightly wavy. I look up at him, trying to decide if it's going to be another good wow like with Tammy or a what-the-hell-just-happened kind of wow.

"That was"—he pauses to clear his throat—"unexpected."

Opening my eyes wider, I peer at him closely, trying to decide if he means that in a positive way or not; I don't know quite how to ask, so I decide the safe thing to do is to simply agree. "Um . . . yes it was." My voice is a bit breathless but I think I pulled it off.

Luke angles his head as he looks at me for a long moment and then says, "Then again, maybe . . . not."

Okay, this time I have to ask, "What do you mean by that, Luke?"

He opens his mouth in order, I hope, to shed some light on the cryptic comment, but then shakes his head. "Let's talk about this on the way home, okay?"

"Sure," I agree, and then begin walking down the stairs while holding on to the handrail as though it's a lifeline. My knees are a little shaky, but I manage the steps with only a slight stumble at the end that I pretend happened because of the rug and not my wobbly knees. "Stupid rug," I mumble, and then realize it's a hardwood floor.

Blushing, I glance up at Luke but he seems lost in his own thoughts. He puts his hand on the small of my back, guiding me toward the front door as we leave the building. I know it's an old-fashioned gesture but it feels so possessive and somehow intimate even though his touch is light and casual. Ever the gentleman, he holds the door open as we exit Jack's and head to his vehicle parked in a lot not far down the street. At one point I remember that we wanted bottles of barbeque sauce but I'm too interested in hearing what he's going to tell me on the way home to ask to go back to the restaurant.

"I was in my truck but Mama insisted I go home to get my SUV," he tells me while fishing in his pocket for his keys.

"I wouldn't have minded the truck, Luke. You know me better than that."

As he opens the door of the shiny black Lexus he says, "Yes, Macy, I believe I do." His tone is light, but again I notice something in his eyes that has me wondering what he's going to say to me. I hate that I'm getting hopeful, but after that hot kiss I don't know what to think. Of course I kissed him . . . or did he kiss me? I'm still trying to decide when we pull out into traffic. For a few minutes Luke concentrates on weaving his way through downtown, but I find that it's an effort to look out the window when I really want to be watching him. Just what is it about a guy driving that's so sexy? Long fingers . . . capable hands, a flex of muscle . . . heaven help me; I want to reach over, run my hand up his arm and then lean over and kiss him senseless.

When he turns onto the interstate he finally glances over at me but for some reason seems hesitant to say what's on his mind. Unable to muster up the nerve to ask, I reach up to turn on the radio, but Luke puts a gentle hand over mine and says, "If it's okay with you, I want to talk."

Glancing down at his big tanned hand covering mine, I can only manage a jerky little nod and a husky, " 'Kay."

"Ahh, Macy . . ." Luke draws out my name slowly but then stops talking. I know this is silly but I simply love it when he says my name. He used to call me Squirt and once in a while still does. I wonder if he's forgotten that his hand is still covering mine, because he seems to be concentrating on something and it's certainly not the rather light Sunday traffic. I'm thinking perhaps he's going to say something important but then again maybe he's just hungover and having a difficult time putting thoughts into words. That happens to me sometimes, but since I left the reception early I'm not feeling all that poorly. "The entire day was unexpected," he finally says with another glance in my direction, but he seems to be talking more to himself than to me.

A little stab of disappointment shoots through me. "Yeah, doing Tammy Turner's hair sure was exciting."

"That's not what I meant," he begins, and I get so nervous at where he might be going with this that the envelope Tammy handed me slips through my fingers and slides to the floor.

"What was that?"

"I think payment for my services," I answer, not really caring. I want to know what the heck he's going to say, doggone it!

"You'd better pick it up so you don't lose it."

"Okay," I answer, hoping that I don't sound impatient. When I lean over and snatch it up, the contents slip out onto my lap. I pick up the loose papers to shove them back into the envelope but when I see what it says I mutter, "Oh my goodness . . ."

"What? Was she generous?"

"Um . . . yeah you could say that."

"I'm not surprised." He reaches over and pats my hand. "Whatever it is, you're worth it, Macy."

I nod because I'm once again rendered speechless.

"Macy?" Luke looks over at me with concern. "You okay?"

"She—Tammy Turner that is—has offered me a job." I look up from the big check and the incredible offer and blink unseeing out the front window.

After a moment of silence he says, "You must have really impressed her."

I swallow and then look over at him. "Yeah, I guess I did. She said something about wanting to hire me because her hairdresser just had a baby but I suppose I didn't really think she was serious."

"Why not?"

"Well because I'm, you know, just"—I pause and shrug—"me."

He takes his hand from the steering wheel so he can reach over and give my leg a little shake. "You don't give yourself nearly enough credit, Macy."

"But Luke, how can I possibly be qualified to work with famous people? I mean, come on . . ."

"Well, Tammy Turner obviously thinks you're qualified," he tells me before turning his focus back to the road. "Jamie Lee always did say that you were really talented and that someday she would lose you to some . . . how did she put it? Oh yeah, some uppity high-end salon."

Jamie Lee. I put my hand over my churning stomach. "Well of course I can't take the position."

Luke looks at me with a slight frown but after hesitating for a moment he asks, "And why not?"

I turn to gaze out the window for a gut-wrenching moment. "How could I ever leave Jamie Lee and the Cut and Curl? My daddy?"

You?

My heart thumps hard while I wait for his answer. When Luke remains silent I turn my gaze from the passing scenery to him. His focus stays on the road and this time he keeps his hands on the wheel instead of reaching over to give me a pat of reassurance. I notice that a muscle ticks in his jaw, making me wonder what's going through his mind. Just when I'm about to ask, Luke inhales deeply and blows out a long breath before turning those intense blue eyes on me.

"Of course the decision is yours, Macy, but it sounds like this is the chance of a lifetime. I know how hard it is to leave home, but would you ever forgive yourself if you didn't give this a shot?"

When he looks at me intently, I nod. I'm having one of those happy but sad moments again.

"Look, there's nothing wrong with cutting hair at the Cut and Curl. It's good, honest work that I know you enjoy. But Macy, think about it. Who knows where this opportunity might lead?" He shrugs. "And if it doesn't pan out, you can always come back home."

I nod again, harder this time. I know he's right and I should be jumping for joy, so why do I feel as if I want to cry? My throat shuts and I look away so he doesn't see me blinking away tears. I understand the reason for my heartache. Just a little while ago I finally kissed Luke Carter and it was knee-buckling, as I knew it would be . . . and now here I am faced with taking a job that will separate me from him. I had hoped that he was going to confess a mutual attraction but here he is basically telling me I'm crazy if I don't take this position. I know he's right, but still . . . if he had just said that he didn't want me to move away, I wouldn't even consider leaving Hootertown, which leads me back to my unhealthy state of unrequited love. I'm probably reading way too much into one little bitty kiss that was meant to be on the cheek for goodness' sake.

"Nashville is only an hour away," he quietly reminds me as if guessing some of my turmoil.

"I know." I force a smile but realistically I know that with busy lives and the price of gas, an hour away might as well be a day. Sure, I'll get occasional weekend visits but if I move from Hootertown to Nashville, my life, my friends . . . *everything* will change drastically. I look down at the paper clutched in my hand and sigh. "Is the opportunity worth it?" I didn't mean to say that last part out loud.

"There's only one way to find out, Macy. You have to take that chance or you'll never know." Luke's voice has an odd quality to it that makes me wonder if we're still talking about my job opportunity but he falls silent for the next several minutes.

Fields of corn are a blur as his SUV gobbles up the Tennessee countryside and we head toward Kentucky. I'm thinking again about turning on some music when I suddenly remember that Luke never finished our conversation that we started in the hallway of Jack's Bar-B-Que. "Luke?" I venture, and he turns to me as if startled out of deep thought.

"Hmmm?"

"You were about to tell me something before when I dropped the envelope and interrupted you. What was it?"

10

This Much I Know for Sure

When an expression of indecision crosses his face I make up my mind that this time I'm going to press for an answer. If Luke has any feelings for me at all, then I want to know before making the choice whether to up and move to Tennessee. Just the thought of it has my head spinning. "Luke—," I begin, but I'm interrupted when my cell phone starts ringing to the tune of "Honky Tonk Badonkadonk." I've been planning on changing it but for some reason that silly song still makes me smile. "Oh my gosh, it's Jamie Lee." I glance over at Luke and then flip my phone open. "Aloha, *Mrs. Sheldon*. What's up?"

"Griff," she jokes. "Has been all day."

"Jamie Lee! Stop!"

"Sorry, but I've been drinkin' some fruity rum concoction with a pineapple spear attached to the rim of the glass. Seriously, he's sleepin', poor thing. Too long a flight and then too much, well, *you know*, and we've only just arrived. I'll admit that I'm tired too."

"Just rest up and you'll be fine."

"I hope! So what's goin' on, Macy-girl? I tried callin' both you and Luke earlier without any luck."

"Hey, little sis," Luke says loud enough for her to hear.

Jamie Lees gasps. "Was that Luke? Are you ... *together*? You finally went after him like you promised? Hand him the phone and lemme talk to him."

I swallow and then glance over at Luke, praying that he didn't hear her.

"He can't talk. He's drivin'."

"Sure he can. I do it all the time."

"Yeah, and last week almost took out Rose Jenkins's mailbox while arguing with your mama about the flowers for the wedding."

"Are you gonna tell her the big news?" Luke asks, but I give him a negative shake of my head and mouth, *No*. I don't want to upset Jamie Lee on her honeymoon.

"Did Luke just say 'big news'?" Jamie Lee asks. "I'm not hangin' up this phone until you tell me. First of all, where are you?"

"Um, Luke is drivin' me home from Nashville."

"What possessed you to drive all the way to Nashville?"

"Well, you're not gonna believe this, but I was at the shop this mornin' messin' around, goin' through inventory since I was antsy just sittin' at home, and Tammy Turner shows up with a hair emergency—"

"Whoa, wait a doggone minute. Did you just say Tammy *Turner*?"

"Yes!"

"Holy cow, I would have been speechless."

"I was! But then I dug deep and pulled my stunned self together."

"So what was her emergency?"

"About half of her hair extensions had fallen out, so I hopped on her tour bus and—"

"Hold on . . . You got on her tour bus?"

I have to laugh. "Jamie Lee, are you goin' to let me tell the story?"

"Sorry. Go on."

"I got on the bus, removed the rest of the extensions by soaking her head with conditioner, and then cut her hair."

"*Wait*, you cut Tammy Turner's hair?" she squeaks.

With a grin I shake my head at Luke who says, "Jamie Lee, let the girl talk!"

"Ohmigod, tell me why Luke is with you. No, tell me about the haircut first. No, I take it back. I want to know why Luke is with you. Oh mercy, just tell me everything!"

"He came to Nashville to pick me up since I got here riding on the tour bus. Tammy Turner asked him to do it."

"No way!" Her voice rises to a higher pitch just like mine does when I get excited. "Wait, are you two making this whole thing up?"

"Now just why would we make this up?" I ask, and roll my eyes at Luke.

"To mess with me. You two have been quite good at it for the past few months while plannin' the wedding."

"Macy's tellin' the truth," Luke shouts with a grin at me. I smile back but it hits me hard that we are once again sounding like and almost acting like a couple . . . but we're not. My mood deflates like a day-old helium balloon when I think of tellin' Jamie Lee about the job offer. Luke's grin fades as if he's reading my mind once again.

"Why'd you get so quiet? Tell me more! Did Tammy like the cut you gave her?"

"Yeah, she did. I added some layers and flipped it out on the ends. She really seemed to love it and got lots of compliments," I tell her with a measure of pride.

"Oh I'm so jealous!"

"Yeah, right. You're in Hawaii for two weeks with the man of your dreams. I'm the jealous one," I tell her, and then want to bite my tongue since the man of my very own dreams is sitting right here next to me making for an awkward moment. I feel a blush creep up my neck but then I remember that he doesn't really know how I feel, so my comment really didn't matter . . . except to me.

Maybe he should know flashes through my brain but I shake it off.

"Speaking of the man of your dreams," Jamie Lee says in a lower voice, "I think that driving all the way to Nashville, especially after a night of partyin', goes way beyond friendship, Macy."

Turning toward the window I hiss, "Jamie Lee!" and then flick a nervous glance at Luke but he seems to be concentrating on the road. "Don't go there."

"I'm just makin' an observation. Promise me when you get back to your place you'll invite him up and maybe *kiss him* or somethin'."

"Jamie Lee!" I hiss again.

"Would you stop sayin' my name like that? You sound like Mama," she complains, but then gasps again. "My God, you already kissed him, didn't you? I can tell!"

"No!" I refute so sharply that Luke looks my way with

raised eyebrows. I know it's weird how she could guess such a thing with no real clues but that's how we've always been. Mercy, I hope that Luke didn't hear her!

"Something wrong?" he asks.

"I think she's been hittin' the Mai Tais a little hard, is all," I whisper, cupping my hand over the phone.

"Ohmigod, Macy," Jamie Lee insists, so loudly that I'm sure Luke heard her this time. "Kiss him again. Make sure you slip him the tongue."

Pulling his eyes from the road Luke asks, "What did she say?"

"Nothin'," I assure him, and then lie, "Jamie Lee, you're breakin' up."

"I am not!" she says because I am such a bad liar.

"Yep, you are," I say faintly as though my voice is fading. "I'll call you later." I think about making static noises but that might be a bit over-the-top, so I simply flip the phone shut.

"Why'd you tell her that? Did she somehow guess about the job offer? It's freaky how you two have that connection."

I consider fibbing but he would most likely see right through me too. "No, but it's likely that it would come up and the last thing I want to do is to put a damper on her honeymoon. Why upset her when it might not come to pass?"

After patting my leg Luke says, "You're a good friend, Macy. But I know my sister well enough to tell you that she would give you her blessing without hesitation. Not that she would want you to leave but she loves you enough to let you. This much I know for sure." He glances over once again and then puts his hand back on the wheel. I get the feeling he wants to say more but falls silent.

"I know," I say quietly, and then sigh. "How can somethin' this amazing be such a difficult decision?"

"Because you care, Macy. For most people this would be a no-brainer. But not for you."

"Thank you, Luke," I tell him, and God help me I want to lean over and kiss him for sayin' such a nice thing. Okay, I want to kiss him regardless but this makes me want to even more. This of course upsets me further, so for the duration of the ride home I'm mostly silent. When I think about all that happened in the span of twenty-four hours I have to shake my head.

"You okay?"

"Yeah, I guess I'm still tryin' to wrap my brain around it all."

"What a difference a day makes, huh?" Luke observes as we pull up to the hardware store.

"You were readin' my mind." I give him a small smile.

"Thought so. Jamie Lee isn't the only one who knows you well."

I widen my smile but his comment sounds like something a friend would say. I'm thinking that I put way too much stock into the kiss and should push it from my brain. Luke certainly seems to have. He puts the SUV in park, kills the engine, and then looks at me with his amazing eyes.

Bedroom eyes.

His mouth is so full and sexy, making me remember how much I enjoyed the kiss, even if it was nothing special to him.

Maybe I need to make it special.

I remember Jamie Lee's suggestion to invite him up and all of a sudden I have the why-the-hell-not attitude. I know I'm bein' wishy-washy but I mean *really*. Why the hell not? I decide to thank him first and then slide in an invitation for a glass of sweet tea on my back deck.

"I'll walk you up," he offers, and I'm glad since it will give me a minute to muster up the courage to invite him in. He opens the SUV door for me and politely takes my duffel bag, easily hefting it from the backseat.

When we reach the top of the landing, I smile when I notice that my petunias are once again perky. Gathering my courage because I've already decided that if I invite him in I will go for another kiss, I inhale deeply and then take the plunge. "Would you like to come in for a glass of sweet tea? I made a fresh pitcher this mornin'."

"That'd be nice. I'm parched."

"Good." While I smile I nod rapidly until I realize that I must look like a Bobblehead but I'm suddenly nervous because of my going-after-another-kiss promise to myself. As I open my door I start having an internal argument, which is kind of silly because come on, whose going to win—me or myself? At that thought a silly little giggle bubbles up in my throat, so I do my usual cough to disguise it.

"You okay?" Luke asks, and I jump at the sound of his voice even though I know he was behind me. I tend to do that when I'm thinking hard about something.

"Sure," I tell him with a wave of my hand.

He nods but doesn't look convinced. "Where do you want this bag?"

"Oh, anywhere is fine," I tell him as I open the kitchen cabinet for a couple of glasses. Because I'm so doggone short I have to stand on tiptoe especially since I'm in my flip-flops.

"Need some help?" Luke asks just as I'm reaching up. Turning to answer, I somehow lose my balance, tipping both sideways and back against the counter. Luke's hands reach out to steady me just as I grab his shoulders for balance . . .

And suddenly we're kissing.

Not just a little brush against each other's lips but a kiss like there's no tomorrow, hungry, devouring, a delicious meeting of our mouths. Because he's so tall I'm still on my toes, so he lifts me up and sets my butt on the countertop. Without really thinking, just reacting, I wrap my arms and legs around him without breaking the lock I have on his lips.

Desire—warm, liquid, potent—has me melting against his chest. I've dreamed about a kiss like this from him but the reality is so much better. He threads his long fingers through my hair while sliding the tip of his hot tongue across my bottom lip before sucking the wet fullness into his mouth. He moans—no wait, that was me moaning— and then tilts my head to the side so he can begin a moist trail of kisses down my neck until he's licking my rapidly beating pulse.

While arching my back I slide my palms beneath his shirt, loving the feeling of his warm, silky skin beneath my hands. When he moans I get bolder and lightly rake my fingernails down his back before cupping his tight butt and squeezing. He sucks my earlobe into his mouth, making me want to rip his clothes off and make wild love to him right here and now.

In fact, I think that's an excellent idea.

"My God, Macy, I'm so sorry. I don't know what the hell got into me," Luke says. He tries to back away but I'm still wrapped around him like a rubber band. Realizing that he wants some quick distance I unhook my arms and legs. As I suspected he takes a giant step backward and rakes his fingers through his hair while looking around the room at everything but me.

"You don't have to be sorry, Luke," I assure him in a small voice. My heart of course has plummeted to my toes.

"Yes, I do. You're in the process of making some important decisions and I shouldn't muddy the waters for you." He closes his eyes, takes a deep breath, and then blows it out.

Tell me that you don't want me to go and I won't. I don't have the nerve to say this out loud but I'm hoping to use mental telepathy to get him to respond. When his eyes open wide he looks at me with a serious expression and for a moment I think that my intense brain waves might have zapped him.

After another long moment Luke says, "I think that because we've been together almost nonstop during Jamie Lee's wedding plans, I started to think of us as . . ." He hesitates as if embarrassed.

"A couple?"

He looks surprised at my observation but then nods. "Yeah."

"Me too. Except for you know, *this* part." Hey, he admitted it, so I might as well too. Could this be going somewhere good? I hold my breath and wait.

"But we're *not* a couple. I need to remind myself of that and keep my nose out of your business. The truth is,

Macy, I have no right to influence you one way or another with this opportunity. The decision is yours." He looks down at the floor as if he doesn't want to hear my answer.

"*Could* we be a couple, Luke?"

His dark head snaps up.

"I'm surprised that I had the guts to say that out loud . . . but I did." Although my heart beats fast and my cheeks feel warm, I bravely hold his gaze.

For a long moment Luke remains silent. Finally, he swallows, takes a step forward, but then jams his hands in his pockets instead of taking me into his arms as I had hoped. "Macy, you know my track record with women." Shaking his head, he laughs without humor.

"I'd like to think I'm different."

"You are." He takes another step closer and tucks a lock of hair behind my ear. Truth is, I've been thinking of asking you out on a real date for a while now."

"Why haven't you? You know what my answer would be." When my voice cracks he closes his eyes and swallows.

"Don't you see? Even the thought of hurting you tears me up. And now with this job on the line . . . ahhh Macy, I can't run the risk of holding you back."

"Life is full of risks. It's about time I took one."

"Yeah, but I'm no good with long-term relationships."

"You *were*. This is because of that—that *bitch* who dumped you when your football career ended. You could never stay in a relationship after that for fear of getting your heart stomped on again. I get that even if you don't. Damn, I'd like to pound her into the ground. She didn't deserve you," I tell him hotly.

He smiles. "You're somethin' else, you know that?"

"You mean that in a good way, right?"

Luke laughs and then nods. "Definitely."

I hesitate to say this but if I'm putting it all on the line I might as well. "I know I'm not an arm-candy Barbie doll–type like you've always dated . . . but Luke, I'm a real woman and I'd treat you right."

I'd love you with all I got and then some.

"I know that," he says, but remains noncommittal.

"I'm willing to give this a shot if you are. If it doesn't work out I can deal. I'm a big girl now."

When Luke gives me a sad smile I know his answer isn't going to be good. He cups my chin in his palm and says, "Ah, Macy . . . the timing is all wrong." With a sigh he then says, "Keep this under your hat, but I have a couple of Division One schools after me to coach football. And even though I said that I shouldn't influence you, I honest to goodness believe that you need to give this opportunity a shot." Looking into my eyes he rubs the pad of his thumb over my cheek. "While I love coaching the Panthers, if I get a Division One offer, I'd be hard-pressed not to take it. And the school could be really far away."

My chest feels tight and my throat is clogging with emotion but I put on a brave face and say, "I understand. It just isn't meant to be."

"Never say never," he answers, and leans in to give me a tender kiss that breaks my heart. "Let's get our lives in order and see where we go from there, okay?"

I want to tell Luke that I'll follow him to the ends of the earth but I don't want him to think I'm some sort of psycho-chick, so I nod slowly. "You're right."

"I should go."

Is it my imagination or does it seem as if he really

doesn't want to leave? It's probably just wishful thinking on my part. I'm an expert at wishful thinking. "That would be best," I force myself to say even though I want to throw myself into his arms.

He pauses, making my heart leap, but then says, "Call me and let me know what you decide and if you need my help in any way, okay?"

"Sure," I tell him as we walk toward the door. He gives me a quick peck on the cheek before leaving. From behind the frilly curtain I watch him get into his SUV and start up the engine. When he doesn't immediately pull away from the curb I think for a heart-stopping moment that he might come back . . . but he doesn't.

With a long sigh that ends in a hiccupping sob I flip down onto the sofa and rest my head in my hands. Wow, how did my simple life suddenly get so complicated?

Deep down I know that Luke is right. It would be crazy to start a relationship under these circumstances. But then my old insecurities rear their ugly heads . . . Maybe the kiss was a moment of insanity on his part and he was letting me down easy? After all, I'm not anything like the women he's dated. He's also right that I should seize this opportunity and hit the ground running. Who knows if something as amazing as this job will basically fall into my lap ever again? Or his?

Yes, before I can give my heart to anyone fully, even Luke, I have to feel good about myself in my own right. With that thought in mind I pick up the phone to dial Tammy Turner's number and tell her that I'll take the job.

"Hello?" My eyes pop open wide when a masculine voice answers. Okay, I *swear* I clicked on Tammy's number in my phone book but obviously I must have hit Luke's number instead . . .

"Macy?" His voice is gruff . . . sexy.

Holy crap, what do I say?

"Um, Luke I . . ." Think, Macy . . . think of something clever, pithy, no . . . sexy. Yeah, sexy.

"Yes?"

"I'm . . . um sorry. I dialed your number by mistake." Well, that answer sucked. I shake my head up at the ceiling.

"No, it wasn't a mistake."

"It . . ." I sit up straight and swallow. Wait a minute . . . what? My heart feels as if it's in my throat but I manage to finish with a breathless, "wasn't?"

"I hope not because I've been driving around aimlessly but I suddenly found myself on your doorstep."

"Oh . . . like you're *here?*"

"Yes. What do you want me to do? Leave or stay?"

11

Just Breathe

I'm stunned for about the millionth time that day, so it takes me a second before my inner voice shouts, *Duh, you big dummy. Ask the man in!*

"What the hell am I doing?" Luke sighs into the phone, and I imagine him running his fingers through his hair . . . and then imagine *myself* running my fingers through his hair. "I should go."

"No!" I squeak in a goofy voice born of desperation, and scramble from the sofa. Skidding to the door like Kramer on *Seinfeld*, I manage to yank it open. For a second we simply stand there and blink at each other.

Finally he says, "I've been thinking. You've got to take the job, Macy."

My heart sinks. So he came back to tell me *that*? "I know. And you might be moving away."

"Yeah." Luke shakes his head. "Plus I suck at relationships."

"Because you were hurt!"

"But I don't want to end up hurting *you*."

"That's silly."

He shrugs. "It's true."

"Yeah well, how about this. I feel like you're out of my league."

His brows draw together. "Now *that's* ridiculous."

I shrug, thinking that if we're getting it all out on the table I might as well be totally honest. "I'm overweight and you're gorgeous."

He steps into the apartment. "That's absurd. No wait . . . that's crazy."

"Which one?"

"Both."

We stand there for a long torturous moment, gazing at each other. The sexual tension hanging in the air is as thick and sweet as molasses on a warm buttermilk biscuit.

After inhaling a deep breath Luke says, "Ahhh, Macy." With closed eyes he shakes his head but fails to finish his thought.

"Luke . . . *please*, just say what's on your mind. Get it all out. You might as well . . ."

Luke opens his eyes and says, "This is going to sound stupid."

"Just say it."

"No."

I fist my hands in his shirt and gaze up at him. "You want me to say something stupid first to make you feel better?"

Luke grins at me and says, "Yeah, okay."

I wasn't expecting him to say *Yeah*. I search my brain for something stupid to say—usually not such a difficult task for me—but when I open my mouth Luke puts a finger to my lips.

"I was just teasing," he says, but then his grin fades. "All right, here goes. Right now I feel as if I'm in the pocket getting ready to throw a Hail Mary into the end zone to win the game. My heart is pounding because I know I'm risking an interception. But releasing the ball also means the chance for a touchdown pass." He looks down at me with serious blue eyes. "I'm excited . . ."

"But scared?"

"Yeah." He appears embarrassed but relieved to admit it.

I tug on his shirt, pulling him closer. "Luke. Throw the damned ball."

When Luke looks up at the ceiling and laughs I decide I might as well go for broke. "So are we gonna forget about all that other stuff and make love?" *Holy cow, did I really just say that?*

"God, I hope so."

I bite my bottom lip and then ask, "Can you read my mind?"

"I wish! But you said that out loud."

"I know."

"Macy, God I . . . ," he says, but then stops and runs his fingers through his hair.

Was he going to say *I love you*? No . . .

I wait for him to continue while my heart beats against my chest. But he suddenly appears so shaken and confused that I gently put a hand on his arm and say, "Luke, let's forget about it all and give each other . . . tonight."

He closes his eyes and swallows. But before he can open his mouth and say something else, I rise up on tiptoe, place my palms on his cheeks, and with trembling lips kiss him softly. "Enough talk," I murmur against his mouth since I don't want to break the delicious contact.

He smiles. "Now you're talkin' . . ."

"Yeah, I know and I need to shut up." While facing him I tug on his hands and start to backpedal down the short hallway. Of course I start bumping into things and stumble.

"Stop, you're gonna hurt yourself." Luke laughs and pulls me into his arms for a hot kiss that makes my legs wobble as though they're made of pipe cleaners. We're laughing, kissing, and untucking clothing until we reach my bedroom . . .

And the mood suddenly changes.

"Macy . . ." He draws out my name as if it comes from someplace deep within before dipping his dark head to kiss me thoroughly. Then, he gently brushes my trembling fingers to the side and starts oh-so-slowly to undress me. Luke kisses each inch of skin he reveals until I'm totally exposed to his intense gaze. But instead of making me feel shy as I'm expecting, he makes me feel sexy.

Beautiful. Wanted.

When Luke cups one breast and sucks a nipple into his mouth, white-hot desire shoots to my toes making my already unsteady legs buckle. I slither to the bed and then have the exquisite pleasure of watching him undress. He takes his sweet time, watching me all the while, caressing me with his gaze.

We don't speak . . . just breathe.

When Luke joins me on the bed, he raises my hands above my head, gently capturing both my hands with one of his. Then . . . he oh-so-lightly glides his free hand over my skin, causing tingling ripples of pleasure everywhere he touches. He replaces his hand with his mouth, swirling his warm, soft tongue over my breasts, and then kisses me all the way to my navel.

"Luke . . ." I untangle my hands from his and thread my fingers through his hair, urging him on. With a deep sigh I bend my knees and arch my back while he makes slow, tender love to me with his mouth. "God!" My release is achingly, intensely sweet and while my heart is still thudding like crazy, he enters me with a smooth, gliding stroke.

"You feel so good," he says in my ear.

"Mmmm . . . so do you." With a deep sigh I wrap my legs around his waist, urging him to go deeper, faster. I make love to him without holding back, giving and taking . . . reveling in the silky feel of his skin, the heat of his mouth, the taste of his body. I slide my hands over his back and squeeze his butt, thinking that I could never get enough of the feel, the taste, the touch of his body against mine. When Luke arches his shoulders and cries out my name I pull his head down for a deep, delicious kiss and ride the wave with him. When we tumble back to earth, I keep my legs and arms wrapped around him, wanting to feel him buried inside me as long as possible.

Afterward, with my head on his chest, I'm content to listen to the steady beat of his heart. He wraps his arm around me and we remain silent for a long time. We both know from our earlier conversation that this could be the beginning or the end, depending on which way our lives lead us. But for right now he's here in my bed and I refuse to think of anything else and just live in the moment.

We doze off but sometime in the night Luke wakes up and kisses me on top of the head.

"Macy," he begins softly, "my car is parked on the street in front of the hardware store. Sweetie, this is a small town and I don't want everyone to know our business. As much as I hate it, I should go."

"You're right," I whisper into the night. "I understand."

"I'll call you," he promises as he eases from my arms and gets up from the bed.

"Do," I tell him, and unable to help myself, I watch him dress. He's magnificent in the shadowy light of the moon filtering through the blinds. Once he's dressed he leans down and kisses me on the cheek, pulls up, but then leans back in for a longer, deeper kiss.

"It is so hard to leave."

I nod and want to answer but my throat closes up when it hits home how hard a long-distance relationship would actually be. As if reading my thoughts, once again he cups my cheek with his palm. For a breathless moment I think he's going to say something more, but then he swallows and withdraws his hand. "Sleep tight," he tells me, and I oh so wish he had said something entirely different. But I nod again and, with tears that I hope he didn't see swimming in my eyes, watch him leave.

Of course I toss and turn the rest of the night arguing with myself. While I want this job so badly I can taste it, I panic at the thought of leaving my friends and family and *losing Luke*. After punching the pillow I decide not to disrupt my life and to tell Tammy thanks, but no thanks. "The stress just isn't worth it," I mutter beneath my breath.

"Are you crazy? You *have* to take this job," I counter

hotly. I think the fact that I'm managing to have a heated argument with myself, out loud no less, means that the answer undoubtedly is yes, I am crazy. Finally, when I'm at a stalemate I close my eyes and determinedly try to fall asleep, but then all I can do is relive the amazing kiss with Luke. With a frustrated little growl I give up and grab the remote from my nightstand. I pretend to channel surf but I know I'll end up at the Home Shopping Network. I rarely buy anything even though for some reason things I have no real interest in always tempt me. It also boggles my mind how really ugly clothing sells out so quickly but I suppose that at three o'clock in the morning even turquoise tunics look appealing to bleary eyes. Plus they have models who would make a potato sack look sexy. I wonder how many people get UPS packages with turquoise tunics, scratch their heads, and mutter, "What the hell was I thinkin'?"

I remind myself of this fact when a chunky burnt orange necklace starts to capture my interest. With an exasperated sigh I click the television off before I end up with an unwanted purchase or two. Snuggling beneath the covers I hope that pure exhaustion will take over . . .

The next thing I know, curling fingers of sunshine are sneaking through moss green curtains that never quite overlap at one spot in the middle. With a groan I squeeze my eyes shut and turn away from the window in an effort to fall back asleep. Waking means making my final decision that's flip-flopped more than a politician on the campaign trail. Sleep, however, is not an option since my stomach wants breakfast and my bladder begins protesting. "Oh, okay," I mumble, realizing that I'm now talking to my body parts.

After taking care of business I pad on my bare feet into the kitchen to start a pot of coffee, adding an extra scoop with hope that a jolt of caffeine will jump-start my sleep-deprived brain. While watching brown liquid steam and gurgle into the carafe, I once again weigh my options. The scale, of course, always tips in favor of taking the job so I begin my list of pros and cons, again hoping that something will change so that I can take the safe option of staying in Hootertown. It's kind of like when Jamie Lee and I would toss a coin to make a decision and then throw it in the air again when we didn't get the result we really had hoped for.

While mumbling to myself, I reach into the cabinet for my favorite jumbo mug that says DECAF SUCKS in big green letters. On workdays I prefer my caffeine in the form of Diet Dew but during my mornings at home I love the smell of coffee brewing. To distract my decision-making process, I head over to the refrigerator for my favorite vanilla-flavored creamer. I'm wondering where in the world it's hiding and tell myself that I really need to clean out and organize my fridge. "There you are," I mutter when I spot the creamer hiding behind the squeezable mayonnaise jar. I know—I'm talking to inanimate objects but I suppose I'm only in real trouble if they start talking back. Just when I'm reaching for the carafe I hear the front doorbell ring.

"Who can that be?" I wonder. With Jamie Lee gone and my daddy on the road, I can't think of anyone who would show up on my doorstep on a Monday morning. When the thought occurs to me that it could be Luke, I panic. "Ohmigod, I'm a mess!" I have serious bedhead from all the tossing and turning, my teeth aren't brushed, and my sleepwear is a shabby Panther's nightshirt! I can't possibly answer the door, so I decide to stand there very quietly and hope that he'll go away and come back when I've showered, shaved my legs, and lost ten pounds . . .

I'm thinking that my plan is a good one until the doorbell chimes bing-bong and then again in rapid secession as if the person on the other side knows I'm standing here hiding in my very own kitchen. Bing-bong!

"Well, hell . . . ," I mutter, and decide that I'll just pour myself a cup of coffee and wait them out . . . but of course now I'm curious as to who might need to see me this early. A sharp knock has me creeping toward the door so I can look through the peephole. Maybe it's Publishers Clearing House with balloons and a big check for a million bucks!

Ha . . . yeah right.

More likely it's the UPS man delivering a Home Shopping Network item I've forgotten I purchased. I hope it's not something ugly or worse, a household gadget that I'll never use. With that in mind I peek through the tiny hole expecting to see a dude in brown shorts, but when big red hair comes into view I have to smile and then quickly unlock the door.

"Why hello there, Mrs. Carter. What brings you here so bright and early?" Like me, Jamie Lee's mama is *not* a morning person.

"Child, when am I ever going to convince you to call me Daisy? I've been trying for years, you know."

I nod. "I think of you as Daisy but there's something ingrained in me that just can't do it."

She pats my cheek. "I understand. It's your proper upbringing. Your daddy raised you well."

"You had a hand in that too, you know."

After patting my cheek she smiles at me tenderly. "Yes, Macy, you know I think of you as a daughter. I will always be here for you."

"I know that," I tell her, and then give her a big hug. After I back away we both take a moment to clear the emotion from our throats. It hits me hard how difficult it would be to leave here, and my decision starts flopping like a goldfish out of water.

"I brought you some leftover cake," Daisy explains as she breezes into my living room. "I wanted to eat some for breakfast but I needed a partner in crime to consume something so sinful this early in the day. Good Lord, child, that coffee smells heavenly. Strong just as it should be. May I have a cup?"

"Why, of course," I offer, but something tells me she didn't show up here just to share breakfast. While her smile is bright Daisy has a determined look in her eyes that I know means business. "Come on into the kitchen and I'll pour you a cup."

"Bless you, Macy," she says with a smile. Although she isn't a morning person, unlike me she looks fresh and cheerful in white summer slacks and a light green cotton blouse scalloped at the edges. Open-toe shoes show off a shiny red pedicure that matches her fingernails, and even though it's a sultry summer morning, not a bead of perspiration has the nerve to pop to the surface of her ivory skin. "Just a splash of cream, if you will."

"It's the flavored kind."

She waves an elegant hand, "Oh . . . that's fine. I'm getting used to the newfangled products. Why just last week I purchased wild rice in a packet that was already cooked! All you had to do was pop it in the microwave and it was ready in seconds! I was skeptical but I have to admit it was quite tasty. So see, I'm startin' to lighten up and try new things. I'm tryin' to branch out and not be so set in my ways."

"Good for you, Mrs. Carter." While I gather together the plates, forks, and coffee, we chat about the wedding and the weather and things in general but I still feel an underlying purpose that she hasn't gotten to just yet. When there's a lull in the conversation I know that she's gearing up to tell me her real reason for dropping by. After swallowing a bite of cake she daintily dabs her napkin to her lips and then says, "So, I hear that you have a wonderful job opportunity."

Ah . . . now we're getting somewhere. "Yes, I do. How did you find out?"

She runs a red-tipped finger over the rim of her coffee mug and looks at me thoughtfully. "Luke told me."

"Oh." For some reason I feel the need to blush. "He did? Well, I guess it had to be him since no one else knows."

Daisy nods. "I hope he wasn't out of line tellin' me but you do know he cares about you, don't you?"

"Of course." I'm not sure where she's going with this but I think that something is weighing heavily on her mind. "Luke and I have been friends for a long time," I venture, and have to wonder if Luke told her about the kiss. I feel my cheeks get warmer.

Daisy inhales a deep breath and slowly lets it out. "Macy, I believe that my son's feelings for you run deeper than mere friendship. I've seen the way he looks at you lately."

At her unexpected comment my pulse beats rapidly. "Mrs. Carter, what are you sayin'?"

She reaches across the table and puts her hand over mine. "I probably shouldn't be tellin' you this, but that's never stopped me before, so here goes. I'm sayin' I believe Luke could be falling in love with you, Macy."

My heart leaps in my chest. "Do you really think so?"

Daisy squeezes my hand. "I think he knows it but is afraid to admit it to himself. We both know he's been through some rough times and I think he's somewhat afraid to put his heart on the line."

I nod because I know she's right.

"I also suspect that you've been in love with him for a long time."

"I won't deny it, but Mrs. Carter, let's be honest. I'm not his kind of girl. I mean, look at me. Luke dates girls who look like supermodels."

"Oh Macy, when will you ever learn that you're a beautiful woman? And sweetie, your beauty radiates from the inside out." She shakes her head. "The funny thing here is that Luke doesn't think he's worthy of *you*. He already cares about you so much that he doesn't want to risk hurting you."

My eyes widen. "What? How can he possibly not think he's worthy of *me*? Have you . . . talked about this?"

"You know I can't keep my mouth shut even though I tried for the past few weeks when you two danced around your growing attraction to each other. I wanted to bang your heads together . . . and now that you're considering this job in Nashville, I felt the need to stick my nose in."

She nibbles on her bottom lip for a moment. "But

here's the thing. Both of you are at pivotal points in your careers. You have to make that part happen . . . be happy in your own skin before a relationship could work."

"Oh Mrs. Carter, I've been wrestling with that very notion." I frown. "So, are you tellin' me to take the job and if it's meant to be between Luke and me, then it will somehow come to pass?"

"Heaven's no. Sometimes you have to make things happen, Macy. Do you think Griff and Jamie Lee would be together without our meddling?"

I shrug.

"Probably not. Fate only gets you so far and the rest is up to . . ."

"Other people messin' with your lives?"

Daisy smiles. "At least where I come from."

I casually lick a dollop of icing from my thumb but my heart is thumping like a base drum. "So, I'm confused. What are you tellin' me to do?"

"I'm encouraging you to take this job, Macy. It won't be the same at the Cut and Curl without you, but at sixty years old . . . ," she says, but when I arch one eyebrow she admits, "Okay, *sixty-five*, I know that nothing stays the same even in sleepy little Hooterville. We'll miss you and I'll shed some tears but we'll be fine. So, don't let that enter into your decision. You got that?"

"Got it," I reply gruffly. "I've been arguing with myself all night long. This is so hard, especially now . . ."

"You go to Nashville, Macy, and give this opportunity your best shot."

I nod, but then ask, "Well then, what about Luke?"

"Find yourself first, Macy McCoy. You have talent and confidence that haven't begun to be tapped. I always knew it. But," she says, and then winks, "go after that son of mine with both barrels. You don't have to give up one thing for the other."

"I know . . . I was thinkin' the very same thing but—"

"No buts, babycakes."

"Oh, Mrs. Carter, I have about a thousand buts rollin' around in my head right now. In the past couple of days my life has been turned on its ear and any moment now I think I might start hyperventilating."

Daisy squeezes my hand once again and says, "Macy-girl, just breathe. Your adventure is just beginning."

12

Rednecks Without a Cause

Three days after my conversation with Daisy my head is spinning and I haven't had a drop to drink . . . Nope, I'm just reeling from exhaustion after three days of whirlwind activity that included up and moving to Nashville. After going back and forth in my decision-making process a few more times—okay more like a hundred—it was my daddy who convinced me to take the job. He said that my mama would be proud and it got me thinking that maybe she's up in heaven playing a hand in all that's been happening to me lately. It wouldn't be the first time I've felt as if she were my guardian angel.

I made Daisy promise not to tell Jamie Lee until after the honeymoon since I didn't want to do anything that would put a damper on her blissful time with Griff. I hate that this decision will bring any kind of sadness to the people I care most about, but when I mentioned this to Daisy, she assured me that it's all part of growing up.

With a sigh I tell myself that at twenty-six I guess it's about doggone time.

Tammy provided a small but nicely furnished studio apartment in a building that she owns near Vanderbilt University. Even though it's just a few miles from the heart of Nashville the campus is a tree-filled green space that's both peaceful and beautiful. Its summertime activity is minimal but I can imagine that the hustle and bustle of backpack-toting students will be a sight to see come fall semester.

But as I look around my living space I'm thinking that it's rather beige and boring, so I'm trying to decide what accent colors to use and perhaps purchase from the Home Shopping Network when my phone vibrates in my pocket, making me jump. There's just something about the vibrating sensation that is unnerving as though it will suddenly zap me or something . . . I know I'm weird that way.

Glancing at the small screen I see that it's Lilly. "Hey there," I answer cheerfully even though I'm too pooped to pop—something my daddy used to say when he arrived home from a long stretch on the road.

"Hey, Macy, whad'ya doin'?"

"Just chillin' here in my new place."

"Well, Sam and I are fixin' to head over to Tootsie's later on tonight. You wanna come with us?"

"Oh, that's my favorite little honky-tonk!" I tell her, but then groan. "Lilly, my butt is draggin'. I don't think I can muster up the energy."

"Oh, come on, Macy. Tomorrow is one of our few days off before hitting the studio. We'll keep it on the down low won't we?" she shouts to Sam.

"Sure we will. Just like we always do," Sam shouts loud enough for me to hear. "We'll be in by eleven—tops."

"Okay, then," I tell them. "Just as long as we don't overdo it. I don't want to start my first day hungover."

"Oh we won't," Lilly firmly promises. "We're not what you would call party girls, are we Sam?"

"Noooo way. Not us. And don't wear anything tight or flashy cuz we don't like to draw attention to ourselves either. We don't care about flirtin' with the cowboys . . . just, you know, listening to the music."

"You're yankin' my chain, aren't you?"

"Sam, are we yankin' Macy's chain? Would we do such a thang?"

Her answer is a fit of laughter followed by a weak, "No . . . course not. We're, um, what do you call it, Lilly?"

"Wallflowers?"

"Yeah . . . that."

By now I'm laughing along with them. "Okay, I'll grab an energy drink but I can't promise how long I'll last."

"We'll come along with a car and pick you up. Boone will drive us so we don't have to worry about drinkin' and drivin'. Plus, if anyone messes with us, he'll give them a ball-shrinkin' glare. It's fun to watch."

"So, he'll come into the bar with us?"

"Yeah. He won't sit with us but watch from a little ways away.

"We'll have a bodyguard?"

"Yep, and he takes it serious. It's totally unnecessary

and I've told him he can just drop us off, but he always insists on staying and keeping an eye on us."

"That's so cool."

"Well I guess, unless he gets too overprotective. Then I have to tell him to back off."

"Yeah, that would suck," I reply, but I personally think that Boone is sweet on Lilly. I've caught him staring at her when she's not looking but I decide to keep my mouth shut. I'm too new in this group to stir up any trouble. In fact, I give myself a warning not to drink too much and get stupid. I'll just have a couple of longnecks to unwind and then back off. "I'll start gettin' ready."

"Okay, we'll see you in a little while."

"Wear somethin' slutty," Sam yells, and then laughs. "Show off the girls. You've got some nice ones!"

"Sam!" Lilly shouts back at her.

"What?" she asks innocently. "She does. It'll get us some free beer for sure. Two words, Macy: low cut."

"Sorry, Macy," Lilly says. "She's outta control."

I have to laugh but then think I'm going to be in for quite a night with the Mason sisters. "Wait, do you two get recognized?"

"Nah," Lilly answers, "not too often, anyway, unless of course we're with Tammy. She comes out with us once in a while but not too often since it's such a hassle for her. Besides, she's pretty much a homebody. Okay then, see you in a bit. Go find your second wind, Macy."

After hanging up the phone I have to smile. While I dearly miss Jamie Lee, these girls are going to be a lot of fun, I can just tell. I'm dying to call Jamie Lee just to talk but I'm so afraid that I'll slip and spill the whole thing that I didn't even take her last call to me.

On my way to the bathroom to primp I snag a Mountain Dew from the fridge but after my lively conversation I'm already feeling energized. I tell myself that it will be fun to go out and flirt and have a good ol' time but then of course my thoughts turn to Luke. Other than a brief conversation after he called to ask if I was settled in, I haven't heard from him, making me feel as if the amazing night we had was some sort of dream I conjured up in my head. I'm really trying hard to take Daisy's advice and to get my own life in order first but my doggone heart refuses to cooperate. Every time my phone rings my pulse races in hope that it's Luke calling to tell me he misses me so much that he just has to come for a visit.

Then, of course, I tell myself now that I'm gone, Luke has moved on and probably doesn't think of me at all. Out of sight and out of mind and all that . . .

I look at my pathetic self in the mirror and sigh. "Okay, Macy McCoy, just wait a doggone minute!" Narrowing my eyes I give myself a well-deserved stare down. I look kind of silly since one eye has mascara on and the other doesn't but I glare anyway. "Stop your bellyaching and take life by the horns." Then I picture myself wrestling with a big old bull and start to giggle. I decide right then and there that I'm being too serious and I need a girls' night out of fun and laughter.

Since it's a sultry summer night and Tootsie's will be jam-packed, I pull my hair up into a loose ponytail, letting locks of hair hang in a deliberate messy way that I hope looks playful and sexy. After a light dusting of hair spray, I touch up smoky-gray eye shadow and add a bit more peach-tinted gloss that Carrie gave me. Satisfied with my hair and makeup, I head to my closet to find something that will show off the girls like Sam suggested. Because I'm self-conscious about my weight I don't have many tight tops, but maybe it's about time I embrace my curves instead of hiding behind loose-fitting clothing. I quickly settle on a jeans skirt but then try on a dozen blouses, hating each one more than the last. "Damn, I don't have anything to wear!"

I'm nibbling on the inside of my cheek and staring at my closet full of crap when my front doorbell chimes. Tugging on a yellow V-neck T-shirt I hurry to answer the door.

"Cute skirt but the shirt sucks," Sam comments as she breezes past me into my bedroom.

Lilly rolls her eyes. "She's in a man-hating mood and I'm not far behind her. I pity the poor cowboy who has the nerve to approach us. He just might get his head bitten off."

"You still having man troubles with that drummer?"

"That two-timin' jackass? I'm *so* done with him."

"Yeah, you've said that before." Sam's voice is muted from the bedroom but her frustration rings out loud and clear.

"I mean it this time."

"Sure you do."

"Bite me!" Lilly shouts in Sam's direction.

"Damn, Macy, don't you have any slutty clothing? I'm gonna have to take you shoppin' at the Opry Mills Mall. Now, get your butt back here and let's try to sex you up."

"What about you, Macy?" Lilly asks as we walk to my room where we find Sam going through my closet like Stacy on *What Not to Wear*. If there were a big garbage can, I do believe my wardrobe would be in it. "You still mooning over Luke? Not that I would blame you."

I shrug. "Sorta."

She hooks her arm through mine. "Well, for tonight join the man-hatin' club. In a sad way it feels kinda good. Empowering even."

"Yeah, but you know it always backfires," Sam says as she holds up a Payton Panthers extra large T-shirt. When we get in one of our man-hatin' moods we sorta radiate it and for some reason we become a challenge, you know what I'm sayin'? I wanna be mean like in the Pink song, 'Leave Me Alone,'" she says with a laugh. "Guys just always go after what they can't have."

So do women, I think to myself.

"Okay Macy, do you actually wear this shirt in public?" Sam wrinkles her nose and tosses it in the growing heap of nonslutty tops.

"No, I sleep in it."

"Well okay." Sam shakes her head sadly. "But that's almost as bad. What would Luke say if he saw you sleepin' in this?"

"We're not goin' there, Sam," Lilly warns.

"He is the coach of the team so he might like it," I protest. "May I keep it, Stacy?"

"Oh you watch that show too?" She gives Lilly a look. "See I'm not the only one who loves *What Not to Wear*."

Lilly shrugs. "I just hate the throwing away of the clothes part, that's all. I wouldn't let anyone toss my very own clothing in the trash."

"But you get to replace it with cool stuff."

"Fancy-schmancy clothes. I'd want my old stuff back."

Sam nods. "True," she admits, but then brightens.

"You know what? I think we need a redneck version of the show on CMC. Wouldn't that be fun? We could have Carrie do the makeup . . . and Macy, you could do the hair!"

"What would you do?" Lilly asks her sister.

"The clothes, of course. I have a very exquisite sense of redneck style," she says with her nose in the air.

Lilly snorts. "I'll give you that, baby sister."

While tapping the side of her cheek Sam says, "You know, we could be on to something."

Lilly snorts again.

"I'm serious," she insists, and I'm thinking she could be right. "We could get our participants at Wal-Mart. You can always find some poor soul in a tube top and go-go boots shopping in Wally World."

"You shop at Wal-Mart?" I ask, and they both nod. "So does Tammy . . . well, she has someone shop there for her," Lilly says. "We all grew up dirt-poor. No matter how much money we make we'll still clip coupons, shop at Wal-Mart, and take restaurant leftovers home to eat the next day. It's just who we are."

"Good for you," I tell them, and mean it.

"Well, Macy," Sam says as she looks at my clothing strewn all over the bed and floor, "a serious shopping spree is in order. Damn, girl, if I had big breasts like yours I'd flaunt those puppies." She tosses a button-down white cotton shirt at me. "Put this on but leave the first few buttons undone."

"But it has long sleeves," I protest.

"Roll them up to your elbows. We'll add some bracelets and a necklace to draw attention to your cleavage."

"I don't want to draw attention to my cleavage."

"Too bad. It'll be fun and get us free beer."

"You can afford your own beer," I remind her with a laugh.

Sam arches one eyebrow. "It's the principle of the thing."

"Well, I don't think you'll have any trouble getting guys to buy you a drink," I tell her. She looks both enticing and sweet at the same time—a combo that drives guys wild. "Your layered spaghetti-strapped T-shirts are too cute and yet manage to be sexy."

She cups her hands beneath her boobs and shoves them upward. "Yeah, like these itty-bitties will get noticed. Ha."

"Hey, I thought we were man-haters tonight," Lilly protests. Lilly is sexy but in a Gretchen Wilson don't-mess-with-me badass way. She's not fooling me, though. I already know that she is a softie beneath her spiky blond hair. That said, I could imagine that she can raise a little hell.

"Oh come on, Lilly, don't get too out of hand. You know it drives Boone crazy. Give the guy a little rest tonight."

"He needs to learn to back off."

"Yeah, right. I think you cause trouble just to get his attention."

Lilly waves a hand at her sister. "Yeah, right. Why would I do that?"

Sam angles her head and says, "You tell me."

"Oh like Boone is my type. Come on, Sam. Get real. I mean he's a nice guy and all . . ."

"And hot as hell."

Lilly shrugs. "If you go for muscle-bound bouncer types. You know I dig musicians."

While shoving my arms in the shirt, I watch for Sam to counter and she does with a laugh. "Yeah, and how's that working out for ya?"

"Bite me."

"You need a shirt that says that," I tell her with a grin.

"Yeah I do."

"She has a coffee mug that Tammy got for her," Sam says, "but a shirt would be better."

"I'd rather have the pleasure of sayin' it. And Boone is not the guy for me," she protests a little too hotly. Something in her eyes tells me that she's at least thought about him that way.

"You want to *do* him. Admit it."

Lilly tosses a shirt at Sam. "I do not want to have sex with Boone!"

Sam winks at me. "Say it, Macy . . ."

I grin at Lilly and say, "Whatever."

"You girls are so wrong."

Sam pushes herself to her feet and steps over the pile of clothes. "He's much more intellectual than he looks, you know, Lilly. He reads a lot of heavy stuff and watches the Discovery and History channels."

"Give it up, Sam."

She shrugs. "I'm just sayin'."

"Speaking of hot guys, Macy, have you heard from that blue-eyed hottie Luke?"

"Not really."

Lilly slaps her jeans-clad thigh. "That does it. It's a man-hater night for sure. We're gonna get beer bought for us and then be snooty bitches. Okay, girls?"

Sam and I exchange looks and then shrug. "Oh, okay."

"Sweet," Lilly says with a this-is-going-to-be-fun grin. "High five, bitches! We're outta here."

"Speaking of Boone, where is he?"

"Waiting for us outside in the SUV," Lilly says. "We should get a move-on."

"How do I look?" I ask Sam.

"Come see for yourself," she says as she grabs my hand and drags me into the bathroom.

"Oh my . . . ," I say as I gaze at my reflection. I thought the plain white blouse would look drab but it off-sets my summer tan. I usually wear my shirts loose in an effort to conceal extra pounds but the shirt tucked into my skirt gives me a waist.

"Here," Sam says, and tugs at my collar, exposing more skin. "Baby, you're hot!"

I giggle, but with my updated makeup and simple but sexy clothing I have to admit I'm feeling a bit more . . . confident. I've always downplayed my breasts but it is kind of fun to flaunt them a little.

"Play up what you've got, Macy. Embrace your full figure. You're a beautiful girl."

I feel emotion clog my throat. "You think so? I've picked up so much weight since high school and—"

"Stop! We all want to be what we're not. Look at me. I'm short and flat chested."

"You're not flat chested."

"Close enough. I've even thought of having a boob job."

"Over my dead body," Lilly says as she joins us in the small bathroom. "You're petite like our mama. Embrace it!"

"I don't wanna be petite. I want curves!"

"Yeah, and I don't want this big ass." Lilly turns around and points to her butt. "Guess what? I'm stuck with it." She turns back around and loops her arms over our shoulders. "Guess what else? Tonight it doesn't matter because we're man-haters."

"But we don't really hate men," I muse out loud.

Lilly laughs. "Yeah, I know. But it gives us a sense of purpose even if it's bogus."

"Tonight we're rednecks without a cause," she explains, and then squeezes our shoulders. "You girls ready?"

"Ready," Sam and I say.

"Good. Then let's go hit the Honky-Tonk Highway."

13

Honky Tonk . . . Badonkadonk

We're still laughing and cutting up as we walk outside to where Boone is waiting. He's leaning against the mean-looking SUV, looking equally big and bad in black jeans and a plain black T-shirt that accentuates his ripped chest. His bulging biceps stretch the sleeves to the limit and reveal Celtic armband tattoos. Dark blond stubble shadows his square jaw and mirrored aviator sunglasses are in place even though the sun is setting.

"Ladies," he greets us in a deep voice, and then reaches over to open the back door. I can't help but notice that he smells as masculine as he looks—something dark and spicy mixed with danger. Okay, I made up the danger part but he really does smell delicious.

"Hey there, Boone," Sam says. "You're looking festive tonight. Where's your cowboy hat?"

"Musta forgot it," he answers dryly.

I greet him with a smile and he gives me a mere twitch of his full lips in return.

"Boone," Lilly says in a rather aloof tone as she brushes past him into the backseat.

Sam gives me a discreet elbow but I had already taken note of the fact that Boone's gaze lingers on Lilly longer than necessary. Sexual tension seems to crackle between them but as usual he has his game face on. It also occurs to me that he takes his job seriously and that we are completely safe in his care—not that Nashville is crime infested, but still it's a protected feeling that's rather nice.

Once we're settled and Boone is behind the wheel, he raises his gaze to the rearview mirror. "Where to, ladies?"

"Tootsie's," Lilly says. "If it's dead there we'll hit The Stage or maybe Legends, but we want to try to snag a table, so let us out in front and then park this monster, okay?"

Boone hesitates. "I'd rather walk you in."

Lilly sighs. "We'll be fine for a few minutes."

A muscle jumps in his jaw but he nods. "Whatever you say, Ms. Mason." After removing his sunglasses he flicks a glance at her in the mirror. Lilly nods back and it's as if they are trying to bait each other. Sam nudges my knee with hers so I know I'm not imagining the exchange. I'm thinking that if the two of them end up in bed—and whether they know it or not it's inevitable—that it will be explosive.

"I'll join you ladies shortly," Boone promises as he drops us off at the corner light on lower Broadway. Even though it's a weeknight the street is buzzing with activity. Laughter and music spill out onto the sidewalk from the bars. Neon signs light up the night and I have to smile when I see the flying pink pigs at Jack's Bar-B-Que. An intense pang of longing shoots through me though since the sign makes me think of Luke and the kiss in the hallway . . . and then the next kiss in my kitchen. I remember how he made sweet and tender love to me. God I've re-lived it so many times in my head, making me wonder whether he has too.

But then it makes me think about the fact that I'm here and he's in Hootertown. Our lives are going in different directions just when there was a chance for something more. Maybe I should swallow my pride and just call him.

"Wipe that sad puppy-dog look from your face," Lilly orders, and hooks her arm through mine. "Tonight is all about fun and games."

"Lilly's right."

"Wow, that's a first," Lilly comments dryly.

"That you're right?" I ask with a chuckle.

"No, I'm always right. It's a first that Sam's admitted it."

Sam pulls a face at Lilly and then hooks my other arm in hers. "Let's go on in for a swaller and a holler."

Lilly grins. "And tip the band a dollar."

I laugh and my mood is immediately lightened. When we approach the entrance to Tootsie's Orchid Lounge a young cowboy greets us. "Sam! Lilly! Haven't seen y'all in a while," he says with a dimpled grin. It occurs to me that even though the general public might not recognize them, these two are still celebrities. "Y'all want the window seat?" I know he's referring to the window in the front of Tootsie's opposite where the band plays. It's a special place of honor that tourists can pay for and reserve, and where they are sometimes joined by country stars.

Lilly waves him off. "Nah. We just want to have some fun. We'd rather keep who we are on the down low if it's all the same to you."

His dimples deepen. "Sure thing. I understand." He looks at me and says, "You a singer too?"

"Only in the shower or my car."

"She's our hair chick," Sam explains. "Macy McCoy, meet Tanner James."

"Nice to meet ya, Macy," he says, and gives me a wink. "Save me a dance for later?"

When I don't answer Lilly nudges me. Oh . . . he was serious? "Um, sure," I stammer.

"Sweet. I'll collect it," he promises with a tip of his black hat.

After we enter the bar Lilly leans over and says, "He's a singer, you know. Pretty doggone good too."

"He is?"

"Yeah, and he can rock the house like Jason Aldean. Country but with a rough, sexy edge," Lilly explains.

"Cool, I can't wait to hear him sing." I then glance over my shoulder at Tanner to see if he's flirting with every girl who comes into the bar. I can't believe he singled me out.

Sam looks at Lilly and then rolls her eyes at me as if reading my thoughts. "Why are you so surprised that he's interested in you, Macy?"

I shrug.

"Maybe it's because you're showing off what you got instead of worryin' about what you're not."

Sam looks at Lilly and they high-five.

"Song idea?" I ask.

Lilly nods and then gives me a nudge. "You're learnin' fast, girlfriend. Oh and FYI, Tanner *will* collect the dance."

"Wait, am I missing something?"

When Lilly and Sam exchange a look and quickly say, "No," I realize that something is up but that they'll never tell me, so I'll just have to find out the hard way.

We snag one of the few tables in the rather small bar that's already getting crowded. There's more room and another stage upstairs but like Sam and Lilly, I prefer the honky-tonk atmosphere on the bottom floor. "Here." I dig a pen out of my purse and hand it to Lilly. "You'd better write that song title down."

"Right!" She sits down on a stool and grabs a napkin.

"I wonder how many hits were written on the back of napkins?" I ask while she writes.

Lilly shrugs. "I do know that many a song has been written right here in Tootsie's. It's rumored that Roger Miller wrote "Dang Me" sitting here at one of these tables. Willie Nelson got his first songwriting job after singing here."

I grin and point to the wall behind. The photos and memorabilia are fondly called the Wall of Fame. "Maybe someday you'll end up there."

"In this business you never know," Lilly says as she looks at the picture-filled wall. "It sure would be cool to write a classic . . ." She holds up the napkin and waves it like a flag. "Maybe this will be it."

A waitress thinks she's being flagged down and hurries over to our table. "What'll it be, ladies?"

"Bud Light," I request.

"Miller Lite," says Lilly.

"Coors Light," Sam responds with a grin.

The waitress nods. "There's nothin' wrong with bein' particular, especially when it comes to men and beer . . ."

"Amen, sister." Lilly gives her a knuckle bump.

"Here comes Boone." Sam nods toward the entrance, not that she needed to announce it since a man his size can't exactly sneak in. Female heads turn in his direction but he doesn't seem to notice, or maybe it's that he just doesn't care. Without making it obvious, he takes a vacant stool at the bar directly across from our table.

"We don't need a doggone bodyguard," Lilly grumbles. "He should just go play pool somewhere and come back to pick us up." She takes a long pull on her Miller Lite and directs her attention to the stage but I notice her sneaking a peek at Boone when she thinks we're not looking.

Sam notices too because she raises her eyes to the ceiling and then leans over and says to me, "We've got to do something to get those two together. If you come up with a plan, let me know because I'm in."

With a shake of her head Lilly says loudly enough for us to hear over the band, "What are y'all cookin' up?"

"Nothin'," Sam says with a fake scowl. "Why do you always think it's all about you?" She circles her hand over her head and says, "Here's the world and here's Lilly."

"Oh shut up." Lilly takes another swig of her beer and thumps it down on the table. "Hey, I thought we had designated this as man-hater night. We need to find us some men and then hate 'em."

"Now Lilly, Macy can't be mean to Tanner, can she? He's too damned cute and promised her a dance."

"Macy?" Lilly asks hopefully. "You in or out?"

"Um, I don't know if I'd be very good at the game anyway."

Lilly rolls her eyes. "Just follow my lead. It's fun. You bait the hook. You reel them in," she explains, and demonstrates as though she has a fishing pole in her hands. "Then toss them back . . . after they buy you a beer."

"It will drive Boone crazy, Lilly," Sam accuses. "I see right through you. Why don't you just go over there and sit on his lap like you wanna do."

"Oh shut up, Sam! Boone's got nothin' to do with it. It's two-timin' Keith I'm pissed at, not Boone. Now, are you playin'? I know you've got man issues, too."

Sam sighs. "Well, okay I guess I . . . holy cow . . ." She breathes and stops in midsentence. "Um, I don't think I could hate anyone who looks like . . . *him*. I could reel him in but I'm sure as shootin' not tossin' him back."

I turn my gaze past the band to the door. "Ohmigod, I know him."

"No way." Sam gives me a hopeful look. "You do?"

"Yeah, that's Brandon Sheldon, the brother of Griff, the guy who just married my best friend, Jamie Lee. I wonder what brings him to Nashville?"

"Maybe it's business. What's he do for a loving—um I mean living?" Sam asks without taking her eyes off Brandon.

"Wow, that sure was a slip of the tongue," Lilly comments with a laugh.

"I'd sure like to slip him the tongue," she says with a grin. "God, he is gorgeous."

"And has bad boy written all over him," Lilly observes. "Macy, am I right?"

"'Fraid so." With a look in Brandon's direction, I sigh. With long, unruly hair that reaches his shoulders, low-slung ripped jeans, and a plain white T-shirt, Brandon is the opposite of his clean-cut, country-boy brother. "You hit the nail on his handsome head. Brandon is a bit of a walk on the wild side. Sam, you've been warned," I tell her, but my warning only seems to intrigue her more, so

I decide to go further. "Oh and after bein' kicked out of two or three colleges he's been workin' with Griff, who owns his own construction company . . . some remodeling but they specialize in building decks. I doubt he's down here on business, but who knows?"

"Oh a man who works with his hands. I *like* it. Well, if he's here for pleasure I'm all over it," Sam announces with a dreamy grin.

"Sam!" Lilly says with a shake of her head. "Whoa there, girl."

"What? I'm just sayin' . . ." She taps her beer bottle to mine. "Macy, call him over here, quick, while he's lookin' this way."

Brandon's face lights up when he spots me. When I wave him over he makes his way through the growing crowd. "Hey Macy! What's up? I saw Luke the other night at Dixie's and he told me the scoop on your job."

"He did?"

"With strict orders not to tell Griff and Jamie Lee."

"Oh, good."

"So what are you up to?"

"We're just havin' a girls' night out," I tell him, and Sam nudges me beneath the table. "Oh, let me introduce Lilly and Sam Mason." I lean forward and say in a lower voice, "They're backup singers for Tammy Turner."

"Wow, I'm impressed." He offers his hand to Lilly and then to Sam, who holds his hand long enough to give him the message that she's interested. "Nice to meet ya."

"So, what brings you to Nashville?" Sam asks. "Business or pleasure?"

I almost choke on my swallow of beer but Brandon doesn't miss a beat. "Definitely pleasure," he responds smoothly. "I'm taking a few days off. I've bid on a couple of projects but other than that I have idle hands." He wiggles his fingers. "I was feelin' a bit restless, so I hopped on my bike and hit the road."

"You have a motorcycle?" Sam asks with a dreamy look. She jumps a bit, making me think that Lilly just gave her a warning nudge beneath the table.

"Yeah, it's my street bike but I do some motocross as well. "Do you ride?" he questions Sam.

"Oh sure, I love to ride," she gushes, but judging by the amused look on Lilly's face Sam has never been on the back of a motorcycle. Sam suddenly jumps as if Lilly's kicked her again and I have to hide my giggle with a cough.

Brandon looks from one sister to the other and then gives Sam a slow grin. "Have you ever been on the back of a motorcycle?"

"No," she playfully admits. "I was trying to impress you. How'd ya guess?"

"From the look your sister gave you. My brother would do the same thing to me . . . ruin my game," he says with a laugh in Lilly's direction.

"Busted," Sam admits. "What I should have said is that I'd *like* to ride but I'll let you in on another little secret."

"What might that be?"

Sam gives him a cute little shy smile that I actually believe is sincere. "I'd be scared to death. I'm not as adventurous as Lilly. Now I've really messed up impressing you, huh?"

Brandon arches one dark eyebrow. "Well, there was no need since I'm already impressed."

Lilly snorts and shoots me a look. "Ohmigod, Macy, is it gettin' deep in here or what?"

Instead of being embarrassed like most guys would be, Brandon tosses his head back and laughs but Sam gives her a scowl. "Watch out, Brandon, she's in man-hater mood."

"You were too until he walked in." Lilly points her beer bottle at Brandon. "Watch out or she'll write a song about ya."

Instead of looking worried, Brandon appears intrigued. "You write songs too?"

Sam nods. "I enjoy singing but it's the songwriting that's in my blood."

Brandon angles his dark head and says, "It must be amazing to be that passionate about what you do for a living."

"It is," Sam admits with another genuine smile at Brandon. Playful banter suddenly seems like real interest and judging by Lilly's thoughtful expression, I'm guessing she's thinking the same thing. I grin at Lilly when their conversation gets deeper and they seem to have forgotten we exist.

Although Brandon has given Griff and his mama fits over the years, I've always had a soft spot for him. I know all too well how tough it is to lose a parent at an early age. But while it was agonizing to watch my mama lose her life to cancer, at least I had the opportunity to say goodbye to her. A tragic farming accident took Brandon's daddy and while Griff was old enough to cope, young Brandon was devastated. I do believe that his wild ways were an expression of grief and I know that such a loss makes it even harder to put your heart on the line . . .

And then it suddenly hits me that I've been doing the same doggone thing. Loving Luke when I knew there wasn't a chance was an easy way to keep from getting hurt. Now that he's showing interest, I'm shying away with excuses that could be overcome if I dare.

"I'm such a coward," I mumble.

"What?" Lilly asks with a frown, but I can only shake my head in wonder.

"I do believe I just had a lightbulb moment," I tell her.

"Oh wow," Lilly says, and grabs my hand. "I've got to hear this."

"Hey, where y'all goin'?" Sam asks when she's able to pry her gaze away from Brandon.

"Outside for a breath of fresh air," Lilly explains.

"Okay," Sam says, and turns her attention right back to Brandon.

Lilly tugs me outside of Tootsie's and leads me to a spot on the sidewalk away from the crowd. "Tell me what you just figured out."

"That I'm an idiot."

Lilly gives me a deadpan stare. "*That* was your lightbulb moment? Come on, Macy. I let my beer get warm for this?"

"Okay, here goes . . . ," I begin, and then take a deep breath of city-scented air while I gather my wits about me to explain. "All these years I've worshipped Luke from afar, telling myself that I'm not good enough for him—"

"Which is a bunch of bull, by the way," Lilly inserts with a little bop of her spiky head.

I nod because for the first time I'm in complete agreement . . . well almost, anyway. "I talked a big game to Jamie Lee tellin' her that I was gonna go after Luke the way she set her sights on Griff."

"But?"

"I was full of—"

"Crap?"

"Pretty much," I admit with a sad shake of my head. "But Lilly, watching Brandon's bad-boy bravado slip there for a moment with Sam made me realize that he wears his leather jacket like armor to keep from getting hurt. See, he lost his daddy just a few years before I lost my mama and . . ." I pause to swipe at a tear.

"I get it," Lilly says gruffly, and swallows hard. "Loving someone means opening up your heart to pain."

I nod. "And I've been hiding behind my weight . . . holding back in fear, telling myself I'm not good enough when I'm really just a coward."

Lilly puts her hands on my shoulders. "You're not a coward and you're certainly not an idiot."

"Yes I am, but not anymore!"

"Well then, Macy McCoy, I do believe it's time for less *talk* and more *action*."

"Damned straight!" I give her a double high five. "So now just how do I get Luke here to Nashville?" I sweep my arm in an arc toward the neon lights.

Lilly taps the side of her cheek and then gives me a slow smile. "I think I might have a plan." She pulls me closer to the orchid-colored brick building. "Now listen up."

14

"Truth or Dare"

"You do know that Boone's been watching us from the entrance to Tootsie's, right?" I ask Lilly before she informs me of her plot to somehow get Luke to Nashville.

Lilly rolls her eyes. "Yes. You'd think he was the Secret Service and I was the president's daughter or something instead of a backup singer nobody even recognizes."

"So, does Tammy send him along or does he do it on his own?"

With a shrug Lilly says, "A little bit of both. Tammy had a stalker a few years back and she's been skittish ever since. If she goes somewhere tonight she'll take Casey with her. It's not a celebrity diva thing. She really was stalked."

"Oh, how awful. Was it a crazy fan?"

With a sad shake of her head Lilly says, "Worse. It was a guy she was dating and then dumped when she realized he was a jealous lunatic."

"Oh . . ."

"Yeah, and she hasn't dated since."

"What about that songwriter dude . . . Colin Reed?"

"We'll get to that after we get you hooked up." She points a finger at me and grins. "I can only stick my nose in somebody's business one person at a time. Tammy's next . . . although I do admit that I've already tried without success."

"Once bitten, twice shy?"

"Yeah, I guess, even though there's not a mean bone in Colin's body," she says as she pulls her cell phone from her jeans pocket. "Sam just sent me a text asking where the hell we're at," she says with a chuckle. "And Boone is starting to look agitated. God, it's fun stirrin' up trouble."

"Should we go back inside?"

"No, let's bug them a bit longer. And besides, I have to tell you of my devious plan." She rubs her hands together. "Shew, it's hot out here . . . humid."

"So, how come Boone somehow ends up with you and Sam instead of Casey?"

Lilly shrugs. "The luck of the draw, I guess."

"*Right* . . . the luck of the draw that he ends up with you. So fess up. Do you like Boone, Lilly? I won't tell."

"This is supposed to be my plan to get Luke on your doorstep. You're diverting my attention," she accuses.

I wring my hands. "That's because I'm usually behind these sorts of plans and not on the receiving end. I'm a pretty good meddler from way back."

"Turnabout is fair play then, huh?"

Suddenly a thought hits me. "Yeah . . . I do believe so."

Lilly takes a step back to let a group of rowdy cowboys pass and then folds her arms across her chest. "Why don't I like the tone of your voice, Macy?"

"What tone?" I bat my eyes.

"The same innocent tone I use when I've got somethin' up my sleeve."

"Okay, you tell me your plan and I'll tell you mine."

Lilly moves to let another crowd of people pass her on the sidewalk. "Why do I feel as if we're playin' truth or dare?"

"Maybe because in a way we are. Divulge this plan of yours."

"It's simple, really. Flirt your butt off in there."

I frown at her, confused. "But Luke's not here."

"Yes, but Brandon *is* and he'll go runnin' his mouth off to Luke in a heartbeat. He'll be on his cell phone before the night is over." She pokes a finger into my shoulder. "You mark my words: Luke will be here by this weekend, if not before."

"You think so? Really?"

Lilly points up at the neon flying pigs. "Are you forgettin' that I witnessed you two together at Jack's? Come on, Macy, the man has it bad for you. Believe it, sister. Now let's get your cute butt in there and start this ball rollin'." She grabs my hand but I tug it back.

"Oh no you don't. First I want to tell you my conditions."

Lilly gives me a deadpan stare. "I'm not gonna like this, am I?"

I hesitate and then say in a rush, "Okay, I'll flirt with Tanner if you kiss Boone."

"What?" She glances in Boone's direction. "You're outta your ever-lovin' mind."

I give her a shrug. "Those are my conditions."

"Your conditions suck," she protests, but I notice that color is high in her cheeks and she licks her lips.

"Truth or dare, Lilly?"

She narrows her eyes and then says, "Okay then, I choose *truth*," she says so that she doesn't have to kiss him.

"Are you insanely attracted to Boone?"

"Yes," she admits through gritted teeth.

"Then I dare you to kiss him."

"That's not how this game works."

I shrug and then angle my head toward Tootsie's front door.

"Macy," Lilly says in a more serious voice, "here's the problem. Boone works for Tammy. She's real fond of him. Do you realize how crappy it would be to start somethin' with Boone and have it go south? Think about it. He's a bodyguard . . . *my* bodyguard. This could get messy."

"Yeah, and it could be amazing."

Lilly closes her eyes and swallows. "You suck, Macy McCoy."

"Bite me."

Lilly opens her eyes and grins. "Okay, you're officially one of us, now."

I give her a knuckle bump. "I'm callin' him over."

"But—"

"No buts! It's time for the little-less-talk part. Boone!" I say loud enough for him to hear, even though he's probably got some expert listening skills and has heard our conversation anyway. They probably teach such things in bodyguard school. Or is it the school of bodyguards? Plus we did get a little loud. I tend to raise my voice when I get worked up about something. When I crook my finger at him he walks our way.

"I'm gonna get you back for this," Lilly says under her breath.

"Make it a good kiss," I warn her, "or all bets are off."

"No, *really*. I'm gonna kick your ass," she threatens, but her eyes are on Boone. I bet her heart is beating fast just thinking about kissing him.

"What's up, ladies? You gonna hang out here all night?" Boone asks, but as usual his eyes are on Lilly.

"Lilly lost a bet and now she has to kiss you." There, I might as well get it all out in the open.

I almost lose it when Boone's badass bodyguard expression becomes comical. I suppose he wasn't prepared for my comment. "Excuse me?" His normal deep voice is laced with disbelief. "You girls been doin' shots?"

"Not yet, but it's sounding like a pretty darned good idea," I tell him, but of course his eyes are still on Lilly. I'm not sure he'd look if Faith Hill walked by.

"What game we playin' here, Lilly?" he questions in a gruff voice. It suddenly occurs to me that he might have arms the size of tree trunks but when it comes to Lilly he's as vulnerable as they come. "So you lost a bet and the payback is that you have to kiss me? Not exactly good for my ego," he comments with a dry chuckle.

"Wow, you have a sense of humor," I tell him, trying to bring some levity to the situation that Lilly and I have created . . . well mostly that I've created, but she started it.

"Yeah, well, Macy, maybe there's more to me than meets the eye," he answers, but is really directing his comment toward Lilly.

I totally get what he's saying. I suppose being a huge,

muscle-bound guy is the male equivalent of being a big-chested blonde. People just assume that you're dumb.

Lilly looks at him thoughtfully but remains silent long enough for him to say, "Yeah, that's what I thought."

She angles her head. "So you think you know what I'm thinkin'?"

A muscle ticks in his jaw. "Are you gonna make good on your bet, or are you just blowin' smoke?" Boone finally asks, and then folds his muscular arms over his wide chest.

"Might as well get it over with," Lilly shoots back with her hands on her hips, and the sparks between them start to fly.

"Come on, *big boy*. Show me what you got."

"Oh no you don't," Boone says, and holds his ground. "The deal was that you were supposed to kiss *me*, remember?"

Lilly looks at me for help. "Um . . . ," I begin, and then wince. "I have to say that Boone has a point. You said that you would kiss *him*."

Lilly narrows her eyes at me. "I am *so* gonna get you back for this."

Boone grins and looks as if he's starting to enjoy himself. "Show me watcha got, *little girl*."

Lilly arches one delicate eyebrow. "You ever heard the saying 'be careful what you ask for'?"

Boone folds his hands and wiggles his fingers toward his chest. "Bring it on."

I jam my thumb in the direction of Tootsie's purple building. "Um . . . I think I'll just head back on in if it's all the same to you guys," I tell them, but neither Boone nor Lilly even spares me a glance. As I walk away, however, I can't help but sneak a peek over my shoulder. I grin when I watch Lilly slowly approach Boone but at the last second she jumps up into his arms. He catches her easily, cupping her butt when she wraps her legs around his waist and then starts kissing her as though there's no tomorrow.

I have to shake my head since neither of them seems to be giving a thought to the fact that they're standing on a public sidewalk . . . but then again this is the Honky-Tonk Highway in the height of the summer. Everyone is partying and having a good ole time, so seeing a young couple kissing wildly on the street corner is pretty much business as usual.

When I get back inside, Tootsie's is wall-to-wall people and hopping with activity. One of the interesting things about the honky-tonks is that the crowd is a mixture of all ages. On the corner stool hugging the bar is a bearded, white-haired dude who appears old as dirt, and then standing near the steps is a circle of college-aged girls in low-slung jeans and belly-button rings. In the mix are always convention-attending businessmen in dress clothes rubbing elbows with farm-raised cowboys in Wranglers and Stetsons. One thing for certain is that everyone seems to be having a fun time.

Tanner James is setting up at the tiny front stage and when he sees me pass he tips his hat and gives me a dimpled grin. When I notice a little more male attention come my way I feel a bit of feminine power . . . and I like it. With a lift of my chin I add a little wiggle to my hips as I approach Sam and Brandon sitting at the round table next to the Wall of Fame.

"Where have you been?" Sam asks, although she

doesn't seem to have minded her time alone with Brandon. Not that I'm surprised, but I am pleased that he's still by Sam's side since it's part of Lilly's making-Luke-jealous plan that I'm not at all convinced will work. "Boone didn't look too happy as he followed you two outside."

"Oh, I think he's smiling, right about now."

Sam's blue eyes widen. "What's goin' on? Spill, Macy."

I angle my head toward the front entrance. "Go look for yourself." When Sam seems reluctant to leave Brandon, I say, "I'll keep Brandon company. Trust me, you've got to take a peek but don't let Lilly know I told you, okay?"

When she glances up at Brandon he gives her a smile that convinces her that he's staying put. "Be right back," she assures him, and then hurries off.

"Damn she's cute," Brandon observes as he watches her weave through the sardine-packed crowd.

"Somebody's smitten," I observe in a singsong voice. "Has the mighty Brandon Sheldon finally met his match?"

"Yeah, right," he scoffs, and then tips back his beer bottle. "You know me, Macy. I'll never settle down. I'm just sayin' that she's hot, that's all."

"You hurt her and I'll kick your butt into next week."

"Wow, you really care about these people that much already?"

"Yeah, I do," I tell him, but I realize that I truly mean it.

Brandon smiles. "I'm happy for you, Macy. Luke says that this is a huge opportunity. You must be ecstatic."

"That's an unexpected way of putting it."

"I do have a vocabulary. I went to three colleges, remember?" he jokes, but then looks a bit embarrassed.

"I'm sorry, Brandon. I didn't mean to imply that you don't."

"No offense taken," he says, and pats my hand so that I know he means it but then shrugs. "With Griff gettin' hitched, you movin' here, and Luke lookin' at Division One colleges, I guess I'm feelin' a little restless . . . like everyone is passin' me by."

"At twenty-three you still have plenty of time to do whatever your heart desires, Brandon. Go back to school if you want to."

While toying with his beer bottle he looks at me with serious eyes. "That's the problem. I'm not sure what direction to take . . . ," he admits, but then shakes his shaggy head. "What the hell am I doin'? I'm here to have fun, not to rag on my sorry-ass life."

"First of all," I tell him as I grab a cold Bud Light from the barmaid, "you don't have a sorry-ass life just because you haven't figured it all out yet, Brandon. Secondly, we'll have all the fun you can handle tonight but I'm always here to bend an ear. You know that, right?"

Brandon gives me a crooked smile. "Sometimes you understand me better than my own family, Macy. Mama's always seemed disappointed in me and Griff likes to preach down to me. I know I've been a screw-off but still . . ."

I point my beer bottle at him. "Look at it this way. Your mama is just worried like most parents. And Griff? Well Brandon, he's just doin' his best to be a father figure to you."

"Yeah, but he can be such a know-it-all pain in the ass."

Griff is one of the nicest guys I know but then again he's not my older brother so I don't argue. "Maybe, but I know one thing for sure—they both love you to pieces."

"I'll give you that," he agrees, and then gives me his usual bad-boy grin. "Even though I've given them reason not to."

"Their love is unconditional, Brandon. Remember that."

He nods. "Yeah well, just the same I think it's about time I grow up, you know? Become more responsible."

"Growin' up is overrated but yeah, I've been thinkin' the same thing . . . about myself that is."

"But let's start tomorrow, okay?"

"Deal," I tell him, and clink my bottle to his. When Sam comes back to our table his face lights up. She's such a cute little thing and as far as I can tell sincere. Lilly says she always goes for the wrong guy and I know that Brandon has some issues but beneath his bad-boy ways is a good person waiting to surface. Maybe the right girl could bring it out in him, I think to myself as I watch them interact. I firmly tell myself not to meddle, ahh but still . . . wouldn't it be fun if they ended up together?

Tanner James starts his set with the Garth Brooks classic "Friends in Low Places." Brandon, Sam, and I join the rest of the patrons in Tootsie's and sing along. "Is it me or does beer make me sing better?" I lean over and ask them.

"It's you," Brandon assures me, and Sam laughs.

"Well, dang," I tell them, but sing loud anyway. "And I've got friends . . . in low-o-o places!"

When the song ends Tootsie's erupts with cheers and whistles. With a grin Tanner reaches down and picks up his beer bottle. "Okay," he shouts, "it's time for a swaller and a holler." He raises his bottle in the air and we follow his lead. "On the count of three . . . One, two, three!" Like Tanner we tip our beers back for a long pull and then shout, "Yee-haw!"

Tanner mixes it up with some old-school Waylon Jennings and then appeals to the young crowd with Kenny Chesney's "Summertime." "He's amazing," I comment to Sam.

"Yeah, Tammy likes him a lot. When he's ready she said she'd listen to some demo tapes."

"Wow, she'd do that for him?"

Sam nods. "She loves to give back."

"It blows my mind that she's stayed so grounded," I comment.

"Oh she has her celebrity moments," Sam divulges with a low chuckle. "But when she does, Lilly and I get her in line."

"Does she get ticked when y'all give her grief?" Brandon asks.

"Nah, she wants it that way." Sam nudges me with her elbow. "Look, here come Boone and Lilly. I guess they finally pried their lips apart," she says with a grin. "It's about time those two hooked up."

"Look," I observe, "he's grinnin' already."

Sam leans in close to my ear so that Brandon can't hear and says, "I betcha he has a big, happy smile on his face before the night is over."

I'm in the middle of a swallow of beer and almost spew it out my mouth. "Sam!"

"What?" She opens her eyes wide. "I'm just sayin' . . ."

Instead of going back to his stool at the bar, Boone joins us at the table. Color is high in Lilly's cheeks and I don't think it has much to do with the summer heat. Boone politely pulls out a stool for Lilly and then scoots up to the table.

"Boone, I'd like you to meet Brandon Sheldon. He's a good friend of mine from Hootertown."

"Hey, Brandon," Boone says over the music, and extends his arm across the table, carefully avoiding beer bottles. "Nice to meet ya."

"Same here," Brandon replies as he grasps Boone's big hand.

While they exchange a few words I lean over and say to Lilly, "Wow, you go, girlfriend."

Even in the dim lighting in the bar I can tell that she's blushing. "Oh, hush."

"You can thank me later," I tell her, but then regret my comment when her eyebrows shoot up.

"And you can thank me when I get luscious Luke knocking down your door. Speaking of which, I do believe it's time to put our little plan into action."

"About that—," I begin, but she shakes her head.

"Oh no you don't. Remember when I said that turnabout is fair play?"

"Um . . . yeah."

"Well, get ready."

15

What a Difference
a Kiss Makes

I'm guessing that Lilly's comment is somehow in reference to dancing with Tanner James since she turns her attention to the stage. After taking a guzzle of my beer I lean close to Lilly and ask in her ear, "Just what am I in store for here?"

When her answer is a grin I start to get nervous, even though I have to admit that this is the most fun I've had in a while. Before I can ask again Tanner's deep voice booms into the microphone.

"Well, for those who don't know me, I'll tell y'all a little of my story. See, even though I've always wanted to sing and write my own songs, I never really considered doin' this for a livin' . . . so I traveled here and there doin' odd jobs like workin' on a ranch in Texas, an oil rig in Alaska, and well, a bunch of other things in between, most of which I pretty much wasn't cut out for."

When Tanner pauses for laughter I glance over at Sam, hoping for a clue as to what's going on, but she's so into Brandon that she doesn't even look my way.

"One thing I did notice during my various stints all over the good ole USA was the beautiful women . . ." He pauses for cheers and whistles. "But I havta tell ya, there's only one kinda girl for this cowboy—one who likes to cruise in her daddy's pickup truck. One who likes to play hard when she's down on her luck." He pauses for cheers and some *hell yeahs*. "One who makes sweet rock and roll while she listens to country songs . . . Y'all need any more clues?"

"A redneck girl!" Lilly shouts, and raises her beer bottle. All the other redneck girls and even those who aren't raise their bottles as well, including me . . . well because I am a redneck girl, after all.

Suddenly I know where this is leading . . .

"Yeah, there's nothin' on earth that turns me on more than a redneck girl. In fact, I've chosen one in particular." He looks in my direction and crooks his finger at me. "Macy, come up here on stage. I want ya to sing and dance with me!"

"Sing?" I squeak at Lilly. "I can't *sing*!" When I hesitate Lilly gives me a nudge and a this-is-part-of-the-getting-Luke-plan wink. I roll my eyes at her but then slip down from my stool and make my way to the front of the bar, high-fiving fellow redneck girls along the way.

"Now, while I'm singin' about my favorite kinda women and dancing with Macy, I want a few other redneck chicks dancin' up on the bar," he requests, and points in that direction. "Boys, take a seat and move your beer bottles outta the way!" Tanner shouts as he reaches out and helps me step up beside him. A moment later he launches into the Bellamy Brothers classic, "Gimme a Redneck Girl," the Southern chick anthem long before Gretchen Wilson's "Redneck Woman" hit the top of the country music charts.

Because I'm basically tone-deaf, I mouth the words while Tanner wraps one hand around the microphone and loops his arm around my waist. He belts out the song so as to be heard over the crowd. "Why don't ya gimme a, gimme a, gimme a"—he shoves the microphone to my mouth so I have to sing loud and proud—"redneck girl!" Luckily my off-key voice goes unnoticed except for Lilly and Sam who are laughing their butts off. Brandon, who is also privy to my lack of singing skills, puts his thumb and pinkie in between his lips and whistles.

"Bring it home, Macy," Tanner shouts. It's a good thing he's holding on to me since the stage is the size of a postage stamp. Spurred on by the cheering crowd and fueled by three Bud Lights, I decide to hell with my horrid voice and belt the song out as though I'm Tammy Turner instead of Macy McCoy. No one seems to care that I suck.

"Let's hear it for Macy!" At the end of the song Tanner puts his hat on my head and raises my hand in the air as though I just won a prizefight. When he leans down and kisses me, I have to admit that I feel kind of special. The redneck girls cheer me on, making me take a bow as if I'm the queen of something . . . although I'm not sure what. Perhaps Bud Light? I laugh at the thought as I place Tanner's hat back on his head where it belongs. He gives me a grin that I swear means he's interested. I smile back even though I know this won't go anywhere since he's handsome as all get out and cute enough to eat with a spoon . . .

But he's not Luke.

Still, he's interested in me. While I know that this is all part of his stage presence, Tanner could have chosen any-one in the bar and for some reason I caught his eye. It's enough to give me a boost of confidence. Tanner doesn't seem to mind my few extra pounds. Maybe being as skinny as a stick is overrated after all.

"God bless redneck girls," Tanner proclaims, and of course is met with cheers. "Thanks for the dance, Macy," Tanner says. I realize that my five minutes of near fame are over but then Tanner leans in close and kisses me on the lips . . . a quick kiss, mind you, but he lingers long enough to get a sigh from the other less-fortunate redneck girls in the audience. If I were bolder I would throw my arms around his neck and give him a good one, but I'm not that brazen. Instead, I feel the heat of a blush creep into my cheeks. But then I remember that I'm supposed to make the most of this situation, so I smile up at Tanner with what I hope is a flirtatious invitation to come sit with me in between sets.

We'll see. Maybe I'm getting a little too overly confi-dent in my cleavage-showing shirt, but then again when I get back to the table there's a cold beer waiting for me.

"From a secret admirer," Lilly announces loud enough to make sure that Brandon hears. I have to wonder if the drink really was from someone or if she's making it up as part of her plan.

"Cool," Sam says. "From who?"

Lilly looks at her and says tightly, "That's the secret part of secret admirer."

Sam frowns. "Yeah but usually—" she begins, and then sort of jumps, making me wonder if Lilly just kicked her beneath the table. Lilly's eyes widen at her sister. "Oh . . . *right*, Macy's been getting that a lot lately." She looks up at Brandon. "Yeah, she's taken Nashville by storm. Haven't you, Macy?"

I'm thinking that Sam is going a bit too far with this but I nod anyway while trying not to snicker. Taking Nashville by storm? What does that even mean?

"Really?" Brandon asks. His lips sort of twitch, making me wonder if he's already got the crazy plan all figured out. "By storm, huh?"

Sam nods vigorously. "Yes sir. I think I'm gonna start callin' her Hurricane Macy," she says, and then jumps again. Poor thing. She's going to have bruised shins. Sam gives Lilly a *what*-I'm-trying-here expression.

"Hurricane Macy . . . ," Brandon muses while rubbing his chin. "Hmmm, I like that. I do believe it fits too." He gives me an I-know-something-is-going-on look but can't quite figure it out. But then his eyes widen just a fraction and he says, "If you'll excuse me, I need to hit the boys room. I'll be right back." He smiles at Sam as he slides from his stool.

"I'll save your seat," Sam promises sweetly, but then pounces on Lilly as soon as Brandon is out of earshot. "Would ya quit kickin' me? You about broke my doggone leg."

"Oh come on Sam. *Hurricane Macy?* What the hell was up with that?"

When Boone snickers, Sam shoots him a glare. "I don't know . . . I panicked. I'm guessin' you're tryin' to get word back to Luke that he'd better get his butt in gear because Macy's got guys lined up around the block? Am I right?"

Lilly hits her forehead with the heel of her hand. "Well hello. Yeah!"

Sam purses her lips. "Pretty good plan, I guess," she admits, but with a bit of skepticism.

"Oh, like you could do better?" Lilly tosses back.

"You didn't ask me."

Lilly leans her elbows on the table and hisses, "Because you're so wrapped up in bad-boy Brandon."

"You should talk. You were wrapped *around* Boone!"

Boone holds up his hands. "Girls, you're veering away from your mission."

"Right," the sisters say in unison, and I have to laugh.

"So, stay on task," Boone reminds them. I notice that instead of snapping back, Lilly nods and slips her small hand over his. What a difference a kiss makes . . .

"Okay, we need to shift this plan into high gear while Brandon's still here," Lilly tells Sam. "It's your job to keep him around for as long as you can, so don't get on his nerves."

"Does it look like I'm getting on his nerves?"

Lilly shrugs. "It's all a matter of time."

"Bite me," Sam says, but just when I think she's serious, Boone laughs and I realize they're just joking.

While they banter back and forth I'm noticing that Brandon's taking his sweet time getting back to the table. Luckily, Sam is deep in conversation about whether they should buy me a long-stemmed rose being peddled by a vendor, so she doesn't immediately notice Brandon's absence. I do, however, and hope that he hasn't for some unknown reason left Tootsie's. It wouldn't be like Brandon to do such a rude thing but then again he seems to have a lot on his mind. While nursing my beer I'm contemplating all of this, including the fact that the jealousy card probably isn't going to pan out anyway, when my cell phone vibrates in my pocket. As usual I'm startled as though I don't know what's tickling my leg.

"Ohmigod, it's Luke," I say, and slide the phone onto the table.

"Answer it!" Sam, Lilly, and even Boone say in unison.

"No!" For some reason I get it into my head that Luke will somehow know about the plot if I answer. Crazy, I know, but I just stare at the phone as it buzzes. Then I can't believe my eyes when Boone—yes Boone—picks up my phone and flips it open. Lilly's and Sam's mouths are hanging open as well.

"Hey," Boone says, and then gives me a startled what-have-I-done look that for any other reason would have been comical. "Um, this is Boone, you know, the body-guard. No, Macy's in the bathroom . . . Yeah, they are too. You know how women go in packs." He winces and then shrugs his wide shoulders. "Yeah, I'm keeping an eye on her. Sure. Okay, I'll have her call when she gets back to the table." He pauses and then says, "Um, yeah, she did sing on stage. No, not too much really, just a few. Okay, will do." He flips the phone shut and then says, "Um . . . sorry. I don't know what the hell got into me."

Again, the apologetic expression on his face would be funny if he hadn't just answered *my* phone. Of course we all start asking questions at once until Boone finally holds up his hands in surrender.

"How did Luke know that I sang with Tanner?" I ask,

and then it hits me. "Brandon! That's why he's been gone so long."

Lilly and Sam high-five. "Are we good or what?" Lilly asks me.

"Wow . . . yeah," I admit with a bit of wonder. My heart starts to pound. "So do you really think he's, like, jealous? Or is it just, you know, brotherly concern?"

"Is he your brother?" Lilly asks, bopping her head so hard that her spikes actually move.

"No."

"Well then, there's your answer."

I blink at her for a moment but then turn to Boone. "I can't believe you just did that."

With a rather embarrassed lift of his shoulders he says, "Sorry. I think I just got caught up in the moment."

Sam snickers. "That totally sounded like a girl."

With an effort Boone reverts to his badass bodyguard expression but even though it's pretty dark in the bar, I swear he's blushing all the way to his bald head. "Hey, I have a feminine side," he says in a high-pitched voice that has us all laughing.

"Right," I tell him.

"I think it's cute," Lilly tells him, and he blushes even deeper.

"Oh gag me," Sam says, but then has no room to talk since she seems to melt like warm caramel when Brandon returns to the table.

"What?" he asks when we all look at him expectantly.

"Where have you been?" I ask him.

"The bathroom."

"Have you been talking to anyone in particular?" I persist, but when he merely shrugs I prompt, "Confess,

Brandon. Luke just called and seemed a bit . . . ," I begin, but I don't have the confidence to say *jealous* because I still can't really believe it.

"Is *jealous* the word you're searching for?"

"Do you think he is?" I blurt out, and then hide my embarrassment behind my beer bottle.

"I was givin' it my best to make him feel that way."

After thumping my bottle down I widen my eyes. "You were?"

"I was pretty much on to y'all's plan from the get-go," he admits. "But for the record, Luke called *me*, so I decided to, you know, help things along." He looks at me and shakes his head. "It's been obvious for a while now that the two of you were fighting your . . . feelings."

Boone grins at Brandon and holds his fists out for a knuckle bump. "Thanks man."

"For what?"

"For sounding like a chick too. See, we all have a feminine side."

I look at badass Boone and bad-boy Brandon and have to laugh. "Yeah, who knew?"

"Don't breathe a word of this to anyone in Hootertown," Brandon requests with a grin. "Don't want to ruin my rep."

"Me either," Boone says.

"You guys crack me up," I tell them with a shake of my head.

"Your secret is safe with me," Lilly says in such a serious tone that Sam snickers, drawing a frown from her sister.

"Oh okay," Sam says, and rolls her eyes. "I won't

breathe a word that Boone is such a softie but I've always known it anyway."

"I'm not a softie," Boone scoffs.

Lilly reaches over and wraps her hand around his bulging bicep. "Personally, I think that it's incredibly sexy when a big, strong guy shows a sensitive side."

Boone grins at her. "Okay, I take it back. I'm a marsh-mallow."

"Oh gag me again," Sam groans, but I can tell she's happy for her sister.

Unable to contain my curiosity one more second I turn my attention to Brandon. "Um, what exactly did Luke call you about?" I keep my tone casual but I'm sure I'm not fooling anybody.

"He wanted me to head over to Dixie's Dance Hall, but I said that I was in Nashville."

"Oh . . ." I feel a stab of disappointment. "So he wanted to go out on the town," I mumble, trying not to sound so pathetically glum, but I know that I do. Of course *I'm* out on the town . . . but whatever.

"Macy, it's Hootertown. What else is there to do?"

I shrug. "I dunno," I mutter, sounding like Eeyore from Winnie the Pooh, but then jump when my cell phone rings. "Ohmigod, it's Luke."

When I stare at the phone Boone says, "If you don't answer it, I will."

Until a little while ago I would have thought Boone was kidding but now that I know differently, I take a deep breath and flip my phone open.

16

Dreamin' and Schemin'

"Hey, Luke," I answer, hoping he can hear me over the music. All eyes at the table are on me. "What's up?" I ask, and then wish I could think of something clever to say. When I can't hear him I put my index finger over my ear but then Tanner starts singing "I Love This Bar" and it's impossible to make out a word Luke's saying.

"Go outside," Lilly suggests, and I nod.

"Luke, I can't hear you so I'm going outside, okay?"

"Good idea," he shouts into the phone.

While weaving my way through the rowdy crowd I get a few high fives resulting from my five minutes of near fame on stage with Tanner. "It was hard making my way through the crowd. Tootsie's is jam-packed," I tell him after I'm finally outside. The fresh air on my face feels good. While staying close to the building I find a more secluded spot. "That's better. I can finally hear you."

"Don't go far," Luke warns with a hint of concern.

"Had I known Brandon was heading down I'd have gone with him."

"I don't think he meant to come all the way to Nashville. You know Brandon. He tends to fly by the seat of his pants."

"Yeah, but he's a good kid," Luke says, and then chuckles. "Well, not exactly a kid anymore. He's all grown up."

"Yeah, me too." Damn, I didn't mean to say that out loud. I really need to work on that . . .

"Um, yeah, I've noticed," Luke surprises me by saying. Maybe he didn't mean to blurt that out either? "So I hear that you've been having some fun tonight," he says casually, but dare I hope that he is just a teensy bit jealous?

While looking up at the flying pink pigs I have to smile. "Me singing into a microphone is not a good thing. But you already know that."

"I don't think you were asked up on stage for your singing ability," he says dryly. Wow, maybe he is jealous . . . "I'm glad that Boone and Brandon are there to watch over you girls."

A bit of my feisty nature surfaces. "Luke, believe me, I can take care of myself."

"Ah, sweetie, I know that, but promise me you'll be careful. You're not in Hootertown, ya know."

Wait . . . hold the phone. Rewind. Did he just call me sweetie? Like in short for sweetheart? I know it's sort of a sexist term but heaven help me, it makes me smile.

"Macy?" he asks, mistaking my melting over the sweetie term for feistiness. "Don't be stubborn about this, okay? Just be careful there in the city."

I want to say, *Call me sweetie again,* but of course I don't. "I will."

"Listen, I'm coming to Nashville on business tomorrow. Would you like to have dinner with me after you get off work? I might be there for a few days interviewing for a position at Vanderbilt."

"Really? My apartment is near campus." *Make an offer for him to stay at your place,* a little voice shouts in my ear but I don't have the nerve. "You should just come over and I'll cook you dinner." *What?*

"That sounds great," he says. "I'll call you later in the day. Thanks, Macy."

"You bet," I tell him, but I'm thinking, *My God, what did I just do?*

"Now get back inside with your friends."

"I will," I promise, but all I can think about is the fact that in a moment of absolute insanity I offered to *cook dinner for him*!

"Good. See you tomorrow."

"Okay," I reply lightly, but then squeeze my eyes shut after I tell him good-bye. *Cook dinner for him?*

Cook dinner for him!

"What was I thinkin'?" I whine loud enough to startle one of those guys painted silver to look like statues. "I can't cook worth a lick," I confess to the silver guy, who reminds me of the tin man. I suppose in the back of my mind I was thinking that if Luke came over for dinner there was a much better chance of him staying the night.

"Sorry about your luck," the tin man says, coming out of character. His silver lips are pink underneath, making him look kind of scary, but I appreciate his sympathy. It's a bit humbling that a street beggar is treating me with kindness. I suppose I should count my blessings.

"Thanks," I tell him, and then toss a dollar into his tip bucket. Then with a little whimper I bang my phone against my forehead. "Now what am I gonna do?"

He shrugs. "Order takeout? Just, you know, put it on real dishes. Or just be honest and tell him you can't cook."

I nod. "Yeah, you're right. So I can't cook. So what?"

"There's the attitude," he says, and then slips back into his statue mode. I have to admit that he looks pretty real . . . and kind of creepy.

Statue guy is right, though. In this day and age I shouldn't be worried about my lack of cooking skills. I mean, who cooks nowadays anyway? Well okay, people in Hootertown still do, not to mention that Luke's mama is famous for her culinary skills. Even so, I should just be up front and tell him the truth.

God . . . but I don't wanna! I want to whip up a fabulous meal that has him raving, doggone it. I suppose it bothers me because I always wanted to be a good cook for my daddy. With all the crappy food he consumed on the road, it would have been nice for him to enjoy a home-cooked meal.

I tried. Really. I read cookbooks and watch cooking shows! Rachael Ray makes it look so easy! But I could never quite put my scattered knowledge into practice. For some reason the kitchen remains a room of mystery and mishaps.

My daddy, bless his heart, would eat whatever I put in front of him but then again I wasn't trying to impress my daddy. With a sigh I head back into Tootsie's, hoping to get some words of wisdom from my friends.

"What's wrong?" Lilly asks when I sit back down on my bar stool. I suppose my misery is written all over my face.

"Luke is coming into town tomorrow for a meeting with Vanderbilt and I offered to cook dinner for him."

Sam angles her head in question. "Wait, am I missing something? This is good news, right?"

"No!"

"Well, why the hell not?" Lilly asks with a frown.

I give them a sheepish look. "I can't cook."

"Oh me neither," Sam scoffs, but then glances at Brandon. "Well, you know, not fancy stuff," she amends.

"No, you don't understand. I really, really suck."

Boone shakes his head. "Well, then why did you say you would cook if you can't?"

"Duh, to impress him," Lilly says, and gives me a look of female understanding. "You should have picked something different, though."

"Ya think?" I ask while tapping my foot to the beat of "No Shoes, No Shirt, No Problems." "It just sort of came out of my mouth! Now what am I gonna do?"

"Easy," Sam says with a wave of her hand. "Just get some takeout from The Loveless Café and fake it." She gives Brandon another glance. "Not that I would ever do such a thing."

With a totally Brandon grin he leans over and says something in Sam's ear, making her laugh. I'm sure it has something to do with not having to fake it.

Lilly, who had been nibbling on the inside of her

cheek, suddenly snaps her fingers. "I think I have an answer to your dilemma."

"You do?" I ask with hope in my heart. "What?"

When we all look at her expectantly she elaborates,
"Well, Tammy is real good friends with Cody West."

"The *Grillin' and Chillin'* chef from the Food Channel?"

"The one and only," Lilly answers. "I don't know if he
could help out on such short notice but even if he can't,
he might know someone who could come over and . . .
you know, *assist* you a tiny bit in the kitchen." She holds
her thumb and index finger an inch apart.

"That would be amazing! All I ever needed was someone to teach me some basic skills. Tell him I'm clueless
but a quick study."

"I'll see what I can do," Lilly promises, and then gives
me a high five.

"What was that for?"

"For being brave."

"Um, you mean stupid?"

"Sometimes it's a fine line," she admits with a wink.
"But you're putting yourself out there, Macy." She lifts
her bottle and tips it forward. "To dreamin' and
schemin'!"

"I'll drink to that," Sam says, and doesn't even give an
apologetic glance to Brandon this time. He, however,
looks at her with a smile and then shakes his head before
tipping back his own bottle. I have to wonder if he's finally met his match. I sure hope so.

"Hey," Lilly says as she glances down at her phone.
"Tammy's callin'. I'll take it outside."

"I'm comin' with you," Boone informs her.

"Okay." She gives in without an argument. "We'll be back in a few minutes."

"Don't forget to ask her about Cody West helpin' Macy," Sam reminds her.

"I won't," Lilly promises.

Brandon leans over and says, "You're lucky, Macy. These girls already care about you. If I didn't know better I'd think y'all had been friends for a long time."

"Oh I know," I agree, but then feel myself get a little choked up.

Brandon reaches over and pats my leg. "But you're homesick."

"Yeah and I miss Jamie Lee and the Cut and Curl." I have to swipe at a tear. "Why couldn't we stay twelve years old forever?"

"It was a helluva lot less complicated back then."

"You can say that again."

"It was a helluva lot less complicated back then."

"Brandon," I say with a laugh, and playfully punch his arm.

He shrugs. "Corny but it got a laugh outta ya."

"Are we gonna be okay?" I've always felt a sense of closeness to Brandon even though we're three years apart in age. He and I have always seemed to be searching . . . aching for something that probably stems from the early loss of a parent. "Sometimes I get so doggone . . . scared."

Brandon places his hand over mine and squeezes. "There's no doubt in my mind that we'll be okay."

I give him a shaky smile and stack my hand over his. "Maybe we should both stop doubting and start believin' in ourselves."

"Sounds good," he agrees with a nod.

"But easier said than done?"

He polishes off his beer and says, "You got that right."

"Hey, I don't want you drivin' that bike of yours. You're welcome to crash at my place."

"Thanks, um, but . . ."

"Oh, I get it. You've got a better offer."

He gives me a grin that's more sheepish than bad boy. I would give him a don't-you-dare-hurt-Sam lecture but when he spots her heading back our way, I can tell there's no need. His eyes light up when she gives him a soft smile full of promise . . . playful, sexual, but I can already sense something deeper simmering beneath the surface.

"Boone and Lilly are draggin' behind," Sam says when she reaches the table. "I'm supposed to tell you that Tammy's got a photo shoot tomorrow morning and that you'll be needed to do her hair. Either Boone or Casey will pick you up and bring you to Greystone Studios."

"In other words we should call it a night."

Sam nods. "Yeah, I don't want to look rough around the edges tomorrow. Tammy will be ticked."

"Gotcha."

Sam gives me a big smile. "She also wanted me to tell you that Cody West will be coming to your apartment tomorrow sometime in the early afternoon."

"Wow!" I put my hand over my mouth. "Um, do I need to go grocery shoppin'? I don't have much in the way of food in my fridge."

"Tammy said that Cody's plannin' on takin' you shoppin'," she says, but the tone of her voice tells me there's something she's leaving out.

"Sam, is there anything else I should know about?"

"Um, okay, you promise not to panic?"

"I promise," I lie. My heart is already beating faster. When someone tells me not to panic it's the first thing that I do. "Okay, now tell me what's goin' on."

"Let's get out of here first. It's too noisy. You're gonna want to hear the details. Lilly and Boone are waitin'."

Holy cow. My panic level rises higher. "Okay." I smile brightly while wondering if this really is my life or if I'm going to wake up here shortly and be in my bed above the hardware store.

Brandon gives me a little poke with his elbow, leans over, and says in my ear, "Whatever it is, Macy, you can do it."

I nod and return his smile with much more confidence than I'm feeling. Once we're outside on the sidewalk Sam turns to me and says, "This is so cool, Macy! Lilly, tell her!"

"Tammy said that when she approached him, Cody West liked the idea of doing a show giving instructions to someone . . . um . . ."

"Hopeless?" I interject.

"Well, not exactly *hopeless* . . . ," she amends, but then with a grin comes clean. "Well yeah, pretty much."

"Okay, let me get this straight," I say as we walk toward the parking lot. "I'm gonna make my ineptness in the kitchen known to all for the entertainment of Cody's viewing audience? I thought this was supposed to be a covert operation to make Luke think I can cook—not to announce to the world that I can't." I raise my hands skyward but I have to admit that it would be kind of cool to be on television. Perhaps I'm going to extend my five minutes of almost fame a tad longer.

"Oh come on, Macy, it'll be fun," Lilly says. "Sort of like a redneck version of *Take Home Chef*. Besides, Luke won't know until after the fact."

"Yeah but Cody is kind of . . . how can I put this politely . . . um . . ."

"Crazy," Boone supplies for me.

I snap my fingers. "That's the word I was searching for. Crazy! He dices and chops and flips stuff . . . Mercy, Lilly, I might lose a finger or something."

Lilly waves a hand in my direction. "You'll be fine."

"Easy for you to say," I tell her, but she just laughs.

"But you're going to do it, right?" Lilly persists. They all stop in the middle of the sidewalk and look at me expectantly.

"Of course. Hopefully I'll learn a thing or two."

"Whoo-hoo!" Sam shouts, and gives me a body bump. "You sure have shaken things up around here."

"Wait a minute, *I've* shaken things up?" With raised eyebrows I point my thumb at my chest. "Just last week I was cutting hair in a small town. Now, here I am in Nashville hanging out with famous people and you think *I've* shaken things up?"

Lilly hooks her arm through mine as we start walking up the hill toward the parking lot. "Yeah, having a fresh face like you around has been fun. I know you miss your hometown, but I hope we've made you feel welcome."

"Ohmigod," Sam says as we reach the SUV. "Macy, you've brought out a softer, gentler side of Lilly. It's a miracle."

"Bite me," Lilly tells her.

"Bite me back," Sam says, but then gives Brandon a sheepish look. "Oops, am I scarin' you away?"

"Not on your life." Brandon shakes his head and gazes at Sam as if he wants to gobble her up. Sam, in turn, looks as though she were melting. I glance over at Lilly to see if she's making gagging gestures but she's too into Boone to notice. A little pang of jealousy shoots through me, making me wish that Luke were here so I could make eyes at him as well. Then I remember he is going to be here tomorrow . . . and I'm cooking dinner for him.

Well, not exactly. I'll be assisting Cody West . . . on television, no less. I have to grin while wishing I could call Jamie Lee and tell her of my adventures. That thought sobers me a bit since it brings home the fact that sometime in the near future I'll have some big decisions to make. But right now I'm not going to even think about that. I'm going to ride this wave until it reaches the shore.

Tomorrow can't come soon enough.

17

Grillin' and Chillin'

Bing-bong! "Oh no!" Of course I'm in my underwear when my doorbell chimes. Isn't that just the way of things? Since it's twenty minutes earlier than when I was told he was going to arrive, I'm praying it's not Cody West and his crew. I'm hoping that maybe it's Sam and Lilly coming over to help me get dressed, but deep down I just know it's going to be Cody and company. Trying not to panic but failing miserably, I look at the heap of clothing on my bed. "Oh God, now what?"

Bing-bong!

"Hells bells!" I actually do a hopping little dance in a circle while desperately trying to remember what outfit looked the best. "None of them!" I whine, closely followed by a pathetic whimper. Even if an outfit did make me look ten pounds lighter the heap is a hopeless mess.

Bing-bong. Bing-bong!

"I'm comin'!" I shout over my shoulder in the general direction of the door, and then giggle. "Oh *no*!" Not the

uncontrollable nervous giggles that usually end up in hic-
cups! "Please, God! Help me out here and I promise . . .
um . . . what? Okay, never to cuss again!"

Bing-bong!

"Damn!" Oh no! "Sorry! It just slipped out!" I squeak.
Reaching into the pile of clothes, all of which make my
butt look fat, I grab something off the top and tug it over
my head. Now of course, my armpits are starting to sweat
and I wonder if I remembered to put on deodorant. I sniff
beneath my arms and, thank God, encounter the scent of
Powder Fresh Secret. I suppose my sweat glands are trying to keep up with my racing pulse.

In the pile I find a pair of jeans that feel a bit too snug
but at this point I have to leave them on. "Shoes!" I locate
leopard print flip-flips—not the best choice but at this
point I'm afraid if I don't answer they will leave.

Just before I open the door I realize that I'm wearing
my WHATEVER shirt and almost say *shit* again but catch
myself. Swallowing a giggle, I take a deep breath and
then after pasting a smile on my face I swing open the
door, hoping that my shoes will go unnoticed.

What? "Luke!" No, he can't be here! Cody and his
crew will be showing up any minute!

"Hey," he says, but his smile falters at what must be an
expression of panic on my face. "Um, I called the studio
and I was told you had come home. I was worried you
might be sick or something."

It enters my mind to pretend a stomachache or something but then duh, it would defeat the whole day if he
doesn't come for dinner. "No, I'm fine." I smile brightly
but don't invite him in. Just how can I get rid of him? Oh

but with Luke in his worn jeans and dark blue shirt, getting rid of him seems like a damned shame.

"Good. Then I thought you might like to go to lunch since you're kind enough to cook dinner for me."

"Um . . . ," I stutter while trying to think. I never was good under pressure like this. Luke frowns and looks past my shoulder into the room as if I might be hiding something . . . or someone. That almost makes me laugh.

"So?"

I blink up him with an innocent expression while my brain races. "Yes?"

"So do you want to have lunch with me?" he asks rather slowly, and then frowns. "Are you *sure* you're feeling okay?"

I snap my fingers when my excuse hits me like a slap to the side of the head. Feeling silly, I snap my fingers again. "Gee, I have Tammy's new song playing in my head. Don't you hate it when you have a song in your head that you can't shake?"

Luke looks at me as though I'm one taco short of a combo but nods politely. "Yeah, um, I do."

"Well, listen, I have to prepare your meal. It will take me a while," I assure him, and nod briskly. I barely refrain from making shooing motions with my hands.

Not taking the hint, Luke leans one shoulder against the door frame and gives me a lazy smile that makes me want to grab him and plaster my mouth to his. "Macy, you don't have to go to any trouble."

I wave a dismissive hand while swallowing a giggle. If he only knew . . . "Oh, I *know*. It's not too complicated, but rather time-consuming."

Luke pushes away from the door frame and brushes

past me into the room. He looks around as if he senses that something is up. Rubbing his hands together he says, "Fine, I'll help. I love to cook. I'll be your sous chef. I can slice and dice with the best of them."

Crap! I do the dismissive hand gesture again. "Oh . . . no. *Really.*" Really comes out high-pitched and goofy, so I clear my throat as if that were the problem. I wave my hand again and then realize I look like I'm swiping at flies. This is not going well. *Gather your wits about you, Macy McCoy!* With a proud lift of my chin I angle my head and say, "Luke, I just want to show you that I can do this on my own." But then I want to swallow my tongue since I'm certainly not doing this on my own . . . at all. What a crock!

Luke looks at me for a long moment and then says, "Okay, I get it. I'll get out of your hair."

Oh God, he thinks I'm blowing him off! "It's not that I don't *want* you to stay . . ."

Luke angles his head in question and I realize I have to finish that statement.

"You would, um, just be, um . . . a distraction." Ohmigod I did not just say that!

"Now that I can relate to." Luke gives me a grin that's so suggestive I think I might have to sit down. Leaning over he lifts my chin with his fingertip and then slowly lowers his head and kisses me. On the mouth. A sweet, lingering kiss that has me fisting my hands in his shirt. Finally, just when I was thinking about grabbing his butt—okay I wouldn't have but I was thinking about it—he pulls back. "Okay," he says in a husky voice that makes me sweat. "I'll leave and let you cook up something special." With another quick kiss on the cheek he straightens up and turns around. With one last wave and another impossibly sexy smile he leaves me standing there with my mouth hanging open.

I finally have the sense to close the door. Several moments tick by as I try to convince myself that this is all really happening to me. But before I can fully recover, the doorbell chimes again. I swallow, paste a smile on my face, and wonder just what's in store for me this time.

"Cody West," the famous chef says unnecessarily but with a friendly smile. "You must be Macy, the real McCoy."

Since I feel a giggle bubbling up, I keep my lips pressed together but manage to nod.

"Nice to meet ya," he says, but when he looks at my T-shirt he laughs.

I feel a blush creep up my neck. "Um, I was in the middle of changing when the doorbell rang. Just give me a second and I'll put something else on."

"No way! I love it," Cody assures me, and raises his palm to give me a high five but I'm so nervous that I miss his hand. He laughs and lifts his palm to try again, this time missing my hand on purpose. "Oops," he says. "See, it happens to everybody." Cody's smile seems genuine and I think that if only I could calm my sorry self down, this really could be a fun experience. He jams his thumb toward his Hawaiian print shirt sporting palm trees and tiki huts. "I'm all about casual and fun. Your outfit works for me, including the flip-flops."

"Really?" When the camera pans down to my feet I barely resist the urge to curl my toes since I could use a pedicure. This also answers my question if we're already being filmed.

Holy cow.

"You betcha. So, way to go, Macy!" Cody holds his palms up for a double high five and this time I manage to hit both of his hands. "Is her outfit okay, Jenny?" Cody turns to a no-nonsense looking woman who sweeps past us into the room.

"*Jennifer* Markim," she announces as she extends her hand to me. "Director of production." I'm thinking she's fairly young but has mannerisms of someone much older. Her eyes narrow behind round glasses while she gives me a once-over. She purses her lips for a second and just when I feel a giggle start to bubble in my throat, she gives me a tight little smile followed by a crisp nod.

"Yes . . ." She draws out the word in a soft voice that somehow commands authority. "She looks casual as if she's going grocery shopping. It will give the show the ambiance of being spontaneous, almost as if you happened upon her instead of this being staged."

"Like a redneck *Take Home Chef*," I supply, remembering my conversation with Sam. But then I want to clamp my hand over my big fat mouth! I look at Cody to see if he's offended but he gives me a huge grin.

"Yeah, I love that . . . ," Cody comments, and I want to fall over with relief. "Jenny, can we somehow use that in the promo? Do a little spoof kind of thing?" I get the feeling she wants to tell him to call her Jennifer instead of Jenny but refrains probably because it wouldn't do any good.

"Won't the *Take Home Chef* guy get upset?" I ask in a small voice. I don't want this to end badly—my suggestions often do.

"Curtis Stone? Nah, he's a friend. We'll probably have

to get some sort of legal permission, though, right Jenny?"

Jennifer does two short nods that are so hard I wonder if they hurt her neck. "I'm on it, Mr. West."

"You know I hate it when you call me Mr. West."

She swallows and then does the two short nods thing again. "Yes, sir, C-Co—"

"You can't do it, can you?" he asks.

Jenny shakes her head. "Sorry, sir," she says softly, her voice so apologetic that I almost laugh.

When Cody loops his arm around Jennifer, two bright pink spots appear on the apples of her cheeks. "Jenny, just when are you gonna learn how to chill?"

"I don't *chill*, sir." I fully expect her to click her heels together and salute but upon closer inspection I have to wonder if she's got a crush on her boss.

"Someday, I'll get y'all to let down that hair of yours," he teases.

As if afraid it might literally happen, Jennifer reaches back and pats the tight bun at the nape of her neck. Satisfied that all is in place, she squares her shoulders. "That's not likely, Mr. West," she responds primly.

"I'd bet my bottom dollar," Cody comments under his breath but loud enough for her to hear. I have to wonder if Cody is merely trying to get her goat or is serious. When Jennifer turns away in what looks like a huff, Cody grins at her back. I'm thinking that there might be something going on beneath the surface that neither of them realizes. Love it seems is certainly in the air in Nashville, Tennessee.

I find that I'm smiling in spite of my nerves and thankfully the urge to giggle has subsided, at least for now.

After picking up a clipboard Jennifer turns around. "Now," she says to me, "I understand that there is a certain gentleman whom you're trying to impress. I do believe it's time to get down to business."

18

A Little Less Talk

Jennifer gestures toward my small oval table, which is off to the side of the galley-style kitchen. The cameraman follows, making me feel as though I'm in a reality TV show. I should tell them that teaching me to cook would view more like a sitcom than an instructional cooking class. "Let's have a seat and discuss what you'd like to prepare for your boyfriend."

"Um, Luke isn't exactly my boyfriend," I amend with a hint of embarrassment. I'm not sure why I felt the need to clarify the relationship other than I don't want Luke to catch wind of this and think that I'm telling the world that he belongs to me.

"He will be after this dinner," Cody promises from where he's checking out my tiny kitchen.

Jennifer taps the pen to her cheek and then asks, "What would you like to prepare for your . . . *friend*?" I'm guessing you'd like to knock his socks off."

"More like his boxers," Cody comments from the kitchen.

Jennifer shakes her head and says to the cameraman, "Remember to edit that out."

"You're no fun," Cody accuses her, and then opens the fridge. "My God, there's nothing in here but beer and sweet tea."

"I just moved here," I explain, even though a month from now it's likely to look the same.

"You're like a bachelor, only way prettier."

"Edit that too."

"What?" Cody says with an innocent look. "I was gonna say with way better boobs."

"Cody!" Jennifer exclaims, and then clamps her hand over her mouth. I wonder if it's because of what he just said or that she totally slipped and called him Cody. With color high in her cheeks she pushes her glasses up on her nose and whispers to me, "Try to ignore him. We need to get down to business."

"I heard that," Cody says from where he's examining my lack of cutlery. "Jenny, we're gonna have to hook her up with just about everything in order to put this meal to-gether."

"I'll make a note of it, Mr. West," she says, and then reverts her attention to me. "Okay, now just what would you like to prepare?"

"Mmm, Luke is a small-town guy from Hootertown, Kentucky. Pretty much a down-home, meat-and-potatoes kind of guy."

"Hootertown?" Cody says with a laugh. "Maybe we should do hot wings and onion rings?"

"And you can wear a little white tank top and orange

shorts," I suggest without remembering that he's a famous person and I'm supposed to be nervous.

Cody points at me and then laughs. "Beat me to the punch. Macy, I like your way of thinkin'."

Jenny gives me a don't-encourage-him look, but for a second there I think she almost smiled. But then she glances at her watch and says, "Time is of the essence. We need to plan this menu, go to the grocery store, and then prepare the meal before Luke Carter arrives."

"Sorry," I tell her, but I'm starting to relax and enjoy myself.

"Okay," Jennifer says as she looks over her notes. "We've decided on hot wings but a healthier grilled and baked version, twice-baked potatoes—not so healthy but one of Luke's favorite foods—celery and blue cheese dressing to cut the spicy wings, and chocolate brownie sundaes for dessert—another Luke Carter favorite." Jennifer looks up from her list and says, "If it's not too bold of me to say . . . Macy you sure know a lot about this guy for him not to be your boyfriend. You know everything down to his choice of beer brand."

"I've known him for a long time. Luke is my best friend's brother."

"Really now, how long have you been in love with him?" Jennifer asks, and then puts her hand over her mouth. "I'm so sorry. I've overstepped my bounds." She looks at the cameraman and says, "Edit that out."

"Does it show that much?" I ask her, suddenly no longer embarrassed. I'm beginning to think it's silly to deny my feelings especially since I seem to wear them on my sleeve.

"I'm afraid so," she says with a sigh. "It's obvious in

the way you talk about him . . . the look on your face when you say his name and, like I said, you seem to know every detail about the man," Jennifer explains with a bit of a dreamy expression, but then seems to catch herself and slips back into professional mode. "Just an observation," she says in her usual clipped manner.

I give her a smile. "Well then, we'll have to hope that this bodacious meal really does knock his boxers off. Bam!" I reach toward my waist and make as though I'm yanking off my pants and tossing them into the air. "Just like that!"

Jennifer's eyes widen and for the first time she actually forgets to be prim and proper, tilts her head back, and laughs hard.

Pointing at the cameraman I say, "Please edit that out too." This makes her laugh harder and after removing her glasses to swipe at tears of mirth, Jennifer looks at her watch and says, "Oh my, time is slipping away from us. We must be off," she says in a laughter-gurgled tone. With a flick of her hand at the crew she starts toward the door but then looks over at Cody who is standing quite still blinking at her. "What?" she asks him. "Did I forget something?" She glances down at her list and then over at him again.

"I don't believe it. You actually know how to laugh."

"Oh stop!" Jennifer shakes her head, "For once I thought you were being serious. I should have known better," she says a bit dismissively, and I see his expression falter for a second before he recovers. I do believe that even though he's always joking, he cares about her more than she knows. *Fear*, I think to myself and wonder how many relationships are ruined or then again never even started because of it. It occurs to me that I'm seeing this in others since it hits so close to home. I make a silent promise to myself that tonight I'm going to push my inhibitions aside and jump without a net. I'm getting my chance and by God it's about time that I stop talking, stop thinking, and take some action.

"Hey there, lighten up, Macy," Cody says as we leave my apartment. "Y'all look like you've got the weight of the world on your shoulders. This is gonna be painless, I promise."

"Oh believe me," I assure him as we pile into the white Escalade waiting at the curb, "I've come so far out of my comfort zone in the past few days that this sort of thing is starting to feel almost . . . normal."

"Welcome to the wacky world of show business," Cody tells me with a crooked grin. "Where normal is pretty much tossed out the window. Right, Jenny?"

Jennifer looks up from her laptop where she had been furiously typing away. "It certainly is where you're concerned," she comments, but then her eyes widen. "Um and of course that's part of your charm."

"Nice save, Jenny," Cody says with a shake of his head.

I notice that Jennifer's lips twitch as though she might smile but then she lowers her head and starts typing away once more. Cody, who pretends to be all play and no work, turns around in his seat and studies his own notes. Like Emeril's energetic Bamm! or Bobby Flay's *Boy Meets Grill*, Cody's bigger-than-life personality is obviously a big audience pleaser, but when we enter the grocery story he walks around with authority, reminding me that he's also an amazing chef and really knows his stuff.

Stuff, I might add, that is a complete mystery to me.

While the crew is setting up lighting, sound, and camera angles, Cody turns to me and grins. "Macy, why is it that you have this look on your face as if you're in a foreign country and can't speak the language?"

I shrug. "I've never thought of it like that but it sure fits. I guess because my mama died when I was young I never got to know my way around the way most kids did. My daddy shopped like a guy—you know, with a little handheld basket." I point to a stack of them and shake my head. "We only bought the bare essentials . . . eating out whenever possible." I raise my hands upward. "Even now I never remember where things are stocked. I'm usually walking around in a zigzag daze." When I demonstrate for him, he chuckles.

"Trust me, you're not the only one."

"My goodness, why do there have to be so many choices for everything? I mean how many varieties of toilet paper do we really need?"

Cody angles his head. "I hear ya."

On a roll now and getting riled up for no good reason, I continue my tirade. "There's just too much room for error, ya know? Low sodium, low carb, sugar free. Chicken raised without antibiotics? I don't even begin to understand that one. And just last week I came home with fat-free sour cream by mistake." I shudder. "Who could eat that stuff? I mean what's the point? That's like caffeine-free Mountain Dew. Ha! That just ain't right."

Cody nods. "I see your point."

I jam my thumb toward my chest. "Now, if it were up to me, I'd simplify things, you know? Put items together that belong together, like bologna and cheese, eggs and bacon."

"Pretzels and beer?"

"Yeah, now you're catchin' on. It sure would save a person some time and effort," I tell him in a serious tone until I realize that he's having a hard time not laughing. "You've been filming this, haven't you?" With narrowed eyes I glance at the cameraman and for the first time notice that a microphone is suspended on a pole above my head.

"Sorry Macy, it was too good not to."

"So this segment is going to be pokin' fun at me?"

"I won't deny the humor, but that's always part of my show. The thing is that you're not alone. You're more representative of women your age when it comes to cooking and grocery shopping than you realize."

"Okay, now I feel a little better."

"Well . . ." He grins as he pulls out his list of items we need to purchase. "I admit that you're at the extreme end of the spectrum, but you mark my words, there will be a lot of viewers who will watch you shoppin' and cookin' with me and who will totally relate. Preparing meals at home is quickly becoming a lost art."

"Yeah but there seem to be more cooking shows on television than ever. What's up with that?"

Cody shrugs. "I've wondered that myself. Maybe you can answer that one for me," he says as he grabs a grocery cart and starts pushing.

As I fall into step with him I think about the question for a moment and then reply, "Well, I suppose I watch cooking shows for that very reason. I rarely cook but I would love to be able to whip up something amazing."

Pausing, I think of Jamie Lee's mama's Sunday chicken dinners. "I don't think there's anything that demonstrates love and caring more than cooking a meal for someone."

"I think you hit the nail on the head, Macy. Which is why I'm going to show you how to prepare something that's simple, easy, and yet delicious enough to knock your boyfriend's . . . um"—he pauses long enough for me to hold my breath but the look of warning he gets from Jennifer has him finishing—"socks off."

Shoppers look on with curiosity, some of them pointing, talking behind their hands, or waving when Cody's recognized. It makes me almost feel as if I'm a celebrity too. Jennifer keeps the onlookers at bay with promises of autographs after we've finished shopping even though we'll have to rush back to start preparing the meal before Luke arrives.

Luke. Just the thought of him sends a tingle of excitement sliding down my spine like condensation on a glass of sweet tea. Now that I've decided upon my no-holds-barred-less-talk-and-more-action approach, my anticipation of his arrival is shooting through the roof. Of course one little problem that I'm going to have to overcome is that when I get nervous, and I'm certain I will be, I tend to talk a million miles a minute or heaven forbid, giggle. With that thought I take a deep breath and blow it out slowly. Just exercise some control, I tell myself. "You can do this."

"Excuse me?" Cody asks as he heads down an aisle as though he knows where he's going, which of course he does. He stops and picks up a bottle of hot sauce without even looking at the other dozen varieties. Impressive.

"Macy, you really need to get over your fear of the grocery store."

I nod, letting him think that I'm nervous about the show and not thinking ahead to my evening with Luke.

He hands me the list. "Here, you're officially in charge."

"Oh, kinda like a scavenger hunt?"

Cody looks at me as though he thinks I'm kidding, so I try to pull a face as if I were, but he's on to me and nods. "It's not that hard, *really*."

"Oh don't look so smug. I just bet you're lost in the feminine hygiene aisle," I toss back at him as though he's not a famous chef and I'm not a hairdresser from Hootertown. *Ohmigod, but he is and I am.* With a gasp I turn to the cameraman and frantically whisper, "Edit that out."

"No, *don't*," says Cody in a high-pitched wheeze because he's laughing so hard. "My *God*, Macy."

"You can't leave that in!"

"We'll edit it out later."

"You are such a liar!"

He nods as he hands me the list. "Yeah, I am. But I shouldn't act so superior. Let's face it; you wouldn't want me cutting your hair, right? I deserved your put-down."

"Okay, you're forgiven." I glance down at the neatly written items, guessing that they are in some sort of order to make things easier as we shop. I try to figure it out as though it's a code of some sort. "Aha!" These are listed in order of where they're found in the store. Am I right?"

Cody raises his hand. "High five!" After I smack his palm he says, "Eliminates the zigzagging that you were referring to earlier."

"The trick is knowing your way around."

"Well yeah. But after cooking dinner tonight, hopefully you'll want to do it more often."

Cody's method, of course works and in no time I've found the items and filled the cart with essential ingredients for hot wings, twice-baked potatoes, celery and blue cheese dressing. I'm about to go down the frozen food section for vanilla ice cream needed for the brownie sundae when I pause to take a sample of raspberry tea offered by a sweet little old lady.

"Thanks," I tell her as I pick up a tiny paper cup. I glance at Cody and shame him into coming over to take one as well.

"Delicious, isn't it?" A big smile brightens her wrinkled face. Sweeping her hand like Vanna White, she gestures to a big display of bottled tea. "Raspberry with a hint of honey. Zero calories and refreshing on a hot day such as this." She thrusts a coupon into my hand. "Can't pass that up, can you?"

"Of course not," I tell her and heft a case into the cart.

"Um, Macy, we're getting off track," Cody warns while smiling politely at the elderly woman.

"Don't you want a case?" she asks Cody.

"Um . . ." When he hesitates I march right over and get another case of tea and plunk it down into the cart. The cameras are rolling but I don't care.

Cody smiles but when we're out of earshot of the tea lady he says, "Macy what was up with that? Did you like the tea that much?"

I wrinkle my nose. "Not especially."

"Then why do we have twenty-four bottles in the cart?"

"Because she's old, Cody! She must really need the job to be working at her age. Do you want her to be eatin' dog food so she can afford her meds?" Okay, I know I'm going a bit overboard but still . . .

"Macy, I'm sure she doesn't get paid on commission."

"Yeah, but what if no one buys it? Do you want that sweet old lady's unemployment on your conscience?"

Cody looks ready to dispute my argument but then he must decide that it's pointless and grins. "No, I suppose not." Pushing the cart farther away from the tea lady he says, "Let's get the ice cream."

I put a hand on his shoulder. "Wait, we have to take a sample of the ham over there."

"No, we don't," he mutters, but pushes the cart over to another old lady who looks bored to tears. The cameraman, lights, and boom stick follow.

"Ham?" she asks in a tired tone. "On special at the deli, today only." She raises a small tray laden with little curls of ham held together by stick pretzels. "Three ninety-eight a pound . . . ," she says, and for a moment I think she might yawn but instead her eyes suddenly widen and her jaw drops. "Oh my, Lord have mercy on my soul. You're Cody West! The *Grillin' and Chillin'* chef!" She puts a hand to her chest and bats her eyes at Cody. "I'm such a big fan! That pork chop recipe from last week?" She puts her fingers to her mouth and makes a huge smacking sound. "Superb! You are a genius!" She thrusts the tray at him. "Here, have a slice of ham. Take two."

"Why, thank you." Cody politely takes a sample and pops it into his mouth.

"A good idea using pretzels," I politely tell her, and she beams.

"It was my idea. Those toothpicks end up all over the floor. Plus, I like the thought of saving a tree," she proudly announces, and looks to Cody for approval.

"Smart thinkin'." Cody taps his index finger to his temple. "Thanks for the tip, Martha."

Her eyes widen. "How'd you know my name?"

Cody grins, "Says so on your name tag."

"Right," Martha says, and blushes all the way to her blue hair. "Hey, am I gonna be on your show?"

"You can count on it," Cody promises with a wink.

A few steps away is another little lady with fresh pineapple chunks. This time Cody doesn't hesitate and heads over for a sample. "Delicious, Velma," he tells her.

"Goes with the ham," I comment with a smile over my shoulder at Martha.

Angling his head Cody snaps his fingers. "You know, you're right." While arching one eyebrow he takes a pineapple chunk from Velma and walks back over to Martha. After picking up a ham sample he slips the meat from the pretzel, rolls the ham around the pineapple chunk, and stabs the pretzel through the whole thing.

"Try this," Cody says, offering me the tidbit.

I nod while chewing up the juicy treat. "Yummy! Ham and pineapple are always a great combo but the salt and crunch of the pretzel make it even better."

"Do you think it might be your tasty tidbit of the week?" Martha asks with hope in her voice.

Cody smiles at her. "Yes, I think so. You really are a loyal viewer, aren't you?"

"You betcha!" she proudly proclaims.

"Just give your name and address to Jenny over there and you'll get an autographed *Grillin' and Chillin'* cookbook."

"Oh, thank you," Martha gushes. "You've made my day and then some."

When I notice that Velma looks a bit put out that she didn't get a cookbook I try to give Cody a discreet little nudge with my elbow but he's already heading in her direction.

"Okay, Jenny says we need to wrap this up and get back to your apartment. So no more sidetracks."

When Cody gives her a mock salute, her chin comes up a notch as if to say she knows her job and what she's doing. I want to tell them that they should give it up and fall into each other's arms like they really want to, but it occurs to me that because of their working relationship there's more at stake than broken hearts.

Oh, why does love have to be so complicated?

"Macy, let's get the ice cream for Luke's dessert," Cody says as we head to the frozen foods.

"Now this is an aisle I'm quite familiar with," I admit as I make a beeline for Häagen-Dazs.

"Ah, discriminating when it comes to ice cream," Cody observes.

"You betcha."

"Life's too short to eat cheap ice cream?"

I have to laugh. "Yeah, *that* and there are too many calories to waste on inferior vanilla."

"Okay then," Cody says as he pushes the cart over to the cashier. "Looks like we're all set and then some. Time to head back and cook up a storm."

19

Timing is Everything

"Oh my goodness, Cody, I don't have a grill!" I suddenly remember this tiny little detail just as we pull up in front of my apartment complex.

"You took care of that, right, Jenny?" Cody asks as he looks up from his notes.

"Yes, of course." Jennifer closes her laptop with a quiet click and then turns toward me. "You've also been stocked up with spices, condiments, beverages, and various kitchen gadgets and appliances that I thought might come in handy. In other words, you're all set."

"Wow, thanks." Unable to help myself I lean over and give Jennifer a big hug. It's obvious she's not a hugger but makes a valiant effort at hugging me back. "Loosen up and go after him," I whisper in her ear. "It's clear that Cody is so into you whether you know it or not." Hey, I figure that someone needs to get the ball rolling between those two. It might as well be me.

Jennifer stiffens and pulls back. "No . . . ," she says, but then whispers back, "You think so?"

I nod. "What you do about it is up to you."

"Yeah, but—," she begins, but I have to stop her.

"There are always roadblocks. Find a way around them."

"Right." She doesn't look convinced but I know I've got her thinking. In the meantime, I've got my own set of roadblocks ahead of me. I really wish I could call Jamie Lee but then I tell myself that I need to be strong and stand on my own two feet. After my mama died everyone felt so sorry for me that somebody was always there to catch me if I fell. But now I'm finally on my own and doggone it, if I fall I'm going to land with a great big splat. But that's okay. It's better than not jumping.

Right?

God, I hope so . . .

When we enter the apartment it's a hub of activity. Cameras, lights, and way too many people are crammed into the small space. A nervous little giggle starts to bubble up in my throat but Cody draws me aside and says, "Hey, don't let this chaos freak you out. In a few minutes it will all calm down and we can have fun cookin' for your boyfriend."

"Is there anything I should know or are we going to play it by ear?"

"Just be yourself, Macy. It's worked so far. Ask questions . . . even if you think it's something stupid because, believe me, there are others in the viewing audience wondering the same thing. We want this to be entertaining and we can edit, so don't hold back, okay?"

"Yeah, I'm tired of holding back," I tell him with a little head bop. "Let's rock this thing."

Cody laughs and holds his fists up for a knuckle bump. "Tammy said that you'd be a riot. She was right. I get the feeling that this won't be the only show you'll be doin' with me."

I'm shocked when Cody says this but I don't have time to dwell on it because suddenly everyone but the small crew scatters and we're told to start cooking. "Just follow my lead and jump right in," Cody says, and then puts on his professional face for the camera.

"Cody West here for another addition of *Grillin' and Chillin'*. In a few minutes I'm going to be cooking up a storm with my friend Macy McCoy of Hootertown, Kentucky. No, I did not make that up. We were inspired by the town's name to do our own version of hot wings, but grilled and then baked until bone tender instead of deep-fried." He holds up a finger and says, "We are however on a special mission. Macy here, is not, how can I say this politely, um, *proficient* in the kitchen."

"All I can say is that you're a brave man. Have the fire extinguisher ready. The smoke alarm tends to be my kitchen timer . . ."

"But you do want to whip up a delicious dinner for a special someone, right?"

"You betcha." I smile at the camera while having no idea where this TV personality is coming from . . . but it's fun.

"Then let's get this party started." Cody turns back to the camera. "We've shopped at the grocery store . . . and by the way, you'll see clips of our adventure throughout the show. Now we're going to throw it all together in hopes of creating an amazing but easy-to-prepare meal."

"You ready, Macy?"

"I think I should be asking you that."

Cody grins. "Just remember that cooking is all about timing. We'll marinate the wings while we prepare the twice-baked potatoes. We'll whip up the brownies and then while the potatoes are baking we'll grill the wings."

"Gotcha."

"Then while the wings are baking we'll mash the potatoes and mix in the ingredients and then pop them in the oven."

"I'm gettin' tired just thinking about it."

"Ahhh, that's where the chillin' part comes in handy. A glass of wine or a cold beer and some music help everything go smoothly."

"And cope when it doesn't?"

"Ahhh . . . yes, you're a fast learner. See, you're gonna pass this class with flying colors. Now, let's get the chicken wings marinating and the brownies in the oven."

"Um . . . what about the chillin' part?" I ask hopefully.

Cody smacks the heel of his hand to his forehead. "Right, I almost forgot." He reaches in the fridge, cracks open a beer, and hands it to me before snagging one for himself.

"Thanks." I accept the bottle but make a mental note to sip the beverage since I really need my wits about me.

After the wings are in Ziploc bags soaking in hot sauce, we mix together the brownies and pop them in the oven.

"The last time I baked brownies they came out like chocolate rocks," I admit as I set the timer.

"The trick is to not overbake them."

"But I followed the instructions."

Cody nods. "I believe you but the baking times are just for guidance. When the brownies start to pull away from the side of the pan you know they are done even if there are a couple of minutes left on the timer."

"Oh . . . okay."

"Yeah, not as easy as the toothpick method used to test cakes," he says.

"Right . . ." I nod as though I know what the heck the toothpick method is all about. "Yeah, not as easy." I add a serious nod for good measure.

To my surprise I continue to assist Cody without any disaster striking. I slice celery with an incredibly sharp knife without drawing blood even though I came sort of close. Meanwhile the scent of chocolate fills the kitchen, making me feel like a bona fide cook. "I don't know what I was so intimidated about all these years," I tell Cody.

"There's the attitude," Cody says with a grin. "Okay, now we're ready to wash the potatoes." He hands me a little round scrub brush.

"All of these gadgets are so cute!" I look at the cameraman as though I'm a star and say, "With the right tools anybody can cook. Even me!" I scrub as if it's my job and hold up the very clean potato with culinary pride as if I've just baked a soufflé.

"Excellent," Cody says. "Now we're going to rub the potatoes with olive oil and then roll them in kosher salt before baking them at three hundred and fifty degrees for about one hour." Cody drizzles some olive oil onto my palms and then hands me a potato. "And what will we be doing while the potatoes are baking?" Cody prompts.

Of course I don't remember so I decide to be cheeky. After all I am the sidekick, right? "Have another beer?"

Cody grins while slathering his own potato with oil. "Well there's that," he agrees with a nod. "But while we're chillin' we'll start grillin' the marinated hot wings.

"Gotcha," I say, doing my sidekick thing.

"By the time the potatoes are done we can bake the wings while we scoop out the flesh to mash with the other ingredients. Remember, Macy, putting together a great meal is all about the timing."

"Of course." I nod with my serious I'm-a-chef-now face going on. "Isn't that the way of everything?" But just when I'm feeling my kitchen confidence begin to build, my potato pops from my slippery hand like a cork from a champagne bottle.

"Ohmigod!" I squeak while making a valiant effort to catch the airborne spud. "I got it!" I shout as if I'm calling for a fly ball, but the potato lands with a loud thump and slithers across the tile floor. Mortified, I let out a nervous giggle and hurry over to retrieve it but the trail of oil makes the tile as slick as ice. "Eeeek!" Like a cartoon character I slip and slide while trying to maintain my balance but in the end fail, going down with a louder thump than the potato. But to my credit, I somehow manage to reach over and pick it up while spinning on my back like a Teenage Mutant Ninja Turtle.

I'm hoping to hear Jennifer yell, *Cut!* but instead the camera is catching my every move. When I finally come to a slow-spinning, tummy-churning stop, I hold up the potato as if it's a fair catch and say as deadpan as I can manage, "Do *not* try this at home."

For a second there's one of those awkward should-we-laugh-or-not moments and to my surprise it's Jennifer whom I hear chuckling in the background. I could be ticked that she's laughing at my expense but I know I'd be pointing and guffawing, so I don't blame her one bit.

"Um, are you okay?" Cody, trying to be the professional host, reaches down to help me to my feet.

"I don't think anything is hurt except for my pride." With a thankful smile I grab his outstretched hands. He yanks me up but since both our hands are slick with olive oil, my fingers slide at the halfway-up point, sending me staggering backward and then sliding into a crabwalk. I swallow my pain thinking that I might have sprained both wrists and both ankles at the same time. I'm the only person alive who can sustain life-threatening injuries baking a doggone potato. Okay, not life-threatening, but you know what I mean.

"Ohmigod, Macy! Sorry!" Cody says, but I swear he's trying not to laugh.

"Just when I thought the kitchen was a safe place."

This time he does laugh along with everybody else in the room. "So glad to provide comic relief," I tell them. "Will someone please yell, *Cut*?" Someone tosses me a dish towel so that I can wipe the oil from my hands. "Okay, just where is the potato?" I wonder out loud. "Don't tell me I've lost the doggone thing after my effort to save it." As I finally hoist myself to my feet I see it between my legs; I look as if I just laid an egg. "Braaach," I say, and flap my wings like a chicken while walking in a circle. I didn't really think it was all that funny but Cody laughs so hard that he has to grip the side of the counter for support.

After washing my hands at the sink I turn back around,

flip my hair over my shoulder, and try to say in a professional manner, "Okay, what's next on the agenda?"

"Grillin' the wings," Cody answers, which thankfully is pretty much all him. After grabbing the bags from the fridge we head out to my small patio, where to my delight there is a brand-spanking-new gas grill. The camera crew follows with the boom stick waiting I'm sure in anticipation of what I'll do next. At this point I'm pretty much convinced that this will be my last venture into *Grillin' and Chillin'* land.

"Oh, the wings smell amazing, Cody," I tell him after the grilling chicken starts to send smoke into the air. My job is to lightly baste every once in a while. Surely I won't mess that up.

"Thanks!" He taps his beer bottle to mine but I'm just taking sips here and there, hoping to avoid another embarrassing incident.

When the wings are lightly charred Cody takes the potatoes out of the oven and replaces them with the chicken, but at a lower temperature. I'm thinking that this cooking thing is pretty darned complicated even though he makes it look easy. I now have a new respect for Daisy's fried chicken dinner that she puts on each and every Sunday without breaking a sweat.

While Cody fries the bacon for the twice-baked potatoes, my job is to scoop the flesh out into a bowl and add the sour cream, milk, and butter. "This I can handle," I happily tell him, and some of my confidence bounces back.

"Not so hard, is it?" he asks while frying the bacon to crisp perfection, neatly turning it without a splatter.

"See, knowing those little details helps."

"It comes with doing, Macy."

And having someone you want to impress helps, I think to myself. The kitchen smells heavenly . . . a mixture of bacon, potatoes, and the hot wings slow-baking in the oven. I can't wait to serve the meal to Luke.

The rest of the preparation goes smoothly except for one little mishap while blending the ingredients with the potato flesh. Note to self: Do not raise the beaters above the level of the liquid or splattering will occur as high as the ceiling if you panic and push TURBO instead of OFF. "You're gonna edit that out, right?"

"Sure," Cody promises with wide innocent eyes. "And the potato incident too."

"Yeah and you're gonna sell me some oceanfront property in Arizona while you're at it."

"Yeah and I'll throw the Golden Gate in free," Cody laughs tossing the line from the George Straight song right back at me. After recapping the recipes and signing off the show Cody turns to me. "Okay, we're outta here, Macy-girl. The rest is up to you."

"Thanks for everything," I tell him with a big hug, and then turn to salute the crew. "One word: Edit." I shake my head. "No, make that two words: Please edit."

Jennifer heads my way and even though it invades her personal space, I don't give a fig and hug her too. "Go for it, girlfriend," I whisper in her ear. "We can compare notes."

Jennifer's eyes widen and she nods her head as if in agreement but I get the impression that she's not ready to take the leap. I understand. It's hard. *Scary.* I glance down at my watch and suck in a long, shaky breath. In about an hour Luke will be arriving on my doorstep.

It's time to put my money where my mouth is . . .

20

A Leap of Faith

Once again I'm standing in my underwear in my bedroom staring . . . no, make that glaring at the heap of making-me-look-fat clothes. I wonder how many women in America are doing the same thing right this very minute. Of course their clothes might not be in a pile on their bed but they are certainly muttering the very same thing: *All of my clothes are stupid!* Then I make the mistake of glancing over at myself in the dresser mirror. "Ohmigod, I cant wear this Hanes Her Way underwear! They're, like, granny pants!"

With a little squeal of frustration I leave the pile on my bed and go over to my underwear drawer and begin searching for something with silk and lace. Soon my granny-pants underwear joins the rest of the heap on the bed.

"Aha!" Finally, I find silky black panties edged with lace and a matching bra that I bought at a Victoria's Secret sale. The price tag is still on the bra. Perfect! I shimmy out of my Hanes Her Way but then hesitate. "Wait a minute." If I'm wearing really sexy panties does it look like I am expecting to have sex? Not that I'm assuming that we will have sex . . . but I am open to the idea. You know, planning ahead.

"I need help." I decide to call Lilly and ask her opinion but my cell phone is missing in action. Great. "Holy cow, it must be beneath the pile of clothing." While totally naked since even my underwear sucks, I start tossing my clothes from the bed to the floor hoping to spot my silver cell. Thankfully, in the midst of my frantic search my phone rings. "Oh, where are you?" I know, I'm talking to inanimate objects once again. "Ah, there!" I locate it beneath my denim skirt that I decide I'm going to wear.

Oh good, it's Lilly! "Hello, thank God you called. I need your advice."

"Okay, shoot."

"What kind of underwear should I wear?"

"Duh, something sexy, Macy," she answers without missing a beat as if this is a perfectly normal question to ask a person.

"How about black silk and lace?" I hold up the panties and wrinkle my nose.

"Sounds like an excellent choice to me, Macy."

"But let me ask you. Wouldn't that be a bit too . . . *obvious*?"

"Guys don't understand subtle, girlfriend. Besides, you shouldn't have anything *other* than sexy underwear. Throw all that other stuff away. Sexy undies give a girl attitude, ya know what I'm sayin'?"

"Oh . . . I don't knoooo-wa. Oh . . . okay." I toss the

phone on top of the soon-to-be Goodwill clothing and slip into the silky undies before picking the phone back up. "They're on."

"Now, look in the mirror."

I look up at the ceiling instead. "Do I have to?"

"Yes! Now check out your boobs . . . now your butt."

"Big and bigger . . . ," I whine with a long sigh, but I have to admit that the black silk and lace are danged sexy.

"Get yourself under control, Macy. Luke's gonna be there soon."

"Don't remind me! Ohmigod, was that my doorbell?" I glance at the digital alarm clock. "He's early! Why isn't anybody ever late anymore? Lilly! Help! I don't know what to wear."

"Girl, just tug somethin' over your head. He won't care . . . oh, but keep the sexy undies *on* and call back with a full report."

"Oh . . ." Bing-bing-bing . . . ! "There goes the doorbell!"

"Well then, hurry your tushie up! Good luck and save me some food."

"Yeah right, there won't be any leftovers." *Oh no, wait a minute . . .*

The food!

"Yikes, it's not the doorbell after all but the kitchen timer telling me that the wings are done and the potatoes need to go in. "Mercy, cookin' is hard. No wonder people eat out all the time!" I shout into the tiny phone, probably breaking Lilly's eardrum. For some reason I always talk too loud into cell phones. I guess it's because they're so small. "Catch ya later."

"Why did I invite him to dinner? I can't even cook

when someone else basically did it for me!" I'm muttering under my breath while tugging on my jeans. I hurry toward the kitchen . . . and quickly learn that hurrying and tugging at the same time is not a good idea. "Whoa!" While hopping on one leg I suddenly lose my balance, stagger sideways, and bump against the counter as though I'm a pinball before I fall down with a thump, followed closely by an unladylike curse. "Well, hell's bells, that's gonna leave a mark," I grumble darkly while rubbing my tush.

"You okay in there?" Luke's voice is a bit muffled from behind the door but I can hear the concern.

"Fine!" I yell back while continuing to rub my tender butt that's already bruised from the potato incident.

Wait a minute . . . Luke is at the door?

It must have been the doorbell that I first heard after all. My heart starts pounding like a jackhammer. "I'll be right there!" I attempt to scramble to my feet but there's a leftover slick spot from the oil and heaven help me, I go down again, landing on my poor battered butt before whacking my head against the cabinet.

"Macy?"

"I'm okay!" I try to shout but it comes out a painful wheeze. Now I know where the term *seeing stars* comes from because I'm seeing them.

"You don't sound okay. Macy, did you fall?"

"Um . . . yeah, but just a tiny spill," I say in a small voice. I decide not to tell him that I almost split my head open like a doggone melon. With a nervous swallow I reach up to the tender spot, thinking I'll encounter blood. No blood, thank goodness, but a cartoon character–sized lump is rising from my skull. A pathetic moan escapes my lips.

"That's it. I'm coming in."

"No . . ." I want to shout but moan instead. "Don't." Unfortunately, the front door is unlocked. A moment later Luke is hovering over me. Looking up I see two of him and think, wow, that would be cool, and then giggle.

Knowing that I laugh at weird moments such as this one, Luke ignores my mirth and frowns at me. "Are you hurt? Anything broken?"

"I think I put another crack in my butt," I tell him, and then wince. "Pretend I didn't say that."

Luke gives me a tender smile that helps take away the throbbing pain in my head. "Since when do you have to watch what you say around me?" After squatting down he offers his hand and assists me to a sitting position. "Okay now, where does it hurt?" he asks with quiet concern in his blue eyes.

"Ummm," I stutter, but hey it's difficult to think with him so close and smelling more delicious than the food, which is pretty darned difficult to do.

"Besides your butt," he says with a crooked grin.

"I might have bumped my head," I admit, and thinking about it makes it hurt worse.

"Where?" he asks, and then gently runs his fingers through my hair.

"Ouch!"

"Sorry, sweetie. Yep, you've got quite a bump there." Easing up to a standing position, he walks over to the fridge and pulls out a tray of ice. "Do you have any plastic bags?"

I'm trying to think but between my pain, the fact that

he called me sweetie again, and that he smells so good, my brain is starting to short-circuit. "Ummm . . ." Think, *ouch*, but thinking hurts.

"Don't worry, I'll find something." When I'm no help, he starts looking around, opening cabinets and pulling out drawers until he locates a plastic grocery bag beneath the sink. "This will do the trick." He dumps some ice cubes into the bag and then knots it shut. "Here you go." Kneeling back down he gently eases my head to the side and places the coldness against my bump. "Hold still. This will keep the swelling down."

"Ouch!" I complain like a wimp and try to suck it up. After a minute the ice dulls the pain. "I guess you know what you're doin', coach," I try to joke, but it really does hurt like the dickens.

"Yeah, I've dealt with many an injury both personally and with my players. I just hope you don't have a concussion. Do you have any pain medication, like Advil, maybe?"

I nod . . . oh mistake. "Yeah, down the hallway in the bathroom next to the bedroom.

"Good. Stay put and I'll get you a couple."

"Thanks," I say in a pathetic full-of-pain voice, and lean back against the cabinet with the bag of ice plopped against my head. The smooth wood feels nice and cool against my bare shoulders . . .

"Ohmigod." While squeezing my eyes shut, I swallow. Don't tell me . . . I had forgotten that my jeans aren't zipped all the way up and I'm in my bra, the black silk one that cups my girls and has cleavage spilling out over the lacy edge.

This cannot be happening!

Okay, *think*, but it hurts my head to do so. Then I get the brilliant idea to cover myself with a dish towel before Luke gets back. Silly, I know, but I'm not exactly thinking clearly. As luck would have it I must stand up in order to snag the towel hanging next to the sink. Of course I decide to do this quickly before he returns, not taking into account that standing up fast would make me light-headed. The ice pack slips to the floor and I wobble like a toy Weeble, except that I think I just might fall down . . .

"Macy!" Luke shouts, and before I bite the dust again, he scoops me up into his arms so easily you'd think I was a skinny stick person. Cool. He didn't even grunt or stagger or anything. "What in the world do you think you're doin'?"

"Gettin' a dish towel." I put my arms around his neck, thinking that maybe the bump on the head was worth it.

"So you were plannin' on dryin' some dishes?"

"No . . . I was gonna cover my, um, state of undress."

"I hadn't noticed."

"Oh . . ." Color me embarrassed.

"But thanks for bringing it to my attention," he comments as he carries me, effortlessly, thank goodness, toward the sofa.

"I wasn't trying to—," I start to protest, but his grin makes me stop and I say, "Wait a minute, you're messin' with me, aren't you?"

"Yeah," he admits as he gently eases me down to the sofa. "I am. I'd have to be dead not to have noticed, and the last time I checked I was alive and kickin'."

I chuckle but then wince. "Oh, that hurt."

"Hey," he says gently, "take two of these." He hands

me two tablets and goes to get a bottle of water. After I down those, I notice that he has a shirt draped over his shoulder. "Okay, now let me help you get this on without hurting your bump." He puts both arms though the shirt to stretch it over my head. "Easy . . . ," he warns as he guides my head through the hole and then tugs the shirt down.

My heart starts to beat faster from the close proximity and when his fingers brush against the sides of my breasts I about jump off the sofa.

"Sorry, did I hurt you?" His voice is husky, making me wonder if this is affecting him as much as it is me.

"No, you're fine." *Are you ever.*

"Good." Luke looks at me for a moment and heaven help me, I think he's going to lean over and kiss me, but just when my eyes flutter shut, he clears his throat and rocks back on his heels. "Those pills should kick in shortly."

"I'm feeling better already," I assure him. *But I'd feel a heck of a lot better if you'd kiss me.*

"Is there anything else you need?"

Yeah, a kiss. "No, I'm good," I tell him, but then change my mind. "Actually a glass of the white wine chillin' in the fridge would be nice."

"Coming right up," Luke says, and I'm disappointed when he rushes from the room as if he wants to put some distance between us. Maybe my he-was-going-to-kiss-me radar was just wishful thinking on my part. Yep, I'm still the reigning queen of wishful thinking!

Or then again maybe I should quit wishing and take some action. Yeah, that's what I'll do. Take some action . . . I'll just drink that glass of wine first. Then I'm all action.

Oh who am I kidding?

Will I ever be more than just talk?

I inhale and then blow it out while I watch Luke deftly uncork the bottle. I'm not sure why I requested the wine that Cody provided instead of a cold beer. Well okay, yes I do. Sipping a glass of wine is sexier than drinking a bottle of beer. Yes, I'm stooping to the use of props. I just hope I don't hate the wine and have to choke it down as if I'm enjoying it.

I watch Luke reach up for a long-stemmed glass and decide that perhaps I should strike a pose on the sofa, like maybe have my arm up over the back. I do this while his back is turned and decide I look goofy, so I snatch it back down. Crossing my legs might be sexy or perhaps I should lean back against the cushions as though I need to be fed grapes. I snicker at that thought and try to come up with a provocative position and then something sexy to say when I glance down at my shirt. "Ohmigod," I whisper. I'm wearing an old Hootertown Hornets T-shirt that is just a little too snug. I inhale a deep breath, making my breasts rise and fall . . . okay, make that way too snug. Holy cow.

"Why the frown?" Luke asks as he hands me the wine glass. "Head still throbbin'?" He sits down beside me and pats my leg. "You okay, Macy? Maybe we should take you to the emergency room."

"My head is already feeling better," I assure him, and truthfully, it is. "I was just wondering where you dug up this shirt?" Of course this stupid question has him looking at my shirt that's stretched like a second skin across my chest.

"From a big heap on your bed."

"Oh . . ." Could this get any more embarrassing? I feel heat creep up my neck and take too quick a sip of wine and start coughing.

"Go down the wrong pipe?" he asks. After taking my glass from me he places it on the coffee table and then gently pats me on the back as though I'm a little kid. I know he's trying to make me stop coughing but this is all going so terribly wrong that I'm just about ready to burst into tears. "Better now?"

I nod and try to smile but it wobbles around the edges.

"You sure?" He tucks a finger beneath my chin. "You know you can tell me anything. I'll listen."

I blink at him for a second while searching for something flirty or funny to say but here I am sitting here in a stupid, too-small high school T-shirt, no shoes, and a big bump on the side of my head. My hair is damp and matted from the ice pack and I never got the chance to redo my makeup from early this morning. Moisture wells up in my throat but I swallow hard, not wanting to humiliate myself further but bursting into noisy tears. God, I am such a train wreck!

"Macy," Luke persists, "if there's something wrong you can tell me. Is it your job? Do you miss your daddy? Jamie Lee? Come on, talk to me."

A little less talk, pops into my head like a banner trailing from an airplane and I think, *To hell with it all.* Taking a leap of faith I place my hands on either side of his face and bring his mouth down to mine for a long, hot kiss. Luke seems surprised at first but quickly warms up to the idea. Carefully avoiding the bump he cradles my head and deepens the kiss. Our tongues tangle, slide, lick . . . lightly and then deeper as we kiss again and again. With a moan Luke scoots back against the cushions and pulls me on top of him, and then we're kissing again as if there's no tomorrow.

21

Get Your Sexy On

The man knows how to drive me wild. First he kisses me with deep, hot strokes that make my head spin and my heart pound, but then he changes the pace with a lick and then a nibble before gliding the very tip of his tongue across my bottom lip. When I moan he continues to tease with butterfly kisses that come closer and closer but never quite reach my mouth. "Luke . . ."

"Mmmm, your skin is so soft." After threading his fingers with mine he concentrates on my chin, my nose, and my eyelids . . . everywhere except for where I want him the most.

"I need . . ."

"Another kiss?" But just when I think he's going to capture my mouth once again, he pauses a fraction away and simply breathes.

"Yes," I whisper. "Another kiss." With closed eyes our warm breath blends, becomes one. Luke's fingers straighten, flex, and then tighten around mine in a simple

yet tender gesture that sinks straight to my heart. With a
sigh I brush my lips lightly over his and then graze back
and forth, teasing and then tasting with the very tip of my
tongue until Luke moans and pulls my head down for another deep, delicious kiss.

"Mmmm," I sigh against his mouth when a hot shiver
of pure need slides down my spine like a snowflake on a
warm windowpane. I don't think I've ever wanted anything more than this, and without even realizing it I find
myself moving my body against his, slow and easy . . .

"Macy . . . God," he says, and then eases my head to
the side so that he can nuzzle the tender skin beneath my
ear. "I've tried to stay away and not interfere with this
amazing career you're beginning . . . ah, but sweetie, I
just can't." When he pauses to suck my earlobe into his
mouth I arch my back, pressing my body as close to his
as I possibly can. "I miss you. Think about you. Worry
about you. Want to be with you. But for the life of me I
don't know what to do about it. Just when I think I have
all of the answers, too many questions pop into my head."

"Luke." I put a finger to his lips. "Just stop."

"Stop what?"

"Talking. We can talk, think, and worry . . . later.
Much, much later."

"What about dinner?"

"It will keep."

"It smells amazing."

"So do you."

Luke laughs and then kisses the tip of my nose. "I
really have missed you so much, Macy. Maybe it took
you leaving town to finally wake my sorry ass up. I'm the
one who needed to get whacked upside the head."

"Well then, let's not waste another minute."

"My thoughts exactly."

After I stand up from the sofa, Luke surprises me by scooping me up in his arms once again. "I'm fine," I protest. "Luckily I have a hard head."

"I want to carry you." He laughs again as he heads down the hallway but then stops at the entrance to the room. "Um, Houston, we have a problem," he says while looking at the pile of clothing. "There is a bed beneath all of that, right?"

"Ohmigosh, there must have been a tornado when we weren't lookin'."

"Right . . ." He grins at me.

"Okay, this is embarrassing but I was tryin' to find the right outfit to impress you and as you can see I was having a bit of a dilemma."

"I kinda like what you have on. It was on top of the pile."

"Oh stop!"

"I'm serious." He eases me down slowly letting my body slide against his. "But I like what you have on beneath the shirt even better."

I wish I had a sexy, flirty comeback but instead I blush like crazy. When I look down at the floor Luke tilts my chin up. "Hey, what's wrong?"

"I'm such a . . . I don't know, a dork."

"For blushing?" Luke tucks a wavy lock of hair behind my ear. "Macy, I'll take wholesome and shy over bold and brazen any day of the week."

"But . . ."

He frowns. "But what?"

I shake my head. "Nothin'." I decide not to point out

that I'm not gorgeous and sophisticated like other women he's dated or that he could be on the cover of a fitness magazine and I'm just . . . me.

"Macy are you having doubts, because—"

"No!" I answer so quickly and firmly that he laughs.

"Good. Now let's toss this mountain of clothing onto the floor."

With a giggle that's not nervous this time but pure joy I start throwing the clothing up in the air as though it's confetti. With a whoop and a holler Luke joins in until the bedspread and pillows are visible.

"Wow, it was made beneath all that stuff," Luke observes with a grin, but when he turns back to me his blue eyes gaze at me with such heat that I really do feel sexy . . . desirable. "Let's add some more clothes to the pile." He tugs his shirt over his head and flings it to the floor.

My, my my . . . I draw in a breath at the sight of his beautiful bare chest. Wide shoulders, powerful arms are the result of years of farm work and football. A light dusting of black hair covers defined pectoral muscles and thins to an enticing line ending at his leather belt. His golden summer tan looks smooth and oh so touchable . . .

Unable to help myself I step closer and run a fingertip down the center of his chest all the way to his jeans. He sucks in a breath, causing a delectable tightening of his abs. "Very nice," I tell him. Because he's so darned tall I have to tilt my head back, but when I withdraw my finger, he reaches out and places both of my hands on his warm chest.

"I like it when you touch me. Do it some more."

"Not a problem." Sliding my hands over his warm,

smooth skin is something I've been longing to do. When I gently rake my fingernails through the dark chest hair, he sucks in another shaky breath. Feeling bold, I lean in and swirl my tongue over one pebbled nipple and then the other while I slide my palms up his back enjoying the ripple of muscle when he moves.

"Macy . . ." He moans my name when I lightly bite his nipple and then soothe it with a moist kiss. "Your clothes need to end up in the pile . . ." He gestures with a sideways nod of his head.

"I know," I tell him with a smile while I squelch the little pang of fear that comes with Luke seeing me . . . naked. Unlike him I would not be on the cover of a fitness magazine . . . okay, or any magazine for that matter. I don't want to be one of those girls whom people point to and say, "How'd she land him?" But I've come this far, wanted him for so long that I refuse to let my insecurities ruin the moment.

"Need help?" Luke asks, but when he reaches for the edge of my Hootertown Hornets shirt I brush his hands away while the sexpot in me that I never knew existed rises to the occasion.

Thank you, God.

"You first." With shaky fingers I unbuckle his belt and slide it through the loops, tossing it to the side with reckless abandon. Then I teasingly slide my fingers along the inside of his waistband until his abs quiver and he moans in protest.

"Macy, you're killin' me," he informs me, but at this point his desire is quite evident. Looking up at him I swallow hard and then slowly slide the zipper over the hard ridge of his erection. His blue eyes are dark and dilated and his nostrils flare when he inhales sharply. Slipping my hands inside his jeans, I slowly ease them over his lean hips and then tug them down his thighs.

Without taking my gaze from Luke's face I run my hands over the soft cotton of his boxer briefs, which are molded like a second skin to his muscular thighs and tight butt. His eyes flutter shut and he clenches his jaw when I close my hand around his erection. I cup him, caress him until his knees seem to give way and he tumbles to the bed.

"Okay, these need to go." Kneeling down I remove his shoes and then tug his jeans the rest of the way off and toss them over my head, nearly knocking over a lamp, but I don't even care.

This is fun.

Luke comes up to his elbows. "Macy, your clothes need to join the pile."

"Not just yet." Instead I lean over, peel his boxer briefs over his hips, and shimmy them down his legs.

Holy cow.

Gloriously naked, deliciously aroused, he looks so doggone masculine against the backdrop of my floral bedspread and ruffled pillow shams. His close-cropped dark hair is rumpled from my fingers, giving him a boyish look that's in direct contrast with the dark stubble shadowing his jaw. "You look good enough to eat." *Oh God, did I really say that?*

He flashes me a wicked grin. "Then do it."

"Maybe I want to save you for dessert."

"Well, ya know," he says with raised eyebrows, "life is uncertain."

"Eat dessert first?"

I put my hands to my cheeks. "Oh wow, I have no idea where this sexpot in me is coming from."

"Do I look like I'm complainin'? Macy, I told you that you can say anything, do anything for that matter." He grins. "And that especially holds true right now."

"What goes down in Nashville stays in Nashville?"

"You could put it that way . . ."

Suddenly grasping his meaning I place my hands to my flaming cheeks. "I should shut up."

"I think you did mention something about less talk . . ."

"Yeah, I did." Out of the blue the Justin Timberlake song "SexyBack" pops into my head and I smother a giggle with my hand. Songs pop into my head at the weirdest times . . . Anything can trigger it.

"What?"

"Nothin'" *Get your sexy on . . .* Justin sings in my head.

"Oh, no you don't. Tell me."

Get your sexy on. "How about if I show you instead?"

"Works for me," he teases, but then says, "Seriously, Macy, just kick back and be yourself. No worries. No inhibitions. Okay?"

"Okay," I whisper to him. Then, with a pounding heart I grasp the edges of my Hootertown shirt and tug it over my head, wincing when the fabric grazes my tender bump. When Luke sucks in a breath I give a silent thanks to Lilly for ordering me to wear the black bra.

"Let me help." Luke pushes up from his elbows and scoots to the edge of the bed. I notice that his fingers have a slight tremble when he reaches for the waistband of my jeans. He makes quick work of the snap and zipper but then takes his sweet time easing the pants over my hips . . . and then again it might be because they are so darned tight, but I'm going with the sweet-time theory.

As soon as my jeans join the pile, Luke puts his hands around my waist and draws me closer. When he kisses me just above my navel I reach out and hold on to his shoulders for support. His mouth begins a warm, moist trail south and when he cups my bottom and kisses me through my black silk underwear, a half moan, half sigh escapes me. His tongue is wet; his mouth is hot and the thought occurs to me that these doggone panties need to join the pile.

"These gotta go." As if reading my mind Luke hooks his thumbs through the waistband and tugs. A moment later the black silk goes skyward, landing who knows where, but who cares? Right now there is only one thing that matters . . .

"Mmmmm . . . ," Luke moans, and when his mouth returns to my bare body I'm shocked at the bolt of sheer pleasure that shoots right through me. With a quick intake of breath I thread my fingers through his hair and press him closer while he arouses me with his firm fingers. He seems to know just where to touch to drive me wild, to make me want him buried deep inside me. This is one of those rare moments in life that I've dreamed about, fantasized about and is actually coming true. Oh, but I have to say that the reality is much, much better.

"Luke!" Just moments later my knees turn to water and I collapse against him, causing us to tumble backward onto the bed. While I'm lying there dazed and trembling, Luke scoots from the bed but before I can protest he returns sheathed in protection.

"You're beautiful," Luke says, and gazes at me with such intense longing that I believe him. When his bare body slides against mine, a hot shiver washes over me, making my breath catch and my heart pound. He kisses my throat and caresses my breasts until I'm arching my back and offering my body to him.

While Luke makes love to me slow and easy, the word *tender* enters my mind but then Elvis starts singing in my head, making me smile. Luckily I don't laugh, which might not be the reaction he's looking for right about now.

Tender soon gives way to passion. "Macy, you take control," Luke offers, and rolls me over so that I'm on top. I moan deep in my throat. I've wanted this to happen again for too long not to give it all I've got and then some. He scoots up, puts his hands around my waist, and guides me, kissing me all the while. I hold on to his shoulders, coming up to my knees and then back down slowly. God, this is so deep . . . delicious. When my legs start to tremble he holds me up, thrusting upward. My breasts brush against his chest and his silky chest hair tickles, teases my nipples, causing heat to build and slide lower. Knowing I'm close, I pull my mouth from his so I can watch his face.

"God, you feel amazing," he says before dipping his head and giving me a kiss that's both hot and sweet. Then with a rumble low in his throat, Luke thrusts upward hard, going deep, and then closes his eyes as he rests his forehead against mine.

"Macy . . ." He pauses, swallows, and I can sense that he wants to say something more to me. My pulse races while I anticipate what he might divulge but instead of talking he rolls to the side, puts my head on his chest, and holds me close, speaking without words. The wild beat of his heart thumps against my cheek and I think to myself that there's nowhere else on earth I'd rather be. In that very moment I know that I love him; that there will never be anyone else for me but him.

My own thudding heart beats even faster. It's exciting to feel love with such intensity but it also scares the living daylights out of me because, let's face it, this changes our relationship forever. From this point forward we will never again be just friends.

A thousand what-ifs spring to mind . . . well, more like a dozen but it might as well be a thousand. I know that I should just be soaking up the moment and not thinking of anything remotely negative. Jamie Lee always complains that I'm such a pessimist : . . looking for the dark side in the best situation, but I can't help it. I understand as an adult that the death of my mother and the absence of my father when I needed him the most have instilled a deep-seated fear in me, and that I need to let go and learn to live for the moment.

I just don't know if I can.

Jump without a net, Macy. Live your damned life, I firmly tell myself, but it sends a tremble right through me.

As if Luke senses my thoughts he rubs a soothing hand lightly up and down my back as though telling me things will be okay. His even breathing, coupled with the steady beat of his heart beneath my cheek, lulls me into a contented state of near sleep. I'm so relaxed wrapped in his arms that I feel as if I'm melting into him. I think of how amazing it would be to wake up like this in the morning . . . every morning. When he kisses the top of my head I almost come undone but I hold it together, thinking that bursting into tears after sex would surely rank up there as one of the top ten ways to lose your lover.

Instead, I inhale a shaky breath and smile when Luke squeezes me in a hug. I'd dearly love to know what he's thinking and it would probably be a good time for us to begin talking, starting with, *Where do we go from here?* But then I tell myself to leave it alone and just take it a day at a time starting with right now. I need to quit analyzing, overthinking and just . . . *be.*

When his stomach growls I chuckle. "Hungry?"

"Yeah, and whatever you cooked up smells awesome. I hope you didn't go to too much trouble especially after working all day."

Raising my head from his chest I manage to keep a straight face. "Oh, it was nothing," I say breezily. "I do have to put the twice-baked potatoes in, you know, to bake the second time," I tell him in a seasoned-cook kind of way.

"I didn't know that you liked to cook," he comments, and I'm hoping he's not recalling the mushy macaroni and cheese I brought to a potluck at his parents' house. Or the previous Jell-O mold that didn't . . . mold, that is.

"Oh I dabble," I explain with a flip of my hand, which is sort of the truth . . . I dabble in culinary disaster. I'll come clean later since, after all, my ineptness is going to be nationally televised. Unless of course Cody West decides it's too much of a train wreck to air, which I'm afraid will likely be the case when he watches the footage. "I'm getting better," I tell him, leaving out the part that explains that I couldn't possibly get any worse. "I watch a lot of cooking shows."

"Me too," Luke says, but looks at me uncertainly, making me wonder if he's recalling the Jell-O incident. "It would be fun to prepare a meal together."

"Sure," I say with an enthusiastic nod. "It would be . . . an adventure." I smile thinking that Cody West might not agree that preparing a meal with me is fun. "Speaking of which, I should put those potatoes in." I reluctantly ease up from cuddling, trying not to feel self-conscious as I shimmy into my underwear and then search for my clothing, although I wonder why I'm even looking for the silly T-shirt. But since Luke seemed to like it I decide to put it back on.

"Here, let me help you so you don't hurt the bump on your head." Luke comes up behind me while I'm picking through the mountain of clothing. I'm serious about giving it to Goodwill and starting fresh with Sam leading the way as my personal shopper. Hey, if I'm going to start living my life, I might as well do it dressed well.

I'm wondering if Luke is naked or in his underwear but I can't bring myself to turn around and peek. Just the thought is enough to make me go weak in the knees yet again. I can, however, feel the heat of his body so close to mine and it's all I can do not to lean back against him instead of raising my arms so that he can assist me.

"Careful," he warns. "We should have iced it longer." Before pulling the shirt over my head he kisses my shoulder and makes his way up my neck. This time I can't help myself and I lean back, loving the feeling of his bare body pressed against mine. "Macy," he says so seriously that all of my senses go on full alert.

"Yes?"

"You might have suffered a concussion."

"You think so?" I'm a little embarrassed that I sound

so breathless. I've discovered that he is wearing underwear but still . . .

He clears his throat. "I should stay with you tonight
and wake you every few hours. You know, for safety's
sake."

Oh how I want him to stay but I'm having a mini–panic
attack at the thought of him sleeping in the same bed. I
mean, what if I snore? Personally I don't think I do but
Jamie Lee has complained about it on occasion. Or what
if I drool? Talk in my sleep? Hog the covers?

Pass gas!

I look at the pile of clothing and know that there isn't
one doggone sexy nightie either. Well damn. Yep, that
whole pile's going to go. And then there's the issue of
him seeing me in the morning. Not a pretty sight. And before coffee or a Mountain Dew I'm just plain stupid.

"Macy?"

I swallow hard. "Um, sure. Yes. You should stay. For
safety's sake."

"Good, I'm glad that you agree. Now, let's eat this
amazing dinner you've cooked up."

I turn around and smile after he helps me on with my
shirt. My head is only a little tender so I'm sure that
there's no danger of my lapsing into a coma or whatever
concussions cause, and I wonder if it was a ploy on
Luke's part to get to stay. Dare I hope that it was an excuse to spend the night with me?

Oh . . . lordy, I'll just have to stay awake so I don't do
anything gross in my sleep. Then I'll sneak into the bathroom early, brush my teeth, shower, and put on makeup
before Luke even wakes up. There now, that's a good
plan. Problem solved.

22

Be Careful What You Wish For

"These hot wings are amazing, Macy. Baking them until they're bone tender is genius."

"Thanks." I'll come clean after I enjoy his praise for a while longer.

He takes a big bite of twice-baked potato and points to it with his fork. "Don't tell her but these rival my mama's."

"Your mother is a wonderful cook. And this might sound crazy but she does it from the heart, you know what I'm sayin'? When I'd come over to your house to eat, which you might recall was pretty often since Daddy was on the road so much . . . it felt as though she was feeding us to please us, not just to nourish us." I shake my head. "Am I making any sense?"

Luke smiles across the small table at me. "Perfect sense."

"It was like a labor of love for her," I add, relieved that he seems to understand and doesn't think I'm crazy.

"Someday, if I ever have a family, I'd like to cook like that," I comment, and then want to swallow my doggone tongue. Talking about having kids right after having sex . . . another surefire way to lose your lover.

If it bothers Luke though, he doesn't show it because after he swallows a bite of his potato he nods. "Family dinners together are becoming a thing of the past. You can blame it on a fast-paced lifestyle but as you know my mother worked and still managed to put a home-cooked dinner on the table."

I arch one eyebrow. "Yeah, but men can cook too."

Luke's eyes widen a fraction but then he smiles. "True, but my daddy would have had a hard time puttin' a meal together unless it involved something on the grill, but not me. I didn't mean to come off as bein' sexist. I just meant that it could be done." He hesitates a fraction and then says, "Just to clear things up, I'm not a caveman. I wouldn't be one of those guys who wouldn't change a diaper, run the sweeper, or cook a meal."

Picturing big football star Luke doing those chores makes me laugh.

Luke puts his chicken wing down. "What?"

"Nothin'."

After licking hot sauce from his thumb and finger, which I find incredibly sexy, he says, "Oh no you don't. What were you thinkin'?"

"I was just picturin' you in a little apron, using a feather duster." I flick my wrist as though I'm dusting.

God . . . now he's licking sauce from the corner of his lip. "Well, I'd probably stick to a baseball cap turned backward and boxers as my uniform but I wouldn't have any problem pulling my weight."

I feel heat creep up my neck. "I shouldn't have jumped the gun, Luke. I have a habit of doin' that."

"Macy, one of the things I love about you is that you speak your mind. When you and Jamie Lee would be hangin' out at the house, you were always gettin' fired up about somethin' or other and I always thought it was cute."

I put my hands over my face and groan. "Your daddy used to say, 'Macy-girl, you're a piece of work.' Most of the time I was just blowin' off steam," I tell him, but it doesn't go unnoticed on my part that he really did pay some attention to me back then.

Luke reaches over and pries my hands from my cheeks. "Hey, blowin' off steam is better than keeping things bottled up inside like I tend to do."

I look over at him and realize that it's true. I've never seen him rattled but maybe it isn't always such a good thing. "Yeah, sometimes it helps to let it all out, Luke."

"I'll work on that."

"Hey, I'll give lessons for free."

He chuckles but then says, "Okay and I don't ever want you to hesitate to tell me how you feel about somethin'. I'd rather know than be in the dark." He dips a celery stick in blue cheese dressing. "Honesty is important in any relationship."

Oh how I'd love to explore the relationship part of his comment but first I have to fess up. "Um, speaking of honesty, I have a confession to make."

"Okay." Luke nods as he crunches through the rest of the celery. While he seems relaxed the wary look in his eyes reminds me that he was dumped by his fiancée when his football career ended. I've been focusing on my own insecurities but Luke must still have a few of his own that he's dealing with. Luke was a mess when Griff hunted him down and dragged him back to Hootertown. Putting his heart on the line again is an issue for him as well and I need to remember that. "Macy? Okay, what's your big confession?"

"Oh, right . . . sorry that I zoned out for a moment." I had been lost in my thoughts long enough to really make him nervous. I make a sweeping gesture with my hand across the small table. "I had a little bit of help preparin' the meal."

"That's your confession?" He appears so relieved that I want to climb over there and hug him. "That you had a bit of help fixin' dinner?"

I clear my throat. "Um, I think I should rephrase it to I helped a little bit preparin' the meal instead of the other way around." I nibble on my bottom lip for a second and then continue. "If you recall, my culinary skills are a bit, well, I guess you could say, nonexistent."

"Ah, yes, now that you mention it." A slow smile spreads across his face. "So who helped you? Sam and Lilly?"

"Actually it was Cody West."

Luke's eyebrows shoot up. "*Grillin' and Chillin'* Cody West?"

"Yep. The one and only. Tammy hooked me up. Apparently she owns the production company that produces his show."

"Wow, Tammy Turner must really think a lot of you to go the those lengths to help you out, Macy."

After swallowing a bite of chicken wing I nod in agreement. "There's more to the story. When Lilly explained to Tammy how in a moment of insanity I said I'd cook dinner for you, she offered to contact Cody. He found the story so amusing that he centered a show around it." I tell him about the grocery shopping event and how Cody came to my apartment with a camera crew. "Yeah, and now Tammy has this crazy notion that I would make an occasional fun sidekick for Cody."

Luke shakes his head in wonder but then an odd expression that I can't quite read passes over his face. "I guess cutting hair at the Cut and Curl seems pretty boring after all that's changed in your life." He silently stirs a celery stick in a glob of dip, making me wish I could read his mind. Finally he looks up over at me. "So are you going to be on his show on a regular basis?"

"I'm thinking that after shoppin' and cookin' with me, Cody must be having second thoughts. Things didn't exactly go smoothly. I was pretty much lost in the grocery store and a disaster in the kitchen. I'll be surprised if they even air the show we did together."

Luke angles his head to the side. "I wouldn't be so sure about that. You have a fun, engaging personality, Macy. I can see how this could work out for you."

I shrug not wanting to make this a big deal at this point. "We'll see. But I really think it's a long shot." I want to change the subject since this is bringing home the fact that our lives are quickly going in different directions, not to mention in separate cities. I don't want what we have to end before it has the chance to even begin. Luke has already admitted that he's tried to stay away, and I know him well enough to know that if he really thinks he's holding me back he'd be gone in a heartbeat. "So," I venture, "how did the interview with Vanderbilt go?"

"Pretty well," Luke replies, and seems relieved to change the subject as well.

"Do you think they might make you an offer?" My heart skips a beat since landing this job would solve the separate-city issue.

While toying with the neck of his beer bottle Luke says, "My biggest drawback is my lack of coaching experience. Division One is a big step up."

I hesitate but I have to ask, "Do you want the job, Luke? I mean, you are such a hero in Hootertown."

"A hero?" A shadow passes over his face. "I haven't always acted in a heroic manner, have I?"

"Don't beat yourself up, Luke. No one's perfect. You went through a bit of a dark time but who can blame you? It's damned easy when life is goin' your way. The true test of character is dealing with the hard times. Believe me, you're thought of as a hero in Hootertown. And you should be."

He smiles but it has an edge of sadness that grips my heart. "Yeah, I had some glory days as a Hootertown Hornet. Made me too big for my britches. I'm surprised that damned helmet even fit on my big head. Maybe I needed a little reality check to make me recognize the important things in life, starting with the fact that I wasn't invincible." With a shake of his dark head he continues. "The funny thing is that I love coaching as much as playing . . . maybe more. The challenge, the strategy, and especially getting a team to find the heart to play over and above their God-given ability is an amazing feeling. When I was playing, it was too much about me—my ego—and now it's about the team."

I reach over and put my hand over his. "You never once came across as anything other than a team player."

"Thanks, Macy. But over the past year I've done some soul-searching and especially recently I realized that for a long time life *was* all about me . . . what I needed and wanted. That's why I shouldn't . . . ," he begins, but then stops and threads his fingers through his hair. I'm not sure what he's going to say but I have the feeling I'm not going to like it.

"You know what?" I ask, knowing I have to lighten things up.

"What?"

"I've got one of your favorite things for dessert. Did you save room?"

Luke gives me a deadpan look and says, "Always."

"Good!" I say with a bright smile and then remembering our earlier *dessert*, I turn away so he can't see my blush and instead thinks I'm flirting. Taking a deep breath I decide I can do the sexy thing . . . I did before. Oh where is the inner sexpot when I need her the most? I try to channel her while reaching into the fridge for the chocolate syrup and the can of whipped cream. When I turn around with one in each hand Luke's eyes widen and it hits me that he thinks I'm going to do something sinfully fun instead of squirting it onto a brownie sundae.

Well, maybe that's a better idea. Luke for dessert and brownies for breakfast . . . works for me.

Now if only I can pull it off.

First, I need a sultry smile and perhaps a bit of a pout. While holding the can and bottle up next to my cheeks I try the smile followed by the pout; then, judging by the confused look on Luke's face, I try again but realize I must resemble a fish gasping for oxygen. Okay, maybe a flirty comment would be a better choice. "Care for some dessert?" I ask, and for some reason decide that my voice needs to be two octaves lower than usual, making me sound like Miss Irma after a cigarette. I clear my throat as though I have something caught there instead of a pathetic attempt at being sexy.

"Sure." Luke nods and looks at me as if he's trying to figure out just where I'm going with this, so I decide that actions would speak louder than words. Arching one eyebrow I set the chocolate down and then suggestively shake the whipped-cream can, totally forgetting that I had removed the lid earlier when I squirted a big dollop into my mouth. Unfortunately, the tip of my finger hits the nozzle and sends a stream of whipped cream in an arc that lands on Luke's upper lip, looking like a fake mustache.

"Hey!" he says, and I try not to laugh since laughing isn't sexy but he looks so funny that I burst into a fit of giggles. This, of course, makes Luke think that I squirted him on purpose.

I'm trying to stop laughing so that I can tell him I'm sorry, but my trigger-happy finger hits the nozzle again and another stream of whipped cream hits him in the chin, making him resemble Colonel Sanders.

"Hey!" he complains again, and then arches a dark eyebrow in what he thinks is a warning but with the whipped-cream mustache and goatee he simply looks comical, so of course I laugh. Taking this as a challenge he advances a step toward me, but since I'm the one armed with the can, I'm feeling pretty confident.

"Not one more step." I shake the cream in warning and when he takes no heed I aim this time and shoot. When a big blob lands on his nose I lose it and would have doubled over in a fit of laughter, but Luke reaches for the chocolate syrup and says, "Game on."

With a squeal I duck and take off running—to where I'm not sure but off I go.

"Come here!" Luke reaches for me and comes up with nothing but air when I zigzag away from him, leap over a footstool, and then turn to zap him with some cream. He tries to avoid the frothy stream but after years of being a beautician I've pretty doggone good aim with a can. I give it some wrist action and it hits him like Silly String. I giggle, feeling as if I have the upper hand, when he reaches for me again without success.

"Gotcha!"

This is one time when being short is an advantage. "Oh really? Ha!" I duck and then hop up onto the sofa, do a cool spin move, feeling like the queen of Whipped-Cream Mountain. "Whoo-hoo!" This strategy, however, quickly backfires since I now have nowhere to run.

Arching a dark eyebrow, Luke advances. "Now whatcha gonna do?" he asks in a low-pitched, taunting voice that might have been intimidating had he not been dripping with whipped cream.

"Not one step closer," I warn, and take aim. "This thing is fully loaded and I'm lethal with an aerosol can."

"Good."

"Good?"

"Yeah . . . I give up." Luke tugs his shirt over his head. "Have at me."

I swallow hard. Oh, my . . . my. "R-really?"

He crooks a finger at me. "Time to put your whipped cream where your mouth is, Macy-girl," Luke challenges, and hands me his weapon—the chocolate syrup. "Or are you all talk?"

I stand there double-fisted while visions of chocolate-covered-and-topped-with-whipped-cream Luke dance in my head. "This could get . . . messy."

He shrugs his wide bare shoulders. "You have towels, right?"

I nod while wondering where would be the most fun place to start. Pool some syrup in his belly button? Slather his nipples with whipped cream? Other more decadent places come to mind and I just about slither off the sofa.

"Good, let's get 'em."

"Get what?" I blink at him for a moment since I'm still contemplating how to best enjoy six foot four inches of hot-man dessert.

"The towels."

"Oh, right, the towels. Follow me," I tell him. He follows me down the short hallway where I snag a big beach towel that says SURVIVED SPRING BREAK 2000 PANAMA BEACH, FLORIDA.

Luke chuckles as he reads the towel. "I don't even want to know."

"Good, cuz I'm not tellin'."

"I do remember that it took Jamie Lee a week to recover and Mama found some pictures that she burned."

My eyes round at his comment.

"Just kiddin'. Although I do remember one of you in a tiny yellow bikini," he admits as he flops down onto the towel.

"Really?" That was twenty pounds ago. I wish I could fit into it now.

"You're surprised?"

"I suppose I never thought you ever noticed me"—I pause with a shrug—"you know, as a girl." I kneel down on the bed and shake the whipped-cream can.

"Oh how wrong you were, Macy. Have you forgotten that you were a Hootertown Hornets cheerleader? Even guys in my grade thought you were hot."

"Yeah, well, back in high school I was a lot thinner . . ."

Luke reaches up and cups his hands over my butt. "There's nothin' wrong with a few curves. In fact, I like 'em. Really like 'em."

I grin down at Luke and tell myself to believe him. After all why would he be here in my bed if he didn't find me attractive? I remember Lilly telling me to embrace what I've got and with that in mind I reach up and tug my T-shirt over my head. Judging by the expression on Luke's face, ample curves aren't such a bad thing after all . . .

"Are you really gonna squirt that stuff all over me?" Luke asks. "We don't have to, you know."

I give him a wicked grin. "I think this is one of those be-careful-what-you-wish-for situations. To answer your question, yes, I am." Leaning in closer I squirt a decorative little swirl of whipped cream over each nipple and then quickly lap it off.

"Um, I think *slow* is the operative word here."

"Are you complainin'? Because as you can see I'm the one with all the ammo." I shake the can and hold up the chocolate. I know that I'm supposed to be doing the sexy thing here, but this is more my style so I suppose he'd better get used to it. To prove my point, with a wicked chuckle I shoot out a stream of chocolate over his chest, closely followed by curls of whipped cream.

"Damn that's cold." He sucks in a breath and I decide it's time to get my sexy on . . .

But when I lean over and start licking the chocolate from his navel, he grabs me and flips me over as easy as if I were a pancake in a skillet. I let out a shriek that could wake the dead and yell, "Oh no you don't."

"Oh yes I do." He squirts my cleavage with cream but I have the chocolate within reach. With a squeal I attempt to get him back but I squeeze too hard on the bottle and chocolate erupts like lava from a volcano. "Ahhhh!" I yell when the cold stickiness slides over my hands and oozes onto my belly.

Luke laughs as he tries to catch my chocolate-covered hand but I manage to swipe brown streaks on both cheeks, making him look as if he belongs in a Mel Gibson movie. When I point and giggle he rises up and looks at himself in the mirror.

"Now you've done it," he says, and narrows his eyes. But instead of retaliating with more goop he leans over and starts to slowly lick the chocolate and cream from my body.

"Um, yeah, I do believe that slow is the way to go."

"Macy, you need to stop talking and simply relax and enjoy."

"Deal . . ." Soon I'm arching my back in response to

his swirling, dipping, licking . . . God . . . sucking. "Luke." I moan his name, forgetting I'm not supposed to talk, which wouldn't have lasted much longer anyway. "This is . . . ahhhhh, nice but what . . . mmmmm, I really want . . . ohhhh."

"Is this?"

A moment later we're completely naked and making love in a slippery, sticky, chocolate-and-whipped-cream mess while laughing and licking in a crazy kind of way. I'm surprised that Luke has this playful side but then again perhaps I'm bringing it out in him. He certainly is bringing out the sexy side of me that I never knew existed . . . oh but thank goodness it does.

After coming to our chocolate-covered conclusion we both flop over and stare up at the ceiling.

"Wow," he says.

"Ditto." After my breathing comes close to normal I rise up on one elbow and look at him, thinking I'll say something tender and sweet, but when I witness his sticky, spiked hair, syrup-smeared cheeks, and whipped-cream-matted chest hair I burst into a fit of laughter. "Look at you!"

"Um . . . I wouldn't be pointing any fingers."

"What?" I sit up and gaze into the mirror. "Holy cow!" My auburn hair is highlighted with streaks of chocolate and sticking up, making me look like I belong in a punk rock band. Dark brown syrup is smeared across my nose and my chin, and is dripping from one earlobe. When I start laughing Luke joins me. I laugh so hard that I snort and taste chocolate. "Ohmigod," I try to explain, but laugh even harder until I flop back down onto the bed in sticky, happy exhaustion.

"We need a shower," Luke says, and my slow-thudding heart kicks it up a notch at the *we* part of his suggestion.

"I think you're right. Now if only my legs will carry me."

"No problem," Luke says as he scoops me up from the beach towel. After turning on the shower to heat up he gives me candy-flavored kisses to, you know, pass the time. When we finally step into the shower stall the tiny bathroom is full of warm, chocolate-scented mist.

Luke stands behind me and squirts a dollop of shampoo onto my head. "Tilt your head back," he requests, and begins massaging my scalp with his long fingers. My eyes flutter shut while hot water pelts the front of my body and I have to bite my bottom lip to keep from making embarrassing purring noises. "Let's rinse." Luke gently tilts my head forward into the spray. The foamy lather slides over our skin, making our wet bodies slick.

"Mmmm Macy . . ." With a deep sigh Luke brushes my hair to the side and starts kissing my neck. Then, reaching up, he grabs the bar of soap and washes my body with his big, capable hands. The soap slides to the floor with a thump but his fingers keep gliding, massaging until I'm pressing my back against his warm, wet skin. "Here hold on . . ." He tugs my hands upward around his neck and then continues his tender assault up and down my slick body, pausing to cup my breasts; then he rubs the pads of his thumbs in little circles over my nipples. A breathy groan escapes me when he licks the tender inside of my neck while his other palm slides down my torso. The warm water pelts my sensitive skin like gentle rain as Luke continues to kiss and caress me.

"Oh . . ." My head falls back against his chest when his fingers slide between my thighs, working sweet magic until I'm melting faster than the sliver of soap on the floor. "Luke!" I cry out while feeling as if I'm made of hot liquid and I could slither right down the doggone drain.

"Mmmm . . . *wow*." When I can finally move I turn around and warn him, "Now, Luke Carter, it's *your* turn".

"I was hopin' you'd say that." We change positions so that I can lather him up. I'm careful not to miss one little bitty inch of his big body, taking special care of certain parts that need extra, um, scrubbing. With the water pelting us I glide my hands over his chest while swirling lower, cupping him, and then caressing the hard length with my soapy fingers. At first I tease him with slow and easy strokes until he groans. "Macy . . ." With a quick intake of breath Luke braces himself with his hands against the tile. Understanding, I go faster, grip tighter while licking droplets of warm water from his back. "Mmmm," he growls deep in his throat, and after catching his breath he turns around to wrap me in a warm, wet embrace.

I will never look at a bar of Irish Spring the same way ever again.

"I do believe I'm clean as a whistle," Luke chuckles, and I have to laugh along with him. I'm feeling so relaxed, so open that it makes me want to smile and just keep right on smiling. I know I must look silly but I can't help it. It helps that Luke has a silly grin on his handsome face as well . . . so it's not just me.

By the time we're finished "showering," I'm as limp as a wet noodle and have to hold on to Luke's shoulders while he towels me dry, carefully avoiding the bump on my head. This time I don't even protest when he carries me to the bed. After removing the soiled beach towel he tucks me in.

"You're staying, right?" I ask in a slurred, sleepy tone. My eyelids feel as if they have weights attached but I manage to open them halfway.

"Yeah, but I'll wake you a couple of times just to be on the safe side."

"Okay," I mumble, and snuggle into the pillow. When Luke joins me in bed he wraps his arms around me from behind and holds me close. "Mmmm," I can't keep from sighing, but at least he can't see the silly smile on my face.

Dinner was amazing.

Dessert was delicious.

Showering was steamy.

But being in his arms like this is sheer bliss.

23

Moving at the Speed of Love

"You radiate happiness," Tammy Turner tells me as she hands me another small sheet of foil. I'm adding some subtle auburn color to her hair that will catch the light for a photo shoot scheduled later that day.

After swiping the fat brush over a few dark strands I pause to look at Tammy in the mirror. "Seriously?"

"Oh yeah, seriously." Tammy nods, causing her head full of foil to tinkle like wind chimes. "You're positively glowin'. Of course if I had that stud muffin in my bed all week I imagine I'd be glowin' too."

Sam snorts from her chair, where she's letting honey-colored solution soak into her hair. She wasn't too sure about it at first but I convinced her that the lowlights would add some depth to her blondness. I'm pretty jazzed that my hairstyles are going to be on the cover of their next CD.

Sam leans over to look at Tammy. "Wait a minute, did you just call Luke a stud muffin?"

"I sure did," Tammy says, turning her foiled head in Sam's direction. "You got a problem with my terminology?"

"Yeah, stud muffin sounds stupid," Sam informs her. "It makes me picture this muscle-bound blueberry muffin makin' love to Macy."

"Oh quit!" Lilly looks up from her magazine to complain. Instead of highlights she wanted bold platinum blond hair and I wasn't allowed to soften her spikes no matter how hard I pleaded. "I had a doggone blueberry muffin for breakfast for goodness sake."

"So did Macy," Sam says, and of course I blush to the roots of my own auburn-colored hair. Actually, this is the longest I've stayed with a hair color, which oddly enough says something for my current disposition. Whenever I'm in an unhappy state of mind I tend to change the shade of my hair. I haven't even thought about it lately.

"Well, I had boring old Cheerios," Tammy complains. "I'd rather have a muffin. Macy, are there any more where that came from?"

"You mean Hootertown?" Lilly asks. "That little ole town must be chock-full of bodacious men."

"Y'all just stop!" I plead, but of course they don't.

"Seriously Tammy, you need to modernize your man verbiage," Sam insists.

"Oh stop flaunting your youth," Tammy shoots back, but then asks, "How about hunk? That better?"

"Eew, no!" Sam whines. "*Hunk?* Who says that anymore?"

"I need a hunka, hunka, burnin' love," Lilly sings in a deep Elvis voice and then laughs.

Tammy sticks her tongue out at them both. "You've

got a hunka, hunka burnin' love," she sings back at Lilly, "and his name is Boone. And Sam has . . . What's his name?"

"Brandon," Sam replies in a dreamy voice.

Tammy nods her highlighted head. "Right, bad-boy Brandon. Doggone it; I'm the only one without a man. This just sucks. I hate all of you."

Lilly swivels her chair in Tammy's direction and points a shiny red, freshly manicured finger at her. "Quit your bellyaching. You could have Colin Reed in a heart-beat."

"I don't *want* Colin Reed. Lilly, we've been down this road before. The man is talented but not my type. Will you please just give it up?"

Lilly looks as if she's going to protest but then with a flip of her hand she swivels her chair back around. "Whatever," she mumbles, but loud enough for Tammy to hear.

When Tammy rolls her eyes in the mirror at me I wince. "Sorry, I got her sayin' that."

"It's better than the very tacky *bite me*," Tammy says loud enough for Lilly to hear as well. I fully expect Lilly to say her favorite phrase right back to Tammy but she has her nose in a *People* magazine and seems as if she doesn't hear Tammy . . . until I see that she is scratching the side of her nose . . . with her middle finger.

"Oh just say it," Tammy tells her. "You know you want to."

"Bite me," Lilly responds, pretending to disguise it with a sneeze.

Tammy laughs. "Now all is right with the world . . . well, at least our little world here in Nashville." She hands me another foil square. "By the way, how are the interviews for the coaching job at Vandy going for Luke? Any word if they've offered him the head coach position?"

While dipping the brush in the goop I say, "All Luke will tell me is that it's going well but that his lack of experience is a factor."

"I can tell by the tone of your voice that there's more."

Lilly and Sam swivel their chairs in my direction after Tammy's question. For a moment I'm silent and then I tell them, "Well, Luke is flying to Florida tonight to interview for another job offer. He says it's just as a backup plan in case he isn't offered the job here in Nashville."

"I hear a but," Lilly prompts.

"I have this feeling that he'll be offered the job in Florida and will take it." I shrug. "I know . . . I'm being such a Debbie Downer but I can't help it. When things go well I wait for the other shoe to drop. It's my nature. It's just that these past weeks have been so incredible but have gone by in the blink of an eye."

Lilly leans my way. "You're just movin' at the speed of love."

Tammy gasps, "Oh I love that! Movin' at the speed of love! CD title?"

"Has it been done before?" Sam asks.

"I don't care," Tammy declares. "We're usin' it. Macy, you are a genius!"

"Hey," Lilly protests, "I came up with that one. How come she gets all the credit?" Lilly complains, but winks at me.

"Yeah but Macy put it in your head." Tammy turns to look at me. "What would we do without you?"

"Well, you'd just be lost, I guess." Of course I beam with pride that Tammy Turner is saying such things to me, but for some reason it makes me wonder how the Cut & Curl is doing in my absence even though Daisy has assured me that all is well. Something else that has me on edge is that Jamie Lee and Griff arrived home today after two weeks in Hawaii. I made Daisy promise that although Jamie Lee is aware that I'm in Nashville, I want to be the one to break the news to her that it's a permanent position at least for now.

That thought bums me a little, making me wonder why everything good has to come with a price.

Tammy meets my eyes in the mirror. "Okay, what's goin' through that pretty little head of yours, Macy McCoy?"

Taking another foil from her I reply, "I was just wondering why everything good that happens seems to come with a big ole price tag."

"I hear ya," Lilly agrees in a tired tone.

Tammy sighs. "Macy, I wish I could dispute that statement but I really can't."

I nod as I carefully fold the last foil square. "So then Tammy, what exactly are you tellin' me?"

Tammy purses her lips and looks to Lilly and Sam for help but they've given her the floor. "Well, sugar, I could say all sorts of clichés like 'Follow your heart,'" she replies, but then hesitates.

"What?"

"Or then again 'Chase your dream' might apply because, I was going to wait to tell you, but Cody West wants you to host a show with him once a month."

I gasp. "Well shut my mouth."

Tammy grins. "He found you refreshingly honest and endearingly charming and he thinks the audience will as well."

"Ohmigod. I'm speechless."

Lilly reaches over and smacks a high five to my gloved hand. "You go, girl."

"Tight!" Sam raises her arms in the air and does a little wiggle. "Pretty soon you're gonna be signing autographs."

"No one will want my autograph," I scoff, but think to myself that it would be pretty danged awesome. I'll have to practice . . . add a flourish of some sort.

Tammy grins. "Yeah! Cody thinks that teaching you a new recipe will be a nice break in his usual routine. Of course we'll have to see how it does in the ratings but Macy, I have a good feeling about this."

"Nuh-uh."

"Yeah baby," Tammy insists with a laugh. "Is that cool or what?"

"Her instincts about this kind of thing are usually spot-on," Lilly informs me. "Congratulations, Macy!"

"Holy cow." My heart is pounding like crazy. "And here I thought Cody would surely chuck the whole thing when he looked at the footage." When I realize I'm nodding up and down like a Bobblehead I swallow and repeat, "Holy doggone cow. And here I was thinkin' that I totally sucked."

"Oh no, he even wants to repeat the grocery shopping as part of the learning process. Of course you don't have to give me an answer right this minute. You can think it over."

"Okay," I tell Tammy, wait two seconds, and then say,

"Of course I'll do it! My goodness, this is another chance of a lifetime. How could I possibly say no?" I proclaim, but then it hits me that if Luke lands the job in Florida it would be almost impossible to give up this new opportunity. "Oh . . ."

Tammy meets my eyes in the mirror and reads my mind. "Let's just hope that Luke lands the position at Vandy and then your decision will be easy."

"Right," I answer with a smile, but the pessimist in me rears its ugly head. Luke is going to take the job in Florida; I just know it.

"Macy, I have a gut feeling that this will all work out," Lilly assures me.

"Think positive thoughts," Sam adds.

I nod. "Thanks, I'm sure it will," I lie, but somehow manage a brave smile. While I finish up their hair the conversation thankfully turns to song choices and I listen, fascinated as the three of them chat . . . well, make that mostly argue over what will end up on the CD they're starting to cut.

The photo shoot itself is tedious and exhausting and by the time I'm back at my apartment my butt is dragging. Luke, bless his heart, brings home a veggie pizza and get this, rubs my aching feet while I eat.

"Mmmm my dogs were barkin'," I tell him with a lazy smile. His strong, athlete's hands are working magic on the balls of my aching feet. "A girl could get used to this," I continue, but then almost choke on my pizza when Luke's hands pause. "What?" I ask in a small voice since my he's-going-to-say-something-bad radar is on full alert.

He licks his bottom lip, hesitating as if contemplating

how to break some rotten news to me. "Vanderbilt offered me a position," he finally responds.

My heart leaps for joy. "That's great. Are you going to take it?" *Please say yes.*

"I'm not sure." He shifts on the sofa and then explains. "They offered me a position . . . but not as head coach."

"But it could lead to that, right?" I ask hopefully.

Luke reaches up and runs his fingers through his hair . . . oh, a bad sign. "Maybe in time." He swallows and then says, "Macy, if they offer me the head coaching job in Florida, then I'd be hard-pressed not to take it. These positions just don't open up that often. And this is a team like the Payton Panthers who could really use me. It would be a rebuilding year . . . a challenge but that's what I love to do."

"You think they'll offer it to you?" I try to sound bright and hopeful when my heart is breaking.

"Maybe," he responds quietly. "But—"

"Of course you have to take it," I quickly assure him. I would hate to be the reason that his dreams aren't fulfilled. He went through such a rough patch that I know he deserves this success. "This might be the chance of a lifetime, right?"

"I wouldn't put it that strongly . . . but in a manner of speaking, yes. But Macy, I thought that—"

"Well then, you have to take it," I interject. When I'm on a roll there's no stopping my mouth. "This sounds right up your alley," I add while the pizza suddenly feels like a ball of lead in my stomach.

"True, but here's the thing . . . I will consider the job only if—," he begins, but we are interrupted by my ring tone, "Honky Tonk Badonkadonk." Luke gives me a small smile. "Go ahead and check who it is. Could be important."

"I need to change the ring tone," I tell him as I pick it up from the coffee table.

Luke shakes his head. "No, don't. It's somehow, *you*."

"The call is from Tammy."

"Answer it," he insists with a gentle nudge.

After flipping the phone open I say, "Hey Tammy. What's up?"

"Macy-girl, I wanted to tell you that I watched the edited segment of you on *Grillin' and Chillin'* and it is an absolute hoot, and yet somehow manages to be informative at the same time. I just had to share that with you. Cody's already planning the menu for your next show. A big congratulations, Macy."

"Thanks." I glance at Luke to see if he can hear Tammy. Her voice is loud so I'm thinking he can.

"I just had to share," she adds. "Oh and we'll be in the studio tomorrow, so it's a ponytail day. We won't be needing you, so enjoy your time off with Luke," she adds before hanging up.

"So do you have some big news?" Luke raises his eyebrows and waits.

"Yeah . . . believe it or not Cody West wants *me* to host a show with him once a month. Apparently he was pleased with the results of the first one." I raise my palms up. "Go figure."

Luke cups my chin with his hand. "Macy, I'm not one bit surprised. You are starting to come into your own. Embrace it and for goodness sake give yourself some credit. Now this truly is a chance of a lifetime. Take it."

I lean my cheek into his palm and remember how

amazing it felt to be cuddled in his arms. My God, could anything be worth giving that up? "Luke, what was the one condition you were going to tell me?"

He drops his hand from my chin and waves his hand through the air. "Oh . . . um . . ." He shrugs and then says, "That they provide a car. You know, since I'll have some traveling to do to visit family . . . and you." He clears his throat and then glances down at his watch. "I should get to the airport soon. I wouldn't want to miss my flight."

"Okay," I say brightly, although I want to burst into tears. "Do you want me to drive you?"

His dark eyebrows come together. "No, that's okay. I'll just park in long-term. I won't be there for more than a few days, I'm sure."

I nod since tears are clogging my throat. I know that I should walk him to the door but my body suddenly feels as if it's made of wood and too stiff to move. With an effort I push up from the sofa and follow him to the door. I realize that he's leaving early and it feels as if he's trying to get away as quickly as possible. I'm hurt and confused but I swallow the tears and pain and dig deep for a smile.

"Have a safe trip."

"Thanks."

"Call me when you make your final decision."

He nods. "They have to offer me the job first."

"I'm sure they will," I tell him, and wonder if it would be horrible of me to pray that they don't. Yeah, I suppose so . . .

When he leans in and kisses me tenderly on the mouth my heart shatters. I want to cling . . . plead, wrap myself around his legs and prevent him from leaving.

"I'll call you," he says, and I nod again, barely holding

it together, but as soon as I close the door I slither to the floor and burst into tears. Usually, I cry loudly but these are silent, gut-wrenching sobs that feel as if they are coming directly from my shattered heart.

I'm not quite sure how long I sit there and cry. In between the sobs I say things out loud to myself like, "I should have stopped him. Pleaded with him to take the Vandy job." I silently sob a bit more and then answer my sorry self, "No, that would have been wrong." Inhaling a shaky breath I say, "I should have said that I'd go to Florida with him. Screw the *Grillin' and Chillin'* gig." Swiping at a tear and my dripping nose I grumble, "I know Luke and he'd never let me do that."

Finally all cried out I swallow, lift the tail of my shirt to dab at my face that's leaking everywhere, and then simply sit there in the doggone dark for goodness knows how long. I know I should get up and go to bed but, somehow feeling the need to suffer, instead I curl up in a pathetic little ball, rest my head on my hands, and fall into a crappy, fitful sleep.

Something thumping has my eyes fluttering, trying to open but after my crying jag my eyelids feel made of lead and my eyeballs as if on fire. Mumbling beneath my breath I try to get comfortable on the floor, which of course is impossible, and then the thumping begins again. I think it could be my head pounding but then it finally dawns on me that it's someone knocking on the door directly behind me.

"Ohimgod." I scramble to a sitting position and push my tangled hair from my eyes. What if it's Luke coming back? Maybe he got to the airport and had this lightbulb moment telling him that no doggone job was worth losing me . . . head coach or not. I just bet he made an illegal U-turn and has come barreling back here to sweep me into his arms and declare his undying love.

Bang . . . bang, bang!

"Okay!" I try to shout but apparently even sorry-ass silent sobs mess with vocal chords, because all that comes out is a froglike croak. I push up to my feet and start to open the door when I realize with mounting horror how dreadful I must look. I can't let Luke see me all puffy, red-eyed with mascara making black tracks down my cheeks, which I'm sure, is how I appear.

Then again, I have to answer the door. But why in such a wonderful moment do I have to look like crap?

Life just is not fair!

"Macy McCoy, open up this damned door or I will be forced to break it down. And don't think I won't!"

"Jamie Lee?" I say in my bullfrog voice as I fumble for the deadbolt. Hopefully at some point my voice will return to normal.

"None other," she answers just as I manage to open the door. She's about to give me a hug when the light from the hallway illuminates my despair. Her eyes widen and she rushes into the room. "Ohmigod, Macy, what's wrong?"

I stumble across the room and flop down onto the sofa. Jamie Lee follows but sits down in a more mannerly fashion and then reaches over to turn on a light. "Tell me what in the world is the matter with you."

"What are you doin' here? You should be with Griff," I say in a wimpy, croaky tone. I'm beginning to get on my own nerves.

Jamie Lee waves a dismissive hand at me. "The man

was with me twenty-four seven for two weeks. Believe me, he deserved a break."

"So that's why you're here? To give Griff a break?"

Jamie Lee nods but I can see right through her.

I narrow my eyes which are burning like tiny little fire pits. "No you're not. Spill."

She shakes her head. "No, you first."

"No way. You drove all the way here at this hour to tell me something . . ." I gasp and put my hand over my mouth. I can think of only one thing that she would want to tell me in person. "Oh." I swallow and I don't know how there is any moisture left in my tear ducts but my eyes well up. "Oh . . . oh, oh! Jamie Lee, are you"—I swallow again and then half squeak, half croak—"pregnant?"

"I think so!" She nods and then puts a hand over her belly. "I did a pregnancy test three times and wanted to do another but Griff put his foot down on that one. They all came back positive. I must have gotten pregnant right before the wedding. Of course I'm tellin' Mama it happened on the honeymoon. I was a few days late, but feeling kinda weird . . . you know, icky and all that. At first I thought it was jet lag but then I had the funny feeling that I might be . . . and I am!"

"Wow, already?"

Jamie Lee shrugs. "We had decided after the wedding not to use protection and just let nature take its course. After Daddy's heart troubles we had discussed not waiting on account of you just never know and thought we'd start trying right away. Of course it'll also get Mama off my back. Yeah, I didn't expect it to happen this doggone quick but Macy, I'm over the moon and Griff is so danged proud of himself," she says with a chuckle. "No seriously, he is ecstatic and my goodness he is going to be such a good father." She rolls her eyes, "Good thing since I have my doubts on my mothering skills."

"You will be an amazing mother," I tell her firmly.

She gives me a deadpan stare.

"With your mama's help of course."

Jamie Lee laughs. "Oh there will be way too much of that, let me tell ya."

"Does Daisy know?"

"Not yet. I'm going to announce it tomorrow at dinner but I couldn't wait to tell you. I just couldn't give you the news over the phone. Griff finally told me to get in the car and head here. I had to get the directions to your apartment from Brandon since Luke didn't pick up his phone."

At the mention of Luke's name I get all teary-eyed again.

"Oh no, don't tell me your state of mind has to do with my brother? I'll kick his ass if he's hurt you." Jamie Lee takes one look at me and says, "Okay, start from the beginning and don't leave anything out. Boy oh boy, I leave town for two weeks and all hell breaks loose."

I try to laugh but it comes out a gurgle. Then inhaling a deep, shaky breath I begin my crazy tale, starting with when Tammy came into the shop even though Jamie Lee already knows that part. I tell her everything except for the amazing sex since Luke is her brother and all . . .

When I'm finished I say, "Just what am I supposed to do? It's like bein' between a rock and a hard place, Jamie Lee. I can't ask Luke not to take a Division One head coaching job."

"Yeah, but Macy, don't you dare give up this opportunity. You could be like the next Rachael Ray . . . well, except for the cookin' part. But your personality rocks. I can see this leading to more and, my goodness, to be doin' hair for Tammy Turner? No man is worth givin' all this up for."

"Really now, would Griff be worth it?"

"Okay, you're not playin' fair."

"I love your brother," I tell her quietly, and then we're both on the verge of crying. "Is anything worth giving that up for?"

Jamie Lee puts her feet up on the coffee table and sighs. "You have a doggone good point but Luke would never let you give it all up."

"See, that's what I was afraid of. I think he just might have been ready to ask me to go to Florida with him when Tammy called and gave me what should have been the amazing news about Cody West wantin' me to do *Grillin' and Chillin'*. Now I'll never know."

Jamie Lees frowns. "Wow, this sucks."

"Royally."

"Maybe they won't offer him the job."

"Oh come on, Jamie Lee. Besides, he seemed pretty confident they would."

"Well, let's just pray they don't."

"Jamie Lee, that wouldn't be right!"

She shrugs. "We can let God decide that one."

I muster up a laugh and then we're hugging. "I've missed you. I hate to leave the Cut and Curl. You know that, right?"

"We're all grown up, Macy. Life changes but we will always, always be best friends. Come hell or high water. No matter what!"

We high-five and do the secret handshake. "Let's get some rest. I'm off tomorrow, so I can be there for the big announcement."

"Okay, but you have to act surprised. If Mama knew I told you first she'd be ticked forever and I'm going to need some serious help with the mothering thing."

"You will not!"

She looks at me with one eyebrow arched.

"Well okay maybe a teensy bit," I admit. "Babies don't come with instructions."

"I know . . . What was God thinkin'?"

We laugh and cry and chat for a little while longer before stumbling dead-dog tired into my bedroom.

Jamie Lee takes one look at the pile of clothes and says without missing a beat, "Couldn't decide what to wear?"

"You know me like no other."

We both laugh until we're snorting and then fall into a deep sleep . . . And I still swear that I don't snore.

24

What Matters Most

Jamie Lee arrives at her parents' house a good fifteen minutes before me since she's a speed demon. When I get out of my car she's waiting on the backyard porch petting Cassie, but when the old collie sees me, she comes bounding down the steps with her tongue hanging sideways out of her mouth.

"Hey there, Cassie girl," I croon to her when she jumps up on her hind legs to be petted. "Miss me, girl?"

"Cassie, get down," Jamie Lee scolds, but Cassie as usual doesn't pay any attention. The only person she obeys is Daisy. "Mama and Daddy aren't here. She must be closing up shop and Daddy is most probably fishin'. Mama's got something cookin' in the Crock-Pot, though. I've got to learn how to use one of those things. You just dump everything in and turn it on, right?"

"I think so." I make a mental note to have Cody do a Crock-Pot show. "And then you come home and dinner is done. You got one at your bridal shower from Miss Irma. She called it the best invention of all time."

"I've got to unpack that sucker. By the way, Griff is heading over."

"Good." After taking a seat on the porch steps I inhale a deep breath of fresh country air.

"Here." She hands me a Mountain Dew. "Thought you might be thirsty."

"Thanks." I take the cold can and pop the top. After it hisses and fizzes I take a long, sweet, and tangy swig. "Jamie Lee, you need to stop drivin' like a bat outta hell. You've got that little bun in the oven to consider."

Jamie Lee puts a hand to her belly and sits up straight. "Ohmigod, you're right. I'm already putting her in danger and she isn't even born yet!" she wails, and her eyes well up in unaccustomed emotion when I fully expected her to come back at me with a smart-mouth remark. "I suck."

I pat Jamie Lee's leg. "I'm sorry. I didn't mean to get you worked up. I was just making an observation. Her? So you think it's a girl?"

"Oh, I don't know but it's fun to let Griff think that he's gonna have to deal with a mini-me." She sniffs and then waves her hand at me. "You won't believe the crap that makes me cry. Television commercials . . . ohmigod, *songs*." She shakes her head. "I'm a basket case. Poor Griff. Yesterday I told him that his aftershave was making me queasy. He immediately went and took a shower!" She chuckles. "It's gonna be a long nine months for him."

"He's gonna be pamperin' you and lovin' every minute of it."

Jamie Lee smiles and then her eyes tear up again. "Oh stop!"

"Stop what? Talkin'? Cuz everything I say makes you blubber."

Jamie Lee puts her hands up in the air. "Darned if I know," she says with a laugh. "Let's head inside. It's gettin' hot out here. Plus we can sample what Mama has in the Crock-Pot. I'm starvin'."

"Sounds good."

"Cassie," Jamie Lees scolds when her dog follows us into the house, but as always she lets her stay. Daisy will grumble but let her stay as well unless she makes the mistake of begging. Then out the door she'll go.

"It smells so good. What's in the pot?"

Jamie Lee lifts the lid and peers inside. Taking a deep whiff she proclaims, "Beef stew!" We both sneak a quick bite. "Yummy. All I do is eat. Weird stuff. I was craving SPAM."

"Ew."

"I know. And this is just the beginning." She shakes her head but then takes another big bite. A few minutes later her mama and daddy arrive.

"Macy!" Daisy says, and gives me a fierce hug for someone so tiny. "My, my but you're a sight for sore eyes."

Her daddy hugs me as well. "Good to see you, sweetie."

"So what brings y'all here on a weekday?"

"A home-cooked meal. Macy had the day off and wanted to visit."

"Well it's a nice surprise," she says with a smile. "I'll just throw some biscuits in the oven and we'll be good to go. Is Griff comin' over too?" she asks, but is answered when the back door opens. He takes his boots off in the mudroom before entering the kitchen.

After greeting everyone he gives Jamie Lee a brief kiss on the cheek but makes the mistake of putting his hand on her belly.

"Oh!" Daisy who doesn't miss a beat puts her hands to her cheeks. "Jamie Lee! Baby girl, are you expectin'?"

Jamie Lee presses her lips together while nodding her head. "Yes, Mama."

"So soon? Well, praise the Lord! Oh!" She throws her hands up in the air and does a little jig that has us all laughing and then doing a silly jig too . . . well, Griff and her daddy refrain but join in for a group hug mixed with tears . . . well, not tears from the guys either, although they both noisily clear their throats and shove each other.

"Hey, what's goin' on?" We all turn to see Luke standing in the doorway with a look of concern on his face. "Everything okay?" My heart of course skips a beat at the mere sight of him.

"You tell him," Daisy says to Jamie Lee.

"Luke . . . I'm gonna have a *baby*."

The worried expression on his face changes to a grin. "Congratulations!" He slaps Griff on the back. "That was quick, you dog, you." He turns and envelops Jamie Lee in a bear hug.

"Careful," Daisy warns.

"Oh!" Luke backs off but then leans in and kisses her gently on the cheek.

"Mama, chill. I'm not gonna break," Jamie Lee scoffs. "You know I'm going back to work tomorrow."

Everyone starts chatting at once and I'm doing my

best not to look at Luke but I have to wonder why he isn't in Florida. Finally his daddy asks for me. "Son, I thought you were on an interview. What gives? Did you already accept the job?"

Okay, now I have to look at him.

He leans back against the kitchen counter for a moment and then explains, "I was on my way to the university when this song, 'Honky Tonk Badonkadonk,' comes on the radio and I knew I had to turn around."

They all look at him as though he's crazy but my heart starts to pound. I put my hands on the back of a kitchen chair for support.

"The song reminded me of what matters most in life."

" 'Honky Tonk Badonkadonk'?" Jamie Lee angles her head at her brother. "Just what have you been smokin', big brother?"

"Jamie Lee," Daisy says in the same exasperated tone she's been using with her daughter every day I can remember, "you know your brother doesn't do that . . . stuff."

"Yeah but . . . ," Jamie Lee begins, and then stops. "Oh . . ." She puts her hands to cheeks and looks at Luke with wide eyes. " 'Oooo-weee, shut my mouth, slap my grandma,' " she quietly quotes the song, and then her face splits into a wide grin.

"Okay I'm lost," Daisy complains, and stomps her foot. "What's this about slappin' a grandma? I'm gonna be one here shortly, so watch what you're sayin'."

"The song Luke is referrin' to is the ring tone on Macy's cell phone," Griff has the decency to explain.

Daisy still looks confused. Cell phones remain a mystery to her. "Ring tone? Oh . . . right. The song that scares the bejesus outta you when your phone rings. Gotcha."

"And hearin' the song on the radio made him think about Macy," Jamie Lee tells her mother.

"Oh . . ." Suddenly Daisy's eyebrows rise. "And caused him to rethink his decision. Now I'm up to speed."

"Am I allowed to speak here?" Luke asks with a smile in my direction. "Macy, this isn't how I had things planned. I had no idea you would be here," he says, and then turns to his family. "Actually, I tried your apartment in Nashville first. Listen, would y'all mind if I spoke with Macy in private?"

"Yes," Daisy replies.

"Mama!" Jamie Lee shakes her head. "It was a rhetorical question."

"Hey, he asked and I answered."

Jamie Lee shrugs. "True. Okay *yes* we mind."

"Griff, Dad, you gonna help me out here?"

His father shakes his head. "We both know how that will end up."

Luke sighs. "Macy?"

"It's okay, Luke."

"They're gonna eavesdrop anyway," his daddy reminds him.

Daisy gasps and puts a delicate hand to her chest. "Why we certainly would *not*. Would we, Jamie Lee?"

Wide-eyed, Jamie Lee shakes her head. "Daddy, how could you say such a thing?" she protests, but has a really hard time keeping a straight face.

"Go on, Luke," Daisy pleads.

Luke clears his throat. "It's probably good that all of you hear this, anyway. You know this town made me out to be a hero because I could throw a football. For a long time it was all that I was, about to the point when I couldn't perform . . . well y'all know the rest of that story." Luke looks at Griff. "I can't thank you enough for draggin' my ass back here . . . sorry, Mama."

Griff waves him off. "You woulda done the same thing. Don't deny it."

"All the same . . . you did that for me, Griff, and I'm grateful. And then coaching the Panthers gave me back my heart and saved my soul. But when we won the national championship, Hootertown made me out to be a hero once again." He shakes his head. "I started to believe it there for minute. I won't lie. I liked being the center of attention . . . in the limelight. Thought I had to move on and go to the big time."

"Son, there's nothing wrong with using your skills to better yourself. You've got a bright future in coaching ahead of you."

Luke nods at his father. "Yeah, Dad, but the key word you used was *yourself*. It always had to be about what's best for me." Luke jams his thumb toward his chest. "But when you fall in love . . . suddenly someone else becomes more important." He turns to me. "Macy, when that silly song started playin', a lightbulb went off in my brain. It hit me like a quarterback sack that you mean more to me than any job ever would. I'd be miserable in Florida without you."

"Luke, we already discussed how the timing was all wrong for us. We're both going in different directions . . . finding our future. I don't want to hold you back." I feel a little weird that everyone is watching but this needs to be said.

"No, I was wrong." Luke takes a step closer to me. "The timing is right. Had we both gone off to wherever . . . we might never end up together and I'd regret it for the rest of my life. The time to do something about it is now."

I grip the back of the chair tighter. "So what are you going to do?" I ask, and everyone in the kitchen looks at him expectantly—even Cassie.

"I'm taking the assistant coaching position at Vanderbilt."

"Luke . . . ," I start to protest, but he shakes his head.

"Macy, I could be standing there winning the Super Bowl but without you in my life it would feel empty."

"Awe . . . ," Daisy sighs, but Jamie Lee shushes her.

Luke takes another step closer so that he is standing right in front of me. "Macy, I've known for a while that I was falling in love with you. It wasn't until I faced the prospect of losing you that I realized just how much you really mean to me."

"Awe . . ." This time it's Jamie Lee who sighs and her mama in turn shushes her. "Hey, I'm pregnant and can't control my emotions," she protests.

"So I'm taking the job in Nashville," Luke continues, and puts his hands on my shoulders. "To be with you and to be close to my family." He arcs his hand through the air. "This is what matters most to me."

"Well come on son, kiss the girl," his daddy urges.

Luke smiles down at me. "Excellent idea."

In that moment when Luke's lips touch mine a peaceful feeling washes over me. I let it seep into my bones and let all my worries drain away. I just know my mama is looking down on me and is smiling. I can feel it.

When the kiss ends everybody cheers and Cassie joins

in with a bark. We laugh and hug until Jamie Lee says, "Hey, let's eat."

"Can I call my daddy first?" I ask.

"There's no need," Daisy says. "He's on his way."

I raise my eyebrows. "When did you call him?"

Daisy holds up her cell phone. "A minute ago in the midst of all the commotion. Hey, I'm learnin'. I've got him on speed dial," she says proudly. "I've got to stay young for this new grandbaby of mine."

"Mama, I'll help you set the table," Jamie Lee offers, and then shoos her hands at Luke and me. "You two go on outside and have a much-deserved moment alone."

"Good idea," Luke says, and draws me outside onto the porch.

After a sweet and tender kiss I put my hands on his cheeks and say, "Are you sure you want to take the job in Nashville?"

"Macy, I've never been more sure about anything in my life. It took me a while but there you were under my nose the whole time and I was too blind to see it."

"It's because I'm so doggone short," I joke. "I flew under your radar."

Luke smiles but shakes his head. "No, Macy, I was just focused on the wrong things. And by the way, you're not too short. You're perfect."

When I open my mouth to protest my perfection, Luke puts a finger to my lips. "You're perfect. Don't even try to argue."

I look up and see my reflection in his blue eyes that are gazing down at me with such adoration. Perfection isn't about dress size or hair color or throwing a touchdown pass. The only perfect thing in this world is love.

"I'd be silly to argue with that," I tease, but then tell him, "You make me so happy."

"Good and I aim to keep it that way."

He kisses me again and we laugh when we hear Jamie Lee and her mama arguing over something. Griff and Luke's daddy are whooping it up over a baseball game on television and a moment later my daddy pulls into the backyard. I wave to him from the porch and laugh when Cassie bounds over to greet him.

When Luke puts his arm around my shoulders I loop my own arm around his waist and hug him close. When my daddy sees this he stops in his tracks and looks up to the sky and smiles. He might have been gone a lot as I was growing up and didn't always know the right things to say to a young girl, but in that moment I realize how much he must have worried and how much he truly loves me.

As if reading my thoughts Luke kisses me on top of the head. "Go on."

I slip from Luke's embrace and run out to greet my daddy. He pulls me into his arms, lifts me up, and spins me around like he used to do when I was little, and I laugh from the sheer joy of it all.

"I love you, Macy. I haven't told you that nearly enough."

"Oh Daddy, some things you just know."

He smiles as if relieved, and I hug him close. Then, grabbing his hand, I say, "Come on inside. There's a lot to tell."

I meet Luke's gaze from across the lawn, and he smiles. He was right. Family. Friends. This is and will forever be what matters most.